Dead Woman's Shoes

Kaye C Hill

CREME DE LA CRIME

First published in 2008
by Crème de la Crime
P O Box 523, Chesterfield, S40 9AT

No cats or dogs were harmed in the writing of this book.

Typesetting by Yvette Warren
Cover design by Yvette Warren
Front cover image by Peter Roman

ISBN 978-0-9551589-9-5
A CIP catalogue reference for this book is available from the
British Library

Printed and bound in Poland EU, produced by Polskabook

www.cremedelacrime.com

About the author:
Kaye C Hill is married with one cat and lives in Guildford. A career involving steel-capped boots, chainsaws and railway embankments somehow inspired her to start writing crime fiction.

Thanks to…

… my mum for teaching me to read before I started school, and setting this whole thing in motion.

I am also very grateful to Lynne, my publisher, for a phone call that changed my life.

Particular thanks go to Jane, and the other members of my writers' circle, who regularly laugh at my work, even though I keep telling them it's not meant to be funny.

My eternal gratitude also to the rest of my family and friends far and wide, for their unconditional support.

I should also mention the shed, where I had my first inspiration.

But my biggest thanks of all go, of course, to Nick, who knew I could do this. He also put my all my apostrophes in the right places – and if someone can do that, you know you're on to a winner.

This is for my dad, Roy Hill.
He always enjoyed a story
about a private eye.

A harmless, necessary cat.
- *The Merchant of Venice*, William Shakespeare

1

Somewhere in the log cabin a phone started ringing.

Lexy Lomax jerked upright in the unfamiliar bed, blinking in the sunlight that stabbed through a pair of faded chintz curtains.

She sat, confused, listening to the persistent *tring-tring*.

Couldn't be her mobile – that played *Born Free*. Anyway, she'd chucked it into the River Orville the previous afternoon. Not exactly environmentally friendly, but satisfying, nonetheless, watching it arc through the air, with Gerard's voice still bleating out of it, and hearing the resounding splash that signified the end of the conversation.

So who was ringing now? She hadn't even noticed a phone when she'd arrived at Otter's End late the previous night.

A small but pointed bark sounded from the end of the bed.

"Yeah, all right pal. It'll stop in a moment."

But it didn't.

Lexy shifted uncomfortably. The sound was starting to unnerve her. Reluctantly, she swung her legs, still encased in jeans, over the side of the bed and eased herself up, aware of a stinging sensation in her left arm.

She padded down a short, dingy hall and pushed open the door at the end.

The living room was flooded with morning sun, making her blink violently. Dust loitered on every surface of the room – dust which must have accumulated over a much longer period than the eight weeks the place had lain empty. Not quite Miss Havisham's wedding, but getting there.

Lexy made her way across the threadbare carpet to a corner table. The green plastic phone was tucked behind a dead pot plant. Hand hovering over the receiver, she hesitated. Her husband couldn't really have tracked her down already, could he?

No. Impossible. But Lexy felt a jab of anxiety. The note she had left, some twenty-four hours earlier, on the mantelpiece of their flat in South Kensington informed him she had left him for good and gone to the Far East.

Now, stuck in this log cabin in Suffolk, with the sea rattling the pebbled beach outside, and the phone implacably ringing, she began to regret her words.

When Gerard discovered what had happened, he was hardly going to leap on the next plane to Hong Kong. He would realise straight away that she wouldn't be able to get through customs, that she would have to stay in Britain. So instead he would be methodically tracing her last movements. At that very moment he might be pondering over the note she left. She could just imagine him muttering *"Far East, Far East,"* and reaching for a road atlas. He would find her, there was no doubt of that.

Not that he would want her back or anything. He'd just be missing his five hundred grand.

The phone must have been on its twentieth ring.

Lexy closed her fingers over the receiver, then jerked them away again as an integral answering machine kicked in.

It was a recording of a mature, rather fruity, female voice.

"Thank you for calling. Please leave your name and number and I'll get back to you."

Lexy took a step back. The recorded voice must belong to the previous occupant of the log cabin. The one who didn't own a duster. The one who'd died.

Her name had been Doyle. Mrs Glenda Doyle.

Lexy had bought the cabin cheap from Mrs Doyle's nephew, from an advert he'd put on the Internet.

"Fabulous little place," he'd said smoothly when she rang him.

2

"Ideal for doing up. Right on the beach, of course. That is," he amended, "only about a hundred yards from the steps down. All on its own, lovely retreat. Needs a bit of work, you understand. But a perfect holiday home."

"Is that what your aunt used it for?" Lexy asked. "A holiday home?"

"No. Actually she lived there," he replied, shortly. "Her choice. Seemed to want to be somewhere remote. Sold her house in Bury St Edmunds and…"

Lived off the proceeds? Lexy could tell that Derek Flint was somewhat put out that his inheritance had dwindled from solid bricks and mortar in a well-heeled town to a run-down log cabin.

"I'll send you the photos," he said.

They were printed from a digital photograph, blown up to ten by eights. OK, she could see that Otter's End was old, and most of the struts were missing from the veranda, and it needed a lick of creosote, and the windows looked like they would clatter in the wind, but it had bolt-hole written all over it. And she needed a bolt-hole. Lexy had cashed in her savings there and then and bought it.

It hadn't bothered her moving into a place where someone had recently died. She wasn't into all that ghost-buster stuff. Even so, it was oddly discomfiting now to hear Glenda Doyle's disembodied voice emitting from the answering machine.

She'd have to wipe that message. She bent over the phone, but before she could even start fiddling with it, there was a click, followed by the inarticulate sound of a throat being cleared.

Lexy remained frozen in position. Someone was leaving a message.

"Er… yes – I'm calling about the advert in the *Clopwolde Herald*. Your discreet services."

It was a man's voice, soft, well-modulated, hesitant. Not Gerard, then. He put a particular emphasis on the word *discreet.*

He recited a mobile number. "I'll be available until one, if you… er… wouldn't mind calling me back." There was a click as he replaced the receiver.

Lexy let out a long breath, grinning at her own idiocy. Had she really thought it would be her husband? It was just some bloke calling about an advert in a local paper.

She pressed the menu key, tried to find a quick way of deleting the message, but couldn't. She'd disconnect the damn thing later. She didn't need a phone anyway. She headed abruptly for the kitchen. What she did need was a cup of tea.

She filled a decrepit beige plastic kettle with water and put it on to boil, took a chipped mug from a hook, rifled through a small bag of provisions she'd left on the worktop the previous night, and realised that she hadn't brought any teabags with her.

Cursing under her breath, Lexy started yanking open the orange formica cupboards. One contained a pot of elderly plum jam. Beside it stood a barrel-shaped tin with scenes from Gilbert and Sullivan operas on it. Lexy picked it up and shook it. Bingo. Thanks, Glenda.

She paced around the kitchen while she waited for the kettle to boil, trying unsuccessfully to stop the events of the previous day drip-feeding into her mind. Maybe she should have gone to the police after all, rather than take matters into her own hands? Perhaps she should have confronted Gerard as soon as she had found out? Or maybe she should have contacted an insider, someone who could have helped her without asking too many questions? But Lexy found she was unable to concentrate fully on these vexed issues, because something else was bothering her, something unrelated to her obnoxious husband, a small, insignificant thing that nevertheless had its hand up in the air.

She frowned.

It was that message she'd just heard on the answering machine. What had the bloke been after? Discreet services? *Discreet* services? What kind of discreet services were we talking about here? Surely not…

With an expression of disbelief, Lexy turned and stared back through the open kitchen hatch into the living room, with its dust and chintz, pink velvet curtains faded to a mouldy green in the creases, and the row of cheap pottery policemen on the mantelpiece above the mock-flame gas fireplace.

It didn't exactly scream bordello.

And she hadn't even started on the bedroom.

OK. Try this. Perhaps Mrs Doyle took her discreet services to her clients' own homes. Wearing the stout brown leather shoes that had been left by the front door of the cabin.

No, that didn't work, either. Lexy shut her eyes momentarily to dispel the image.

Whatever services she offered, it was clear from the message that the local newspaper was still running Mrs Doyle's advert.

Well, great.

Lexy stalked back into the living room, and turned to a caramel-coloured chihuahua, source of the earlier pointed bark, who was now sitting like a miniature Sphinx on the arm of the grubby sofa.

"Better sort this out right now, Kinky, or we'll be getting calls from every neglected husband between here and Lowestoft," she said grimly. "And somehow your name doesn't help."

She picked up the receiver and punched out the number the man had left. She'd send him packing, then ring the local paper and cancel the advert.

The phone was picked up almost immediately.

"Hello?" It was the same civil, tentative voice.

"Hi. I'm returning that call you just made about discreet services," Lexy announced matter-of-factly. "I think I should tell you…"

"Er… I want a surveillance job done," the voice cut in, nervously.

Surveillance job, eh? She'd never heard it called that before. "As I said," she reiterated coldly, "I think I should tell you…"

"I'll pay over the odds for a quick result."

Lexy's mouth set. Quick result? She'd give him a quick result, all right. "Look – you're talking to the wrong person, mate," she snapped.

"It's my wife. I think she's… up to something. I just need you to follow her when she goes out."

Lexy stopped in the act of forcibly replacing the telephone receiver.

"Follow her?"

"Er – I did phone the right number, didn't I? Discreet under-cover investigations?"

Lexy closed her eyes slowly. The poor sod wanted a private detective, not a private massage.

She snapped them open again. If that was the case, why was he calling Otter's End? Lexy hadn't quite recovered from the notion that Glenda Doyle might have been an ageing call girl. The idea that she could have been an ageing private eye seemed, if anything, even more bizarre.

But it would at least explain the presence of a large magnifying glass in the kitchen drawer.

She had to quell a sudden snort of laughter.

"As I said," continued the voice, "I will pay over the odds."

Lexy hesitated. If Glenda really had been a private investigator, and this injured ego thought he was talking to her, and, more to the point, was prepared to hand over some cash, it might not do any harm to play along for a minute. Just see what the deal was.

"So you need your wife… tailed?" she queried.

The relief in the man's voice was almost tangible. "That's right. I just want to find out… you know… what she's doing. I'll give you fifty in advance, and two hundred pounds to follow if you can get me some photographic evidence. Cash in hand."

Two hundred and fifty pounds? For following a woman about for the night? Lexy whistled under her breath. Could she get away with it? It would certainly get her out of a tight spot. She only had a handful of loose change to her name.

Not counting the half million quid in the suitcase under the bed, of course. But she couldn't touch that – she had some morals. Anyway, she didn't want to risk getting her prints on it.

Through the open kitchen hatch she glimpsed the near-empty larder. The chihuahua was watching her intently. He was down to his last can of Pedigree Chum. And it was a small one.

"All right – make it a round three," said the voice, sounding slightly exasperated at her silence.

Lexy took a deep breath. How difficult could it be to spy on a straying housewife?

"Three fifty. A hundred in advance. That's my last offer."

"OK. I'll do it," Lexy said quickly. She resisted saying that she'd throw in a private massage, too, at that price.

"Right – I'll bring the details over. Where's your office?"

Office? Lexy was thrown. "Er… I work from home, actually. Otter's End. Top of Cliff Lane." Damn. She shouldn't have given her address out.

"Fine," said the voice. "I'll be there in an hour."

2

Lexy stared incredulously at Kinky, the green plastic receiver still in her hand.

"And I was worried we'd starve to death in this shack. It's not even nine-thirty and I've already made three hundred and fifty quid."

The chihuahua gave her a dubious look, then, large bat-like ears pricked, he jumped down from the sofa and trotted up to the door leading out to the back veranda, looking round at her expectantly.

"Oi, you might show a bit of interest," Lexy chided. "We're talking here about the first proper job I've ever had, and all you can think about is your bladder."

He gave her a toothy grin.

Kinky had belonged to Gerard's mother until she had become too ill to look after him, a year back. Her dying wish had been for Gerard and Lexy to take care of the dog, but when the time came and Kinky was deposited at their house in a small wicker dog basket, Gerard was all for taking him straight to Battersea. He'd never liked lap dogs. Lap dancers – now, that was different.

Chihuahuas weren't really Lexy's cup of tea either, but to her a promise was a promise. The relationship was on a strict under-standing, though.

"I'll come clean with you," Lexy had told him. "I don't like small dogs. And they don't come much smaller than you, pal. But I'll make you a deal. You yap, you go. You don't yap, you stay. And for my part, I promise that, unlike your previous owner, I won't tote you around in a shopping bag and I won't make you wear a designer coat. Or a necktie. Or a retractable lead."

Kinky looked as if he could stand the offer, so an uneasy truce had mellowed over the months into respectful friendship.

In fact, in many ways, Kinky was the perfect companion, always polite, sympathetic and loyal. There was just the one small problem.

Still, thought Lexy, eyeing him apprehensively, perhaps the calming influence of the countryside would help him grow out of that particular habit.

She replaced the receiver and followed the dog. As she unbolted the door and pushed it open a wall of heat and brilliance hit them.

When Lexy's eyes adjusted, the view that met them eased the disturbing events of the past twenty-four hours aside like a soothing bedtime lullaby.

Otter's End had been built on the very edge of a cliff. In front of Lexy lay the jade green sea and forget-me-not blue sky of a child's painting. There was even a round yellow sun at the top right hand corner.

She took a few more steps forward, gazing at the smooth muscles of water rolling hypnotically towards the shore. It was tempting to clamber down the cliff face there and then, rip off her clothes and run straight in. But the salt water, she mused, would play havoc with her new tattoo.

She stretched out her arm, twisting it this way and that, to admire the intricate Celtic knot work. Gerard would have hated it, she thought with satisfaction. She was tempted to send him a photo.

She made her way around the veranda, her ebullient mood only mildly quashed when she discovered that the cabin itself wasn't such a pretty sight.

Its wooden side panels were bleached and rotten, strung about with unpleasant grey skeins of long-abandoned spiders' webs. The roof on the leeward side was green and slippery with lichen, patched up in several places with polythene sheeting.

The guttering sagged ominously below the eaves. Still, she could fix it up. She'd bought the place for a song, so she couldn't expect much. And that view was second to none. But, a small voice annoyingly reminded her, the cabin had still cost her all the money she possessed. All the money she had inherited when her dad died last summer.

Lexy moved swiftly off again around the cabin. On the far side she found a complicated-looking electrical junction box, together with a large, ugly red gas cylinder. It was half-empty. She'd have to find out how to get it refilled, or replaced. She didn't even like to think what the sewage situation might be.

The cabin had a garden of sorts, long-neglected, enclosed by a low picket fence. Beyond lay a tangle of gorse, heather and young birch. Lexy threaded her way through an open gateway to a small grass clearing. Nearby on the cliff edge she could see the top of a set of wooden steps that she assumed led down to the beach. All pretty much as Derek Flint had described. But not quite as she had imagined.

Something was missing.

People. There was no trace of any other log cabins, or for that matter any sign of human habitation at all. But she wasn't complaining. As it happened, it would suit her very nicely to live in splendid isolation. It reminded her of when she was a kid, living in the caravan, picking the quietest spots they could, the places where they were less likely to be moved on.

"You know, I haven't stayed by the sea for years, Kinks," she mused. "Except abroad, of course." She felt a spear of guilt. The Caribbean Islands, Acapulco Bay, Madagascar. All-inclusive, sanitised resorts where the illusion of paradise was unspoilt by the inconvenient sight and sound of the native people. "No – the last time was about eighty-seven, when Dad and I fetched up in Norfolk. That was a great summer."

She was thinking about her dad again, and an upbringing she

had vowed to forget, when, thirteen years ago, she turned her back on him and the caravan. The day she let herself be driven away in a flashy Range Rover by Gerard Warwick-Holmes, like some exotic artefact he'd discovered in one of his precious attics.

"She's got gypsy blood, you know," Gerard would murmur suggestively to his friends, as if that made her dynamite in the sack.

Well, that novelty soon wore off. With a snort, Lexy scanned the grass margins, where yellow tormentil flowered in profusion. What did her dad call it? Blood-root. Another memory from her childhood: she and her dad collecting wild plants, making ointments, salves and lotions and selling them from the van. Must have been good, too, because the same people came back for them year after year, as the caravan did its annual rounds.

But then there were the others, the people who called them gyppos and pikeys. Smug, ignorant hypocrites who didn't understand the nomadic way of living.

Lexy kicked at the grass, angry that she'd allowed herself to be persuaded that the travelling life was something she had to be rescued from.

Lexy's grandmother, Lal, had come from a old Kent Romany family. Lexy had the blood running through her veins, all right. Thing was, Lal chose to settle with a *Gorja*, a non-gypsy man. It wasn't the accepted custom to marry outside the Romany community, so rather than give her man up, her grandmother had become estranged from her roots.

Lexy's dad, Lal's only child, never knew where he fitted in. He didn't belong with the Roma, nor with the New Age traveller set; but he still had an instinct to hit the open road. He bought a caravan and made a living doing anything he could – carpentry, gardening, making and selling potions, stewarding at the summer festivals. He met Lexy's mother, Angelica, at Glastonbury. Admired her humanitarian principles and lustrous black hair. Nine months later Lexy was born in a tent, with the sound of an anti-hunting demonstration kicking off in the background. Angelica, by all accounts, had been pretty annoyed to miss that demo.

Martyn Lomax handed on to his daughter everything that Lal taught him about the countryside from the old Romany knowledge. It seemed like a long time since Lexy walked with him in the woods at dawn and dusk. But she hadn't forgotten. Neither had she forgotten how she used to spend hours on end tracking badgers, foxes and owls, trying for candid shots with the old SLR camera her dad had given her when she passed her exams. Secret surveillance. A skill that might come in handy in the near future.

In fact, one might even say that she had a talent for that sort of thing.

Half an hour later Lexy was washed, dressed in her spare jeans and a clean t-shirt, and gazing at the selfsame camera from her youth. She hadn't taken a shot with it for years.

The sound of car wheels scrunching along the rough gravel path outside made her look up sharply.

"Here we go then," she said to Kinky, taking a deep breath. "Try to look like we run a professional outfit here. No scratching or leg-lifting."

She placed the battered old camera out of view.

A car door was slammed, and moments later there was a quiet rap on the wooden door.

Lexy opened it, Kinky sitting watchfully on the arm of the sofa.

A small, bald man in a blue suit stood on the threshold, clutching a Jiffy bag.

"I called earlier," he said. "About my wife. Name's Roderick Todd."

"Lexy Lomax. Come in." She offered her hand. His was both damp and limp. Lexy dropped it quickly.

"I've never done this before." Mr Todd stepped into the living room.

Join the club, mate.

Up close he had eyes as large, soft and violet as pansies, in a face that was the colour and texture of a field mushroom. He was probably, guessed Lexy, in his mid-fifties, and, judging by his nervous tic and champed nails, he wasn't comfortable in the role of injured spouse.

"Have a seat," she offered. Some minutes earlier she had hastily whisked the living room surfaces with an old flannel she'd found in the bathroom, and plumped up the cushions on the chintz sofa.

They now seemed to be moving in a world of dust, thousands of disturbed motes swirling lazily in the sunlight that striped the living room. She fervently hoped Roderick Todd didn't have an allergy. He'd be leaving Otter's End in an ambulance before he even had a chance to say 'marital infidelity'.

"Is he all right?"

Lexy wrenched her mind from the dust. Mr Todd, hovering by the sofa, was indicating Kinky, who was regarding this stranger with genial interest. "I mean, he won't bite or anything?"

"No – he's fine with… people," Lexy assured him, but she shooed Kinky from the sofa anyway. He sat in the middle of the room instead, and began scratching himself loutishly.

Lexy gave him a murderous look, and turned back to Mr Todd, who was struggling awkwardly in the sofa's sagging embrace.

Pretending not to notice, she sat opposite him.

Once he'd gained an upright position, Mr Todd, looking discomfited, opened his Jiffy bag, shook the contents on to the coffee table and slid them towards her. A couple of glossy photos and some handwritten notes.

"Self-explanatory, really," he mumbled. "The pictures of my wife, Avril, are fairly recent – last year, in fact, at the Clopwolde-on-Sea summer fete."

Lexy examined the photos. It had obviously been raining heavily that day. Summer fete, England, stood to reason. The woman pointed out by Mr Todd was a big, beefy type, with a pile of rust-coloured hair and a blue two-piece outfit. She was one of the tallest in a group of drenched and wry people, overshadowing her small, fretful husband, who stood next to her, by at least four inches. And she was the only one not cracking a smile.

Lexy glanced up at Mr Todd with a new sympathy.

"Does she still look the same?" she asked. "You know, hair, that sort of thing?"

"Her hair never changes," said the man, almost defensively.

"Oh," said Lexy, rubbing her spiky crop ruefully. "Not like mine then – halfway down my back and champagne blonde yesterday morning."

"Good heavens," he replied, politely.

Lexy bit her lip. He didn't need to know that. This wasn't about her, and anyway, she was meant to be on the run, in disguise, lying low.

"So – you'd like me to follow her?" she said. It wasn't like the woman was going to be difficult to spot – she was the size of a prize heifer.

"That's right." He seemed relieved to be getting to the nitty-gritty. "She goes out every Friday night, sometimes on Wednesdays, too – tells me it's to do with the amateur dramatics committee, but I've found out that they only meet monthly." He leaned forward, gazing at Lexy intently. "I need to know where she's going the rest of the time. She might be getting into something she can't control. In fact, I'm very worried she's going to get into… trouble."

Lexy tried to hide her astonishment. What was he trying to tell her? That his wife was prone to unrestrained bouts of illicit passion and might end up pregnant as a result? She tried not to snort out loud. Avril Todd was fifty-five if she was a day.

Aware of her silence, and of Mr Todd still gazing at her, Lexy tried to think of some appropriate questions to ask.

"She done this sort of thing before?" Straight away she realised the question was impertinent. But Roderick Todd answered readily enough.

"Yes – in fact that's why we had to move from London."

Lexy blinked. Avril was obviously a regular little raver.

"And why it's so important that I nip it in the bud now," continued the cuckolded husband. "I don't want to have to move again."

Lexy nodded. "Yup – I can understand that." Actually, she couldn't understand it at all. But she wasn't here to do psychoanalysis on this oddball.

"Er… does she always go out at the same time when she goes off on these… meetings?" The word on her tongue was 'jaunts'.

"Oh, yes – eight o'clock on the dot," he replied, promptly. "Takes her car. It's a blue Volvo saloon. I've written the details down for you." He indicated the sheet of printed notes.

"And does she always return at the same time?"

He shrugged. "Usually between ten and eleven. It's in the notes."

Lexy regarded him uncertainly, trying to get his measure. Your average red-blooded male would be positively frothing at the mouth if he suspected his other half was playing away from home.

"Any idea who she's meeting?" Perhaps that would get him going.

"It's… more about what she's doing," he said, hesitantly.

Lexy's mouth formed a circle, suddenly comprehending.

He knew who she was meeting, but he didn't know how far things had got. Strolling hand in hand along the beach? Canoodling over a candlelit meal? Or was it directly to a hotel room, without passing Go?

"So basically, you just want me to tail her and…"

"Get some photographic evidence," Mr Todd supplied, earnestly.

"No problem." Lexy glanced at the kitchen where her elderly camera sat just out of sight.

"You can send the photos mobile to mobile, if you like." Mr Todd held up a slim silver lozenge. "My number's there in the notes. Or email them to me."

Lexy gave him a sickly smile.

Her companion stood up, obviously relieved to conclude business.

"Right, I should be on my way. I expect you're busy?"

"Well…" Lexy made a balancing motion with her hands.

"Make a good living from it?"

Lexy looked around. "Keeps me in small china policemen."

He gave a quick smile that faded almost as soon as it appeared. "You're not exactly a stereotypical private detective are you?"

"You mean a chain-smoking, alcoholic, divorced, overweight middle-aged bloke?" She shook her head. "But I'm working on divorced."

"As long as you aren't working on middle-aged bloke. I… er… don't recommend it."

He reached into his jacket pocket. "Here's the deposit. One hundred pounds. And I need you to follow her tomorrow night. Friday, you see."

Tomorrow?

He had caught her involuntary look of alarm. She was so not prepared for this.

"That will be all right, won't it?" he said, urgently. "It's just that I think things are coming to a head."

It wasn't the best way to put it, Lexy thought, considering the circumstances.

She eyed the roll of notes.

Although Roderick Todd looked like an ordinary business-man, there was something about him that made her feel… Her shoulders gave an uncontrolled twitch.

"If it turns out your wife is doing what you think she is," she said, "have you any idea what you're going do about it?" She didn't quite know why she'd asked him this.

The question caught him by surprise, too. "W… well, I'd have to put a stop to it, wouldn't I?" One pale hand went to his mouth, and he nibbled softly at an already half-consumed nail. "Once and for all, I mean."

Lexy's eyes couldn't help flicking back to the banknotes that Mr Todd was still gripping in his other hand. "C'mon!" they seemed to be shouting.

"How, exactly?" she asked.

"By getting her some help or something, I suppose. Is this relevant, Miss Lomax?"

"It's Ms, actually."

He acknowledged this with a conciliatory nod.

"Just like to assure myself that everything's under control," Lexy continued smoothly. "You'd be surprised at how some people react when faced with the evidence." She was so busy congratulating herself on her own quick thinking that she nearly missed Mr Todd's response.

"Oh… yes, I see. Well, it's not as if this is the first time." He gave a small laugh. "But I'm not contemplating violence, if that's what you mean. So – will you do it?"

Try as she might, Lexy couldn't think of a rational reason why not. She nodded, and he thrust the notes at her.

"Oh – I forgot to mention." Mr Todd rubbed his smooth chin.

"She might be out a bit later than usual tomorrow night. I'm… er… going to be at an old school reunion in Lincoln, you see. I'll be heading off tomorrow afternoon, and I won't be back until… er… lunchtime on Saturday, in fact. I'll call you sometime Saturday morning, if that's all right?"

"Fine," said Lexy vaguely, wondering if she was going to have to spend the whole of Friday night sitting in her car outside a cheap hotel.

"Right, I'll be off, then." Roderick Todd rubbed his hands as if glad to be rid of the money and navigated back through the dust cloud to the front door. Moments later Lexy heard his car door slam and the crunch of gravel under receding tyres.

Kinky got up, shook himself, sneezed loudly and trotted through the kitchen on to the veranda.

Lexy stared into the silence.

After a while she followed Kinky outside. She needed to talk over this Avril Todd thing, even though it was almost certainly going to be a one-way conversation. "You there, pal?"

But there was no answering patter of tiny feet.

The wild, sunlit garden had an Eden-like quality about it, and she leaned on the warm veranda railing and lifted her face, eyes closed for a minute. She might have a few problems to deal with, but this was a good place to be dealing with them. No one was going to bother her here.

Nevertheless, a quiet rustling nearby made her eyes snap open again.

"That you, Kinks?"

But it wasn't.

Lexy felt her pupils contract in surprise.

A red deer stag had stepped from the scrub. He stood at the end of the garden and eyed her calmly, branched antlers poised above his head like carved driftwood.

Lexy gazed, captivated. You didn't get this in South Kensington.

18

Then all hell broke loose.

Kinky, snarling like a miniature Tasmanian devil, hurtled across the garden.

"Oh crap," said Lexy.

The deer wheeled around, startled, and lowered its heavily armoured head.

"Oi!" Lexy leapt down from the veranda. "Leave it!" She didn't know if she was addressing Kinky or the stag.

The chihuahua had almost reached his antlered quarry before the latter made a snap decision and leapt hugely but neatly over the picket fence and bounded away. Kinky forced his way through a gap and continued the chase.

Lexy gave a frustrated shout. Stupid little mutt. Never did know when he'd won.

She was standing with hands on hips when Kinky returned, still emitting small snarls. One of his ears sported a long, bloody gash, no doubt from the tangle of gorse and bramble he had raced headlong into. Lexy rolled her eyes, swept him up, and carried him to the kitchen sink to bathe the wound.

"This is going to need stitching," she groaned, as a mixture of blood and water streamed down the plughole. "When are you going to learn, dunderhead?"

The chihuahua gave her a reproachful look, but Lexy wasn't in the mood to be reproached. Last time Kinky had to get an ear stitched, the day he went for an Afghan hound in St James's Park, it had cost her a hundred and fifty quid and a shed-load of grief from the owner.

She eyed the dog speculatively. Perhaps if she made a healing poultice of tormentil? It wasn't called blood-root for nothing – it had mild coagulating properties.

But this was more than a surface wound. Trudging to the bedroom, Lexy shrugged off her now bloodstained t-shirt and pulled on yesterday's again.

3

Minutes later Lexy closed the front door behind her, an unrepentant Kinky tucked under one arm. She considered taking the car, then rejected the idea in case the parking was a nightmare in Clopwolde-on-Sea. Anyway, Kinky wasn't about to bleed to death. In fact, he was looking rather pleased with himself. So instead Lexy strode down the steep gravel lane, through open heath, towards the pastel-coloured seaside village spread out below her on a sparkling bay.

As she drew closer, her stride faltered. She had been expecting something rather more down to earth: one of those ubiquitous British scruffy-but-cheerful seaside resorts, perhaps with an amusement arcade or two, and a bunch of cafés on the seafront selling pie and mash. Somewhere she wouldn't look out of place wearing ripped jeans and sporting a tattoo.

Clopwolde, however, appeared to have been designed specifically with chocolate box lids in mind. Each rose-entwined cottage vied playfully with the next for preposterous prettiness. The names said it all. Buttercup Cottage, Coot Cottage, Mudpuppy Cottage, Pumpkin Cottage…

The meandering high street confirmed her apprehension. It had a rash of cutesy gift boutiques, bijou art galleries, an olde worlde inn bedecked with hanging baskets, a 1930s memorabilia shop called Gentler Times, a generous sprinkling of tea rooms and, somewhat incongruously, an Internet café.

Above it all a large white windmill smirked on a grassy knoll.

Lexy groaned. Passers-by were throwing her sideways looks. Glancing down, she noticed blood leaking through the dishcloth serving as a bandage for Kinky's ear. She stopped outside a dinky stone edifice called Periwinkle Cottage. A woman in crisp green linen was just turning out of the gate, accompanied by a beribboned Yorkshire terrier, which Kinky eyeballed beadily.

"Scuse me," said Lexy. "Is there a vet in Clopwolde?"

The woman's stony eyes swept over Kinky, and met Lexy's with an almost audible clack.

"That dog should be in a basket," she stated.

For a moment Lexy thought she meant a shopping basket. Sod that. She was about to tell the woman that in that case, gay little Fido there ought to be in a handbag.

"It might run off and do further damage to itself," continued the woman. "You people have no idea."

"You people?" Lexy spluttered.

"Go straight along the high street and the surgery is about halfway down on the left, in a little alley," continued the woman, in her loud brittle voice. "That is your dog, I suppose?"

Several passing holidaymakers slowed down, faces agog.

"Yes, thank you," snorted Lexy, hurrying off before she got herself lynched. The supercilious bat had obviously decided that Lexy was some sort of low-life who had just nicked an old dear's pet chihuahua. Anyone would think she'd asked her where the nearest fur glove-maker was.

Lexy rapidly negotiated the drifts of tourists that were starting to fill the high street. She had to dodge out into the road at one point to get past a clot of grey-tops clucking over a billboard in the shape of a palm tree.

It proclaimed, in foot-high letters, a forthcoming production of *South Pacific*, by the Clopwolde-on-Sea Players. Lexy shook her head despairingly. This was so not her kind of place.

Within a minute she was turning from the end of the high street into a side alley which bore a sign announcing that G Ellenger, Veterinary Surgeon, resided in the unexpectedly shabby end building.

As soon as she stepped into the reception area, Lexy became aware of an atmosphere that didn't have anything to do with disinfectant or dogs.

A large woman with a pile of rust-coloured hair stood at the counter holding an indignantly mewing wicker basket in one hand and a small white plastic tub in the other.

Lexy melted into a corner behind a stand of magazines about worms and tetanus.

The woman was reading out loud from the label on the tub. "… and apply frequently to the affected area, blah blah." She had a flat, penetrating, confrontational voice. "So that's what I did. And what happened? The rash got worse."

Lexy glimpsed the receptionist behind the desk, to whom this tirade was being addressed. She was about thirty, hollow-cheeked with quietly furious eyes.

"I'm sure the aloe vera cream wouldn't have made Horace's rash worse, Avril." Her voice shook under the distinctive Suffolk lilt.

Avril. It was Avril Todd. Lexy thought she'd recognised those granite features from the photographs.

"So now I have to pay for antibiotics," Avril continued, ignoring the receptionist. "This quack remedy was a waste of time and money."

Lexy frowned. No need for that.

"Perhaps the rash had reached the stage where it needed something stronger," said the receptionist. "But if you carry on using the cream alongside the medication, it will soothe the inflammation, and make him more comfortable."

"And I suppose when this tub runs out, there will be plenty more at eighteen pounds a go?"

A spot of red appeared on each of the receptionist's hollow cheeks. "Avril, we will happily refund the money if you don't want the cream."

"No, I'll take it," replied Avril Todd, as if she was conferring some kind of favour. She dropped the tub into her handbag and turned to go.

The other woman closed her eyes briefly.

"But," Avril threw over her shoulder, "I'm starting to wonder if the trading standards people might be interested in what's going on here."

The receptionist's face froze.

Lexy's mouth twisted. What a bitch! What bloke in his right mind would be having an affair with someone like that? As she watched Avril Todd's broad back disappear from view, she suddenly found the prospect of tailing her strangely intriguing.

She put Kinky down and emerged from behind the magazine rack.

The hollow-cheeked woman jumped. She had a badge on her tunic that proclaimed her to be Hope Ellenger, Veterinary Practice Receptionist. Was this nervous wreck the vet's wife?

"Er… hi… I'd like to get my dog looked at," said Lexy, somewhat disconcerted by the fact that Hope Ellenger was still looking beyond her to the door through which Avril Todd had just passed. "It's his ear."

"His ear?" The receptionist's voice was vague.

"Yeah. It's torn quite badly. I think it needs stitching."

"Stitching?"

"You know. Needle and thread." Lexy made a sewing motion in front of the woman's nose.

The receptionist focused properly on Lexy for the first time, taking in her cropped hair and tattoo. She managed a thin smile. "Yes. OK. Not a problem." Up close her eyes were bloodshot; she looked like she could do with a good night's sleep.

"Great," said Lexy.

"But I'll have to ask you for the money in advance." She glanced down at a list on her desk. "Ninety-eight pounds, I'm afraid."

Lexy swallowed wordlessly at this unwelcome news, feeling her fingers curl around the roll of fivers nestling so comfortably in her jeans pocket. She brought it forth and handed it over.

Hope Ellenger counted it out with hands that shook a little, and gave Lexy a pound coin and two fifty pence pieces. Lexy regarded the change dismally. At this rate she wouldn't be treating Kinky to a can of Pedigree Chum; she'd be fighting the little git for it.

"I assume you're from the camp?"

"Camp?" Lexy started, giving the woman a hard stare. "I'm not a …"

"Pleasurelands holiday camp?" interrupted the receptionist. "In Marshlands-on-Sea?" From her tone of voice, Marshlands-on-Sea sounded like the sort of place that Lexy should have chosen from the start.

"No – I'm not on holiday. I… live in Clopwolde." Unfortunately.

"Really?" Hope Ellenger's eyes narrowed as she studied Lexy. "You're not Pam Bridgend's daughter are you? Back from India?"

"No. I just moved here. From the city. Escaping the rat-race and all…"

But the receptionist's face had set, and Lexy's voice tailed away.

"You'll be expecting to register with us then?" Her voice was tight.

"Well, yes, please."

"Name?"

"Lomax." Lexy racked her brain, trying to work out why Hope Ellenger was eyeing her so rancidly.

"Dog's name?"

"Kinky," she muttered, wishing, not for the first time, that her mother-in-law had plumped for Prince. Or Lucky.

Hope Ellenger's lips pursed in distaste as she tapped at the keyboard in front of her. "Here you are then." A registration form was passed over the desk. "Where is the animal?"

"Here." Lexy held Kinky up above a display of flea powder packets.

At the sight of him, Hope Ellenger appeared to experience another kind of inner struggle. "A chihuahua," she pronounced at last.

"Yeah – is that OK?" said Lexy, irritability finally bursting through. Perhaps the receptionist would have preferred it if Lexy had turned up with a sodding great elephant.

"The vet has four chihuahuas."

"What's he want – a round of applause?" said Lexy, under her breath.

"I beg your pardon?"

"Er… is the loo through those doors? I need to get some paper to mop him up." She indicated Kinky's bloody ear.

Hope Ellenger ripped some tissues from a box next to her and handed them wordlessly to Lexy.

Lexy made a final grim attempt to smile at the woman. "Will I have to wait long to see Mr Ellenger?"

"You'll be next." She glanced at an appointment book. "When my brother has finished with Floppy."

Brother and sister act then.

Lexy plumped herself down heavily on a plastic chair to fill in her form. How the hell was she going to survive on two pounds until she saw Roderick Todd again? And what if she didn't manage to get a single snap of Avril and lover boy anyway? And where, she added darkly, did Hope Ellenger get off on being so condescending? She wouldn't be in the least surprised if the woman was related to the arrogant cow from Periwinkle Cottage. In fact, everyone in Clopwolde was probably inbred. She should never have fled to this one-pony village. She should have gone to a big, anonymous town and got a cash-in-hand job in a bar, or a factory.

But wherever she went, Lexy thought with a sudden wave of misery, the truth was, she was going to be pretty much alone now.

Except for a tiny mutt with a death wish.

Her black musings were interrupted when a door opposite her opened. Through it emerged a pale, lofty man holding a lop-eared rabbit awkwardly out in front of him. Kinky's lip immediately curled, showing a small fang.

That'll be Floppy and his owner, then, thought Lexy, gripping the chihuahua a little more tightly under her arm. Don't need to be Miss Marple to work that one out.

The man headed towards the receptionist's desk, looking around the surgery as he went. His sombre grey eyes met Lexy's. To her horror she saw them suddenly snap open with the involuntary surprise of recognition.

She immediately turned away, aware of him still staring.

"Don't come over. Don't come over," she heard herself whispering frantically into Kinky's neck.

Lexy had never seen the man before in her life, but she knew that look.

Some while ago she'd made the mistake of appearing in *Heirlooms in Your Attic*, Gerard's long-running TV show. Lexy had been a kind of glamorous sidekick, climbing up loft ladders and helping him forage through boxes of old tat – anything, in fact, that involved her bending over in tight jeans. A number of men began emailing Gerard's website, asking for her vital statistics. One or two had even recognised her in the street. Gerard cut her out of the next series. He couldn't bear to be upstaged. But the damage was done. She had a feeling that this miserable-looking specimen might be a member of the fan club, judging by the way he was gazing at her.

Then Lexy frowned. She kept forgetting. She wasn't a glamorous blonde in tight jeans any more. There was no way on earth this man could have recognised her from the show. So, how else…?

"Kinky Lomax," repeated the receptionist loudly, indicating the surgery door.

Lexy leapt up, keeping her head turned from the strange, disconcerting man.

She dropped her completed form on the reception desk, rapped on the surgery door and bundled quickly through it.

Lexy had already made up her mind what the vet would be like. Irritable, balding, harassed, probably nursing a peptic ulcer. Which is how anyone with four chihuahuas was going to be. She was heading that way herself with just the one.

If he was as offensive as everyone else she had met so far, that was it. She wasn't going to take any more crap from…

"Hi there." He was large and handsome, with wavy golden-brown hair, clear luminous eyes and a perfectly good-humoured countenance. Rather like a well-groomed Labrador, in fact.

"Ms Lomax?" He smiled, showing a flash of even white teeth and healthy pink gums. "I'm Guy Ellenger."

Temporarily nonplussed, Lexy plonked Kinky on the examination bench, unwrapping the dishcloth from his head. He had said Ms. He was a man, and he had called her Ms – without prompting.

He took hold of Kinky confidently. "Let's have a look at you then." His voice had the same Suffolk lilt as the receptionist, although there any resemblance with her seemed to end. "You know what, you're just like my Juan."

"One?" Lexy found herself exclaiming accusingly. "Your sister said you had four."

He flashed that smile at her again. "Yes, that's right. Juan, Jose, Chico and Gomez. I inherited them from my godfather."

"Oh," said Lexy. "I inherited this one too. From my mother-in-law. Ex-mother-in-law, that is." She wasn't sure why she added that last detail.

"What a coincidence!" Their eyes met briefly. "So, are you new to Clopwolde?"

"I moved here yesterday." She watched him closely for signs of disapproval but his smooth face remained neutral.

Probably can't afford to be choosy about who he treats – he obviously needs the money, she thought, looking at the shabby lino and peeling paintwork on the window frames, which in turn reminded her of Otter's End, and her own financial dilemma.

The vet was peering at Kinky's ear. "Nasty cut."

"Yeah. He was chasing a …" Lexy hesitated. She wasn't going to tell him that Kinky had been chasing a chuffing great stag. It was embarrassing and almost certainly illegal. "…a cat."

But she wished she had stuck with the buck. The vet's expression had changed to one of consternation. "Chasing a cat?" he almost snapped. "Did he harm it at all?"

"God, no," said Lexy, suddenly anxious. "Look at the size of him! Any self-respecting cat could deck him with one whack. In fact, that has been known to happen. Thing is, he's always chasing things. He's never actually bitten anything. Main problem is he keeps getting *himself* duffed up. Went after a police horse once and got kicked into the Thames. Had to fish him out with an umbrella. Never learns." Lexy realised that she was babbling.

Her incoherent speech had seemed to work, though, and the vet's former pleasant expression had returned.

"Never bitten anything, you say?"

"That's right."

"Good, good." He nodded vigorously and turned back to Kinky. "Right, I'd better put a couple of stitches in this ear." He tipped some clear liquid on to a wad of cotton wool and dabbed it on the wound, then turned away to rummage in a tray of instruments.

Kinky looked at Lexy dubiously.

She winked at him. It wasn't as if this was the first time he'd faced the needle.

She stared around the room. Mounted on the wall, above the vet's head, was a huge yellowing bone.

"Femur from a St Bernard, that one," said the vet, turning back and seeing the direction of her gaze. "Found the skeleton on the beach."

Lexy swallowed.

"What brings you to Clopwolde, anyway?" he continued, conversationally.

She jumped. "Er… my work."

He smiled genially at her. "And what do you do?"

"Do?" Lexy stared at him. He had eyes like melting toffee. Say something, for heaven's sake.

"Private investigations, actually." The words blundered out like so many Keystone Cops.

The vet stopped in the act of pushing a length of surgical thread through a needle head. His straight dark eyebrows shot up. "Seriously?"

Lexy nodded, internally berating herself.

"Hold him steady, will you?" Guy Ellenger advanced on Kinky. "This shouldn't hurt him."

With practised ease he slid the needle in and gently sewed the gash together. Kinky appeared to be gritting his teeth.

"Um, this private eye business," the vet murmured, as they bent over the chihuahua together. "Is it all muck and bullets, or do you stoop to finding lost cats?"

Lexy could only stare at him.

"It's just that the Carodocs, this couple who live next door to me, are missing their cat. They suspect my dogs."

In spite of her confusion at this sudden turn of events, Lexy nodded to herself. That would explain the vet's earlier third degree about Kinky's homicidal tendencies.

29

"Absolutely ridiculous, of course," Guy Ellenger continued. "Every time they so much as glimpse her through a window they dive under the shed."

"Big, is she?" Lexy tried to imagine a moggy that would make Kinky dive under a shed.

"No. But she is ugly." The vet gave an apologetic shrug at Lexy's expression. "Not her fault, of course, poor thing. She was the runt of a litter of farm cats, and unfortunately she came out rather... well, deformed, to put it bluntly. The farmer dumped her in a ditch when she was about three weeks old. Don't you just love some people?" He shook his head despairingly. "Anyway, she was rescued by my next-door neighbour Tammy. Tammy heard her crying when she was out walking, found her, took her home, and she and her husband have had her there ever since. I'm surprised the cat pulled through, actually, but she seems perfectly healthy now. In fact, I think she's turned into a bit of a handful. They don't let her outside, but I quite often see her climbing the curtains, and running along the windowsills." He grinned. "She adores Tammy. Sticks to her like Velcro when she's allowed. Scares the life out of visitors when they knock on the door and Tammy answers with Princess Noo-Noo draped around her neck like the scarf from hell."

"Princess Noo-Noo?"

"Yes – the names some people give their pets, eh?"

Lexy smiled weakly. "How'd she go missing, then?" She was interested in spite of herself.

The vet gave her an enigmatic look. He snipped the end of the thread, and Kinky stopped gritting his teeth. "I've got some thoughts on that," he said. "I just need a bit of help in proving it."

He flashed another of those white-toothed smiles at her, and reached into a box behind him.

"This'll stop him scratching it, by the way." He fitted a small plastic funnel around Kinky's neck. The chihuahua stared at

Lexy in outrage.

"And crush one of these up in his dinner. One a day for ten days."

He stuck a label on to a brown plastic bottle.

"And… um…" He handed her a white tub. "Dab a bit of this gently round the wound every morning. Help it heal faster. We usually charge extra for this but you can have it for nothing."

"Thanks," she mumbled. She wasn't going to ask why he was handing out the freebies, but as he was in the mood…

"He's started to be a terribly fussy eater." She nodded at Kinky. "Is there anything you can recommend?"

"Let's see." The vet rummaged in a cupboard. "Thought so. One of our suppliers, Doggy Chomps, has brought out a new range of all-singing biscuits – you know, the sort that provide all the nutritional needs. Would you like a sample or two?"

"Yes, please." She smirked at Kinky. "Better take one of each flavour, knowing what he's like."

As Lexy was dropping four packets of dog biscuits into her bag, the door to the surgery suddenly clicked open. A tall, unsmiling teenage girl shimmied in, pulling on a white coat over her cropped top and designer jeans. Lexy glimpsed an expanse of taut tanned stomach and a glittering belly-button jewel. A shiny silver badge pinned to the girl's white coat identified her as Sheri-Anne Davis, Trainee Veterinary Nurse.

"Sorry I'm late," she said, tonelessly. Her blank, leonine face was deeply shadowed under expressionless dark eyes. She looked as if she hadn't slept in a month.

"Don't worry." Guy Ellenger turned to a computer on the table behind the examination bench. "There have only been three so far and…" He gave a sudden exclamation. "Aw, look at this stupid machine. It's doing that thing again."

He pointed to a small flashing icon in the corner of the screen. "Look…"

"S'all right. I'll do it," the girl replied nudging him away. She probed at the keyboard with fingernails that had been beautifully manicured, but looked as if they had recently been chewed at the ends. Like Mr Todd's.

Throwing Lexy a complicit grin, the vet took a disinfectant wipe from a box and started to clean the bench around Kinky.

"Three customers?" Sheri-Anne Davis looked up briefly and dismissively at Lexy. "Who were the other two?"

Guy Ellenger, Lexy noted, seemed unfazed by his trainee nurse's abrupt, familiar manner.

"Man called Milo. Had a rabbit with an eating problem. Gave him some of our tonic."

The girl continued to look at him.

"And, er…" Guy Ellenger's voice tightened. "Avril's been in. Horace has developed a rash." Sheri-Anne Davis was silent, but Lexy had noted her lip curl with distaste at the mention of Avril Todd. She gave the keyboard a final prod. "Right, it's sorted." She moved away and Lexy saw her own details appear on the screen. The receptionist must have entered them already from her application form.

"You angel," exclaimed Guy. "Oh – and if you're going out the back now, can you bung this in the fridge, please." He handed her a foil-wrapped package. "Preferably not next to the urine samples this time. Oops!" This last was directed at Lexy. "Don't let anyone know I keep my sarnies in the surgery fridge."

"Your secret's safe with me," Lexy smiled. Actually, it wasn't. The foil-wrapped package was a forcible reminder of her growing hunger. She was practically salivating looking at it.

She was suddenly aware of the veterinary nurse's long-lashed, expressionless appraisal.

"Er – can you make a start on the drug inventory, please, Sheri?" Guy Ellenger bent down to open a cupboard.

"No problem." The girl headed into a small annexe leading off from the consultation room. Lexy watched the foil package disappear with her, heard a fridge door open and close, then saw Sheri-Anne collecting bottles from a shelf, grabbing at one that almost fell. Despite her inscrutable face, the girl emanated nervous tension.

"Tell you what," she heard Guy Ellenger say. "Why don't you bring this fellow round to my place on Saturday afternoon to meet the boys? About two o'clock, say?"

Lexy almost heard Sheri-Anne's ears snap to attention.

"You could look for clues," he added.

Clues? "Are you hiring me then?" she said in an undertone. Surely this wasn't happening to her. Not twice in one morning.

"If that cat isn't found before Saturday I think I'll have to. What are your rates?"

Lexy thought fast. "Waive your bill if I find it." She was aware that she was talking out of the side of her mouth.

"Done," said the vet, without hesitation. "Well worth it to get the Caradocs off my back."

Lexy wished he wouldn't talk quite so loudly. She also wished she'd had this conversation with the vet before she'd handed his sister ninety-eight pounds. It wasn't like she could go and ask for it back. Not straight away.

She scooped Kinky from the examination bench, aware of how still the veterinary nurse had become.

"Er – where do you live, by the way, Mr Ellenger?" she murmured, *sotto voce.*

"Guy. Call me Guy," he said, resonantly.

"Lexy," she returned.

"Gorse Rise – it's a private road off the south end of the high street, by the church. Backs on to the heath. My place is about halfway along. Kittiwake, it's called."

He opened the surgery door for her.

"OK. See you Saturday afternoon, then," she mumbled,

passing into the waiting room.

"Look forward to it, Lexy," he sang, closing the door.

"My brother isn't on duty on Saturday afternoon," snapped Hope Ellenger as Lexy approached the counter. She had obviously overheard their last exchange.

"I know," said Lexy. "Mr Ellenger... er... Guy and I are meeting... socially."

The receptionist stared at her with an expression that seemed to combine incredulity and loathing. It was a look that went way beyond simple native distrust.

She's jealous, Lexy thought with a sudden rush of insight. She doesn't want to share her precious brother with anyone else, even for an afternoon.

"I see you have some additional medication." Hope was looking at the tub of cream that Lexy was holding. "That'll be..." She glared down at the screen. "Wait – Guy hasn't entered that item."

Before Lexy could explain, the receptionist had stomped towards the surgery.

Lexy hung on nervously, hoping that Guy Ellenger wasn't going into detail with his sister about deals made with private investigators. At this rate the whole village would know.

But Hope reappeared almost immediately and said through clenched teeth, "I understand there will be a settlement when you bring your dog back next week for a check-up." She returned to the counter and rattled at the computer keyboard venomously.

"Fine. Bye, then." Lexy made a dive for the door.

She paused outside, aware of Kinky glaring at her accusingly from inside the plastic funnel.

"It'll be OK," she said bracingly. "I'll get the money back. Hey – all I have to do is find a missing pussy cat. How hard can that be?"

4

As Lexy approached the end of the alley, followed grumpily by the chihuahua, she saw that their way was obstructed by the tall, pale man she had seen earlier. He was standing beside a white estate car, examining a plastic bottle with a label similar to the one on the tub of cream the vet had given Lexy.

The rabbit was sitting upright, peering pensively out of the back window of the car. A small growl emanated from inside Kinky's funnel.

The man stiffened as he saw Lexy approaching, and put the bottle on the car bonnet.

"Mind if I just squeeze past?" she said.

He gazed at her for a long moment, almost hungrily. Oh, great. A weirdo. With a rabbit. And he had definitely recognised her, in spite of her disguise.

"OK, what do you want?" she asked, wearily.

"Er…" He groped inside his jacket.

Lexy heaved an internal sigh. He was a bit old for this sort of thing, but anything to make him go away.

"Look, I'll give you an autograph, right," she said, "but you have to pretend you haven't seen me. I'm down here on a secret project."

Her companion raised an eyebrow.

Lexy found herself looking at an identity card, embossed with a silver crest.

"DI Bernard Milo, Lowestoft CID. Mind if I ask you a couple of questions, madam?"

Lexy felt her face redden, then blanch, then turn a sickly yellow, like a chameleon trying to blend into a trifle.

"Er – what's the problem?" she enquired.

"No problem. Just carrying out some enquiries."

"W… what sort of enquiries?" She could already guess. The sort that would involve him asking her if she knew the whereabouts of a suitcase containing a significant sum of money. She tensed, glancing behind her. The alley was a dead end.

DI Milo pressed his fingers against his forehead, as if he was trying to push a headache away. Lexy stared at him in agonised anticipation.

"I need to confirm what treatment your dog received from Mr Ellenger," he said at last.

What treatment Kinky had received? Lexy almost yelped out loud with relief. She didn't know what in hell this was about, but it wasn't about her.

"He had a cut stitched up." She indicated the chihuahua's neatly sutured ear with a flourish and smiled at DI Milo.

The look of approbation that met her was almost like a physical blow. There was an awkward silence. Lexy tried to ease the tension. "So what was the matter with Floppy?"

"Eh?" The policeman's expression changed to one of alarm.

"Your rabbit?" she reminded him.

"Oh. Yes. Him." He hesitated. "Eating problems."

They looked over at Floppy, who stared back in mid-chomp, a lettuce leaf dangling from his mouth.

"That bag of tricks worked quickly, then." Lexy indicated the plastic bottle on the bonnet, giving the policeman a challenging stare, but his head was now bent over his notebook.

"Have you been registered with this veterinary practice for long?"

"About half an hour. Why are you asking?"

"Can I take your name?"

"Why?" This was so not what she needed.

"Just tell me your name," he said.

Lexy struggled with her conscience. How much of a good

idea would it be to lie to the police?

"Lexy Lomax." Only one way to find out.

"Address?"

Lexy's eyes narrowed. That was going a bit far. For a moment, she considered making up an address, but her wits had temporarily flown.

"Otter's End, Cliff Lane," she mumbled, reluctantly.

As he wrote down the address, his pale forehead slowly wrinkled into a perplexed frown. Lexy stared at him apprehensively. Now what?

She cleared her throat loudly. "Right, I guess I should get on now, if that's OK?" She began to edge past the car.

"Hang on. How much were you charged for that?" He pointed at the tub of cream Lexy was holding.

"Why do you want to know?"

"Just answer the question, please."

"All right. Nothing. I agreed to do Mr Ellenger a small favour in lieu of payment."

The ice-grey eyes opened a shade wider.

"Not that sort of favour," she snapped. "I'm helping him out with a cat problem."

"Are you a pet psychologist, or something?" he enquired, making it sound like 'con-woman'.

"Something like that. Look, I really have to go now."

Determinedly, she squeezed past him. "Come on, Kinky."

"I'm sorry?"

"My dog. I'm calling my dog," she said through gritted teeth, stooping to pick up the chihuahua.

"Oh. Well, thanks for your help. I may see you again." He handed her a business card.

Not if I see you first, mate, Lexy thought. She shoved the card into her jeans pocket, feeling the policeman's unfathomable eyes boring into her back all the way down the high street.

As she hurried on, Lexy started wondering if it had just been coincidence that Avril Todd had been kicking up about the herbal cream she'd been given for her cat's rash, and a police officer had started making enquiries too. A high-ranking one, at that. The rabbit had obviously been a cover. Lexy squinted at the tub the vet had given her. The label just said *For soothing inflammation – apply three times daily.*

She paused in the doorway of a bookshop that appeared only to sell books about Clopwolde, twisted the lid and sniffed at the cream, rubbing it between her forefinger and thumb. Aloe vera, obviously, and something else... smelt like chamomile. Lexy gave another sniff, and nodded. Cloves, too – no mistaking that. It all figured. Aloe vera to soothe, chamomile to reduce inflammation and cloves as an antiseptic and pain-killer, all mixed up in a cream base. The kind of stuff she and her dad used to make. Homemade, in other words.

Lexy shrugged as she replaced the lid. If the Ellengers were selling it for eighteen pounds a go, good on them. They were probably making a tidy little profit. No law against that, as long as it was all legit. She returned the medication to the bag and continued along the high street, examining every shop carefully. When she reached the Co-op, which was housed in a tastefully converted chapel, she produced a small chain and attached one end to Kinky's collar and the other to a convenient low bar outside the shop.

"Right, I'll be back in a sec. Don't... start... any... trouble."

A gnarled old man gaped at her. "He ain't a fighting dog, is he?"

"I had to pull him off a stag earlier."

The pensioner hurried by, giving several looks behind him.

Lexy pushed open the door, mentally prioritising what she could buy for two quid and a handful of coppers. Brown rice and lentils came to mind. That sort of thing. Bit of a contrast to her champagne and ciabatta lifestyle in London.

She picked up a copy of the *Clopwolde Herald* and quickly scanned the Personals column.

Although she was expecting to find it there, it still gave Lexy a strange jolt to see the advert actually written out in black and white.

Private Investigations
Discreet Service – Anything Considered

The Otter's End telephone number was printed underneath.

So Glenda Doyle really had been a bona fide Sherlock.

When they arrived back at Otter's End and Lexy opened the door, it felt like she was entering Death Valley. She fanned the air in front of her and began throwing open windows. Would have been nice to have a cold drink waiting in the fridge.

She checked the answerphone. No new messages. With some misgivings, Lexy picked up the receiver and called the advertising department of the *Clopwolde Herald.*

"Hello. My name's Doyle. I'd like to check on a small ad I have running in Personals."

"'Ang on a mo'," said a bored-sounding female voice. After considerably longer than Lexy's understanding of a 'mo' the voice returned.

"Mrs G Doyle is it?"

"Yes," said Lexy, smoothly.

"I got the original order here. Repeat until September first it says. It's on a bank order. All paid for."

"Right. Thanks."

She replaced the receiver thoughtfully.

Glenda Doyle's ad would keep running for three more months.

5

Lexy went into the kitchen and unpacked her meagre shopping. She needed something fresh and green to supplement it. And she knew exactly where to get that.

She went back out into the midday sun and cast around, collecting soft young leaves from a hawthorn tree, dandelion greens from a flowering clump growing near the cabin, and a bunch of tender nettle tips, protecting her hands to pick the latter.

Lexy gave a wry grin. If only Gerard could see her now, transformed from yesterday's sophisticated city blonde to a dishevelled ragamuffin, revelling in the delights of Mother Nature. She'd gone full circle.

Lexy had met Gerard Warwick-Holmes thirteen years ago, when she'd just turned sixteen. Angelica had left for China, intent on joining an ongoing campaign on behalf of beleaguered wildlife, and she stopped writing after a while. Lexy's dad went into a decline, and became snappish and withdrawn, neglecting his awkward teenage daughter just when she needed him.

As they did the annual rounds in the caravan, Lexy took to visiting towns on route, just to watch the other teenagers – the ones who had homes and normal parents, and went to regular schools with their friends. The ones who wore trendy clothes, and always seemed to be laughing and joking, as if they were enjoying some hilarious party that Lexy couldn't go to.

One day, a scorcher in mid-August, Lexy was mooching around a Sunday market in a small county town near their pitch. Her dad hadn't wanted to walk the two miles into town and back – he was trying to fix the tow hitch or something. There was always something.

Lexy, wearing a dowdy old hippy skirt and a t-shirt which had seen better days, was looking at the second-hand video tapes. She glanced over to the next stall, a big one, selling bric-a-brac. A man was examining a stack of old pictures. Her glance turned into a stare. Wasn't that…?

He turned around and clocked her. A smile hovered over his lips. It was an expression she would get to know very well.

"Hiya." He wore expensive-looking pre-faded jeans, with a white shirt open at the collar. His white-blond hair was gelled into fashionable untidiness, and little rectangular glasses framed his pale blue eyes. He looked like an advert for Gap, except he was about thirty. And he looked even taller in the flesh than he did on the box.

Because it was definitely Gerard Warwick-Holmes, from *Heirlooms in Your Attic* – the antiques expert currently making a name for himself discovering lucrative hidden treasures in people's lofts, attics and cellars.

Lexy swallowed and managed to mumble a greeting. She'd never met anyone famous in her life. His sheen of glamour instantly put everyone around him into the shade.

He was giving her a long stare now. "Have you got a name?"

"L… Alexandra."

"You've caught me doing a bit of research, Alexandra. What do you reckon to this?"

He didn't even bother to introduce himself, so confident was he that she recognised him.

Lexy focused with difficulty on the framed painting that he was holding.

"It's a… p… print," she faltered. "Probably only worth a couple of quid, but the frame's a good one. You could get a tenner for that."

"I can tell you're a fan of the show."

She nodded, letting Gerard Warwick-Holmes think she'd learned that stuff from him, rather than from her dad, who'd been to a few antiques sales himself in his time.

Gerard took a quick look at his watch. "Lunchtime by my reckoning. Would you like to come for a drink with me, Alexandra?"

She reddened. "I'm only sixteen."

He stepped back, glancing around. "Sorry. Sorry. You… look older."

"Yeah, well, I've had a hard life."

He smiled at that, not realising that she wasn't joking, then caught her bleak expression. "OK," he said, seeming to understand, obviously thinking rapidly. "How about a trip to London instead? Tomorrow? See the sights. And I'll get you back by bedtime. Your bedtime that is," he added, hastily.

"Are you kidding?" Lexy blurted. She had only been to London three times, all for demos. It had been kind of hard to see the Trafalgar lions from the middle of a yelling, placard-wielding crowd of peace protesters.

"No. I mean it. We can get a boat trip down the Thames, stop off at the Tower, go up the West End…" His pale blue eyes were hypnotically persuasive. That was the trouble.

Lexy felt her entire spirit soar at the thought of doing all those things with Gerard Warwick-Holmes. He was quite a bit older than her, but that didn't make it bad, did it? It wasn't as if he was married. Lexy knew that, because his divorce from a TV soap star had been all over the tabloids. What she couldn't understand was why he was asking her out when he could have anyone. But why worry about that when…?

Then a problem far more pressing than Gerard's age and recent history enveloped Lexy like a shabby old anorak. "I can't come," she said dully. "I haven't got anything to wear." And there was the small matter of her dad.

"Don't worry," Gerard said, quickly. "We can fix that. Quick trip to Monsoon or somewhere, before we get the boat. What are you, a perfect size ten?"

No one had ever described her as perfect before.

He left her a mobile number and prowled away through the stalls like an albino tiger, throwing her back a meaningful blue glance.

Lexy sneaked out of the van early the following morning, leaving her dad a note to say she was going to town. She just didn't specify which town.

When she got back that evening she was wearing designer jeans, a funky blue sequinned top and jewelled flip-flops. A new mobile phone resided unseen in a new beaded shoulder bag. Gerard had dropped her off in a quiet lane a couple of hundred yards out of sight and sped off immediately. He seemed to relish the cloak and dagger stuff.

"Good time?" her dad asked. He was leaning on the van door, smoking a roll-up.

"Yes." Lexy gave him a brilliant smile.

Her dad squinted at her. "Those new clothes?"

"Just a couple of things."

"How much?"

"A few quid. I got them from the cheap shop. Used my bracelet money."

Martyn Lomax looked almost convinced. He was aware that Lexy braided brightly coloured bracelets in the evenings, and sold them for cash where she could. He hadn't questioned her any further, and she and Gerard Warwick-Holmes managed to meet a few more times behind his back. Lexy even visited his smart South Kensington flat one afternoon.

That was all until her dad picked up a newspaper and saw a photo of his daughter and Gerard Warwick-Holmes in the gossip column.

TV's Mr Heirloom seems to have acquired a bijou treasure of his own, the column ran. *But she's no antique…*

After a barrage of furious questions about how and when and where they had met, and how the hell long it had been going on, and how the hell old Gerard was, Martyn Lomax had finally thrust the paper in her face.

"Has this bastard tried anything on with you?"

"Nope," Lexy replied, brick-red and unblinking.

"So why don't I believe you? Oh Lexy – he's got you lying already. We're talking about someone who lives in the shallow, material, narrow-minded world that we rejected years ago."

"That you rejected," Lexy burst out. "I never got a chance. Anyway, you're happy enough to watch his shallow, material, narrow-minded TV show every week."

"That was before I realised he'd been screwing my sixteen-year-old daughter."

There was a horrible silence.

At that moment Lexy hated her dad, hated him for making what she and Gerard had sound grubby. She just wanted to hurt him, and keep on hurting him. "Actually, he's asked me to marry him."

Martyn Lomax went pale. He glanced down at the crumpled newspaper again, spoke quietly. "What would your mother think?"

"This would be the mother I haven't heard from for eighteen months because she's more concerned about saving the planet than being with me?"

It was too close to the truth.

Lexy stared at her dad's receding back, already regretting her words, but too proud to admit it. Her campaigning mother was never coming back, and they both knew it. She was probably in the Philippines by then, trying to stop illegal logging. Or chasing a Japanese whaling boat. Stuff Lexy used to care about. But what was the point? We were all going to hell in a handcart anyway – at least that was what Gerard reckoned. Might as well enjoy the trip. Lexy groped in her beaded bag for her mobile phone.

"Can you come and get me? Now?"

She never saw her dad again.

Lexy walked slowly into the log cabin, washed her green bounty and simmered up a pan of couscous.

"I'm gonna make a hedgerow salad just like we used to in the van," she called to Kinky, a little too brightly. "And it's as well my old man taught me my aconite from my elder, or you might be following Mrs Todd on your own tomorrow."

When she had finished eating, Lexy leaned back on the sofa next to Kinky, and picked up her old camera again. It had a new film in it, never used. Touching the wooden coffee table for luck, she took off the lens cap.

"Smile," she said to Kinky. He glared at her, but she took the picture anyway, relieved to hear a familiar click.

Lexy leaned back, allowing Roderick Todd to swim into view. She wasn't able to pinpoint exactly what she found wrong with the man, but he was definitely odd. One of his oddities, she decided, was the way he had phrased things when talking about his wife's transgressions.

She might be getting into something she can't control.

Lexy scrunched up her face. Avril Todd looked like a woman who was entirely in control of her world, definitely not the sort to make a fool of herself with a bout of uninhibited passion.

She checked out the photos again. They hadn't quite done Avril justice. She had been a lot more morose in the flesh – one of those perpetually discontented middle-aged women, with scowling eyes and a mouth permanently wedged down at the corners. The sort of woman who always looked at the cloud, never the silver lining.

But someone other than her husband must have discovered a quality in Avril that floated his boat.

And what else had Roderick Todd said? Something about wanting to nip it in the bud there and then? Not wanting to have to move again.

Move? If everyone moved because their partner had an affair the whole country would be in perpetual motion.

Lexy frowned. Mr Todd even seemed to know who his wife was meeting. What he really wanted – and this was the other strange thing – was photographic evidence of exactly what they were doing. As if he couldn't guess.

But at least Roderick Todd had been civil during their exchange, unlike Hope Ellenger.

Even though Lexy had met the receptionist on what was clearly a bad day for her, she had been inexplicably rude. Particularly when she discovered that Lexy had moved to Clopwolde from London.

Lexy shuddered when she remembered the singular look of hatred the woman had thrown at her when she realised that Lexy was 'seeing' her brother that coming Saturday. Even though this was genteel Suffolk, it occurred to her that she was a tad exposed up here on her own with half a million quid under the bed and the world's smallest guard dog.

She shifted uncomfortably. She really ought to do something about that money, but she needed a contact. Perhaps the vet could help out there. He probably knew the right people.

Guy Ellenger, Lexy considered, seemed to be everything that his sister wasn't. Engaging, kind, funny, understanding. And he had called her Ms. He was almost too nice.

Although, when she had accidentally blabbed that she was a private eye, he had been quick enough to take advantage of it and ask if she could look into the disappearance of that deformed cat. It was clearly preying on his mind. Lexy was no cat expert, but she knew from the number of posters on lamp-posts she had seen in her life that cats had a tendency to disappear from home, even those kept under lock and key. And how would a pampered moggy like that fare in the countryside around Clopwolde, if that's where it ended up? Finding the thing might prove a little more tricky than she first thought. She rubbed her nose. With any luck it might turn up of its own accord before Saturday and save her the trouble. It wasn't that she didn't want a full refund on the money she gave to the vet – just that the iniquities of Avril Todd were more than enough to cope with for someone only pretending to be a private investigator.

She found herself squinting at the Todds' address again.

4 Windmill Hill, Clopwolde-on-Sea.

"Better take a quick trip over there this afternoon and check out where this house is," she said to her canine companion. "Don't want any wrong address balls-ups."

Kinky's eyes conveyed the information that he wasn't going anywhere with this stupid funnel on.

"Hope she doesn't drive too fast when I'm following her," Lexy went on, now pacing the living room restlessly. "Her Volvo'll leave the Panda standing. How embarrassing would that be?"

Lexy had spotted the lime green Fiat Panda in a driveway in Ealing a few days ago. She needed a car as part of her escape bid, and this one was taxed, MOT'd and a bargain at one hundred and fifty pounds. She bought it on the spot with her rapidly-dwindling cash reserve. Didn't drive as well as the Mercedes Coupé she'd been used to, but she wasn't going to keep anything Gerard had bought her. Anyway, it got her to Suffolk in one piece. Just about. Protesting a lot.

She glanced down at Roderick Todd's notes again. Perhaps this whole private surveillance gig might not be quite the piece of madeira she had originally thought. She could do with a bit of advice right now, as it happened. How would Glenda Doyle have gone about it? She began to pad around the cabin, checking what Glenda had left, as if that would give her some kind of clue.

47

There wasn't much. A brown waxed jacket, size sixteen, hanging in the hall cupboard. Might come in handy if Lexy put on a couple of stone and lost all her dress sense. A knobbly walking stick propped up by the front door, looking like it had been made from the root of some alien vegetable. The stout brown brogues. All seemed to suggest a lot of footwork. The large magnifying glass in the kitchen drawer, of course, although Lexy had a feeling she wouldn't need that on her first job, unless Avril Todd had hooked up with a very inadequate lover.

And that seemed to be about it.

Lexy arranged her own meagre pieces among Glenda Doyle's. A few clothes, all practical – jeans, t-shirts and a fleece, which she hung in the empty wardrobe; some bathroom necessities; a copy of *Culpeper's Herbal*; a slim, oddly-shaped musical instrument case; a portable CD player and half a dozen CDs, a small bag of essential oils, and a compass.

Finally she withdrew from her rucksack a framed photograph of her mother being manhandled by the police during a dockside demonstration against the export of veal calves. Lexy had always thought this photograph caught Angelica Lomax particularly well.

She put the photo in the very centre of the mantelpiece, above the fake flame gas fire. "Go Mum," she said, "wherever you are."

6

After a restless night, Lexy awoke early and sloped down into Clopwolde, a still-sulking Kinky in tow. A silvery haze hung over the village, promising another day of brilliant sunshine, and in anticipation café owners were already pulling down striped awnings and setting out tables on the pavements.

Lexy was studying the adverts in a newsagent's window, when a voice hailed her. "Ms Lomax?"

She twisted around, alarmed.

"Hello… again." It was Hope Ellenger, the vet's receptionist, standing stiffly behind her.

"'Lo," replied Lexy warily, hoping she wasn't in for any more grief from the woman.

"How's your dog?"

"My walking lampshade, you mean?" Lexy threw Kinky a sardonic glance. "He'll live."

A tentative smile hovered on the receptionist's lips. "Look, I want to apologise to you for being so rude yesterday," she said.

Lexy hadn't been expecting that. "Don't worry about it," she replied gruffly.

"No, really." Hope Ellenger grasped hold of Lexy's arm. "I've felt awful ever since. You caught me in a really bad way, I'm afraid."

Lexy nodded mutely. Hope had caught her in a really bad way too. She didn't want to start screaming, but if the woman gripped her new tattoo any harder, Lexy thought she might have to.

"I don't want you to feel that Clopwolde-on-Sea is an unfriendly place. Please, let me buy you a coffee. There's a really nice café over the road." She darted anxious glances at Lexy as she spoke.

"But I've got…" Lexy inclined her head at Kinky, managing to free her arm.

"Not a problem. Tuck him under the table – they won't even notice him. You'll behave yourself, won't you, poppet?" This last was directed at Kinky, who was looking distinctly truculent, having just noticed a doberman approaching.

"OK… thanks," said Lexy, looking back at the newsagent's adverts. There was one offering work at a local plant nursery. A nice sensible job that didn't involve stalking sex-crazed women or searching for mutant cats. Someone else might have called about it by the time she got back.

"Great!" Hope herded Lexy across the road. Kinky followed reluctantly, emitting small snarls from his funnel. She opened the door of a gingham-themed café called Kitty's Kitchen. Lexy leant down to pluck up Kinky, concealing him under her shoulder bag as best she could.

The aroma of freshly ground coffee hit them as they went in, mingling with a pleasant low murmur of chat and chink of crockery.

"Let's sit over there," said Hope, indicating a dark corner behind an oak pillar.

Lexy thrust the still irritable Kinky under the long white tablecloth, and watched while Hope fussed with her serviette, picked up and put down the menu several times and seemed at a loss for words. Her eyes, Lexy couldn't help noticing, were every bit as red and bloodshot as they had been the day before, and her cheeks seemed even paler. She obviously didn't get that good night's sleep.

"Are you all right?" Lexy asked, bluntly.

"Yes, yes. I'm fine," insisted the receptionist, with false brightness.

An awkward pause followed.

"Look, this isn't about me going to see your brother at home

on Saturday, is it?" Lexy said. "Because it's not like I've got any…"
Any what? Designs on him? Intention of seducing him?

But Hope Ellenger was frowning uncomprehendingly. "I never thought… no, this is something else. It's rather difficult, actually."

Lexy stared at her with new consternation. What was rather difficult?

"I…" Hope broke off. A stout woman in a gingham apron had materialised at Lexy's shoulder.

"Hello, Kitty." Hope's voice was as brittle as a charcoal twig.

"Hello, dear. What can I get you and your friend?" The woman peered curiously at Lexy.

"Er…" Lexy glanced distractedly down the list of beverages. "Just a black coffee, thanks."

Hope glanced quickly up at Kitty. "Double espresso for me, please. And… I don't know… chocolate croissants?"

The woman nodded. "Anything to eat for you, dear?" she asked Lexy.

"No – I'm fine, thanks," Lexy replied, tersely. She just wanted the woman to be gone, so that she could hear the worst.

Hope waited until Kitty had bustled out of earshot.

"I have this problem," she said, in an undertone.

"OK," said Lexy, slowly. Why was Hope Ellenger coming to a total stranger with her problems?

"I…" Suddenly a tear shivered in each of Hope's eyes.

"Hey, don't get upset, now." Lexy cast around nervously, wishing that she could pass the woman on to someone else. "If it's a… personal thing, isn't there someone you can tell who can really help you?"

"Yes – I'm telling you," Hope rejoined, wiping her eyes fiercely. Her voice dropped to a whisper. "You're a … *private investigator*, aren't you?"

"What? I'm not exact… who told you that?"

"Guy, of course. I got it out of him, actually. I knew some-thing was up when you said you were going to visit him. Anyway – I want to hire you."

"To do what?" This couldn't be happening. Not three times in the space of twenty-four hours. What was it with this village? She eyed Hope. What could this be about – another lost animal? Money missing from the RSPCA collection tin on the reception desk? Or some scam involving…

"Find out who's sending me poison pen letters," whispered Hope.

"Poison pen letters?" That was a turn up. Despite herself, Lexy was interested. "What – nasty ones?"

"Is there any other sort?" Hope's lips pulled tightly inwards in a way that told Lexy more tears were approaching.

"How long's it been going on?"

"I got the first one six w…weeks ago."

"How many have you had?"

"Three."

Lexy considered, while Hope picked up a paper napkin and blew her nose. She and her folks often used to get anonymous letters shoved under the van door, or chucked through the window. Pretty unpleasant ones, too. Stuff you don't forget.

"You told the police?"

Hope shook her head violently. "I want to keep this as low key as possible. It could have… implications. Anyway, I just couldn't bear to have it raked up again." She put her head in her hands, looking at Lexy through splayed fingers.

"You told anyone about them? Your brother?"

"No one. You're the only person I've told. It would devastate Guy. He does a good impression of a grounded human being, but he's really a mass of neuroses."

Was that a fact? Lexy filed this unexpected piece of information away for later analysis.

52

"Any idea who's sending them?"

"No. But it's either someone who knew me and my family a long time ago, or someone who's been deliberately doing some research. Either way, it's someone who really wants to hurt me."

"Can I ask what took place – you know, in your past?" Lexy eyed her steadily, expecting a rebuff.

Hope was silent for a moment, then, eyes cast down, she began speaking in a low voice. "We were brought up on a big old farm outside the village."

Something in her voice gave Lexy a prickle of fear.

"Our f… father…" Hope swallowed hard. "He was a drunk, an alcoholic." She closed her eyes. "He was abusive to our mother – violent. Accused her of all sorts of senseless things, from not cooking the dinner to his liking, to sleeping her way around the entire neighbourhood. Any excuse for him to lay into her with both fists." She paused. "Basically, he was ill and needed help, but Guy and I were too young to understand that. We hated him. We kept telling mum to leave him. But she wouldn't. She was too frightened of causing a scandal. Can you believe that?"

Lexy shook her head, saying nothing, just letting Hope get it out. She felt torn between sympathy, morbid fascination and guilt because the receptionist was only telling her all this because she thought she was talking to a real private detective.

"No one except us knew what he was like," Hope went on, her voice now hoarse with emotion. "He only used to drink at home. He was never drunk in public. He was a respected man in the community. Can you imagine that? A pillar of the local Rotary Club, Farmers' Union, you name it…"

She shook her head. "Anyway, to cut a long story short, one night, twenty-five years ago, when I was eight and Guy was ten, he got paralytic on a litre of whisky someone had given him, and started beating the hell out of mum." Hope's eyes went dark. "Then he dragged her upstairs by her hair like a bloody caveman, while she screamed the place down."

She began shredding her napkin, her hands shaking. "I was hiding in Guy's room. I always used to when he started drinking. We'd listen to music through a shared set of earphones so we didn't have to… you know…"

"Yes," said Lexy, thinking about her own father, a world away from this. And a world away from her, now.

"Well, this time Guy and I decided to call the police. I had got as far as dialling 999 on the upstairs phone, while all this screaming was going on. Guy was behind me… we suddenly heard this awful crashing, thumping sound." Hope paused, her eyes wide, and unfocused. "The bastard had fallen downstairs and broken his neck. He was stone dead."

"Christ," said Lexy, softly.

"When we realised he was dead, we were all crying," Hope continued, speaking faster now, as if she wanted to get the words out before they stuck in her throat. "But Guy and I were actually crying with relief and hugging each other. Is that awful?"

"No… no." Lexy passed Hope another napkin.

"Our mother thought we were wicked to be rejoicing," said Hope. "She called an ambulance, and the police came, and there was an inquiry." She gave a humourless laugh. "Even after death he kept hurting us. They didn't accept that it was an accident. We all had to give statements. Guy and I… we didn't see what had happened. I think the police thought our mother had pushed him, because it was obvious he had been drinking, and there had been some sort of scene. But that was never proven. In the end the verdict was death by misadventure."

She pushed back her hair. "But the damage was done. Local people, who had no idea what our father was really like, started whispering, saying that mum really had pushed him. They reckoned she did it deliberately so she could hook up with another local farmer she was friendly with. Then a hate campaign started in earnest. Mum couldn't take it. She sold up, put the money in trust for us, brought us to Clopwolde to our godparents, who had just moved here, and then she walked into the sea down near Sizewell and drowned herself. Like she was finally admitting guilt for what she'd done." Hope nodded, emphasising this last fact.

"I'm sorry," said Lexy ineffectually, appalled by the tale. "Do *you* think she was guilty?"

Hope looked down. "I do think she might have been having an affair. But Guy and I didn't see what happened, so I guess we'll never know."

"Can't have been easy."

Hope gave a faint smile. "We survived. Local people gradually forgot, and new faces replaced old ones. Our godparents were wonderful, considering they'd had a couple of screwed-up kids dumped on them when they were looking forward to a peaceful retirement.

"Anyway, as time went on, Guy did well at school and decided to become a vet. We settled here and eventually bought the practice with the money we'd inherited, and we bought our two properties, and we've been happy ever since." She paused. "At least I *was* happy…"

She opened her handbag. "Then I got this. The first one. Delivered by hand to the surgery." She gave Lexy a small white envelope.

Lexy, resisting an urge to pick it up with the corner of a napkin, took it reluctantly.

Hope threw her a warning look. Kitty was approaching with a tray.

"There we are, my dears. One black coffee, one double espresso, and two chocolate croissants."

Hope immediately grasped her cup.

"How are the driving lessons, going, dear?" Kitty asked.

Hope grimaced. "Bit of a struggle." She glanced sheepishly at Lexy. "I had my third one this week – I think the instructor is even more afraid than I am."

"Well – keep at it." Kitty waddled off, and Hope gave a nervous giggle which was cut off as Lexy, with some trepidation, slid out a sheet of paper from the envelope. It was pasted with an assortment of letters cut from magazines. If there was a text-book on how to construct and word a poison pen letter, this one would have illustrated it.

I KNOW WHO KILLED YOUR FATHER

Lexy stared at the words, feeling a chill slice through her.

"And you've had two more?"

Hope nodded. She drained the last of her coffee with a grimace.

"Same wording?"

"Pretty much." Hope's face crumpled.

"It's OK. We'll figure something." Figure something? Figure what? What was she saying?

Lexy replaced the letter distractedly in the envelope and handed it back to Hope.

"Were all the letters delivered by hand?"

"Yes."

"Any pattern – like were they all delivered on the same day of the week?"

"I'm not sure. I'll try to remember. All three I've picked up on the mat with the morning post, I know that."

"Can I see the others?"

A strange, guarded look suddenly came over Hope's face. "They're much of a muchness," she said.

Lexy studied her. "I can't help you if you don't tell me everything."

"I've told you a lot more than I've ever told anyone else."

"I need to know every last detail if I'm going to make a plan."

"A plan, eh?" A sudden fruity, jovial voice made Lexy and Hope jump violently. "The plan's the thing!"

A floridly handsome man had materialised at their table. He had a shock of rich chestnut hair which he now flicked from his eyes with what seemed like a practised gesture. Lexy was aware of the rapid appraisal he gave her.

"Bloody hell, Tristan," Hope put her hand to her chest. "You nearly gave me a heart attack."

"Guilty conscience, obviously," he purred. "Anyway, who's this you're conspiring with?"

"I'm Alexandra Lomax," said Lexy coldly, annoyed at this intrusion. Hope seemed temporarily fazed by the man's arrival. Lexy wondered how much of the conversation he'd heard. "I've just moved to Clopwolde," she added.

"And you are a most welcome addition," said the new arrival, turning the full force of his copper-coloured eyes on her.

Lexy gave him a weary smile. A tea-shop Lothario. All they needed.

"Er… Lexy, this is Tristan Caradoc," said Hope, recovering herself. "He and his wife Tammy live next door to my brother."

Oho. The couple with the deformed cat. Or rather, without the deformed cat.

"That's right, Hopeless. Ruin any chance I might have had of sweeping this girl off her feet by telling her I'm already married." He was almost maniacally cheerful.

"And I thought it was me you were trying to sweep."

"Oh, that was last week, darling. A man can only take so much rejection." He turned to Lexy. "Don't mind us, we're always like this. How are you finding our little village?"

"Bit by bit and slowly," said Lexy. "I only arrived yesterday."

"Then you must let me show you around," he said, throatily. "I do a marvellous ghost walk." He waggled his fingers next to his face. "Very scary."

Hope cleared her throat.

"Tammy and I moved here ourselves about ten years ago," he went on, quickly. "Got rather jaded with the city theatre scene."

Lexy saw a look of despair pass across Hope Ellenger's face that she sensed had nothing to do with anonymous letters.

"Tammy was actually rather a well-known actress," Tristan continued. "You may have heard of her… she's been in *Lovejoy*, and *Bergerac* and numerous Beeb dramas. And… ahem… I've been known to tread the boards a bit, too."

"Really?" said Lexy politely.

"Do you try your hand at all?" he continued, appearing not to realise that she didn't know him from Adam. "We could do with some new life in our little am-dram group here in Clopwolde. We're doing *South Pacific* this season. Perhaps you should come along for an audition."

Lexy had a sudden insane vision of herself singing *I'm Gonna Wash That Man Right Outa My Hair*.

"We're a very small group," Tristan went on. "But perfectly formed. We have to rope in the local school kids for the crowd scenes."

"Maybe when I've settled in a bit," Lexy demurred. Or when hell freezes over.

He gave a mock-pout, and turned his attention to Hope. "So, are you ready for the annual bun-fight tonight?"

Hope's hand flew to her mouth. "Oh, Triss, I'd forgotten. I don't know if I'm going to be able to make it."

He cast up his eyes. "It's going to be a very poor showing at this rate, because Tammy won't go anywhere at the moment, of course, and she won't allow me out socialising either." He preened himself. "Not unescorted anyway, with my reputation – ha-ha! So I thought to myself – Tristan, you might as well do your ghost walk and earn a few quid instead. I mean," he went on quickly, "I'm just as cut up as Tammy about poor little

Princess. But we all have our different ways of dealing with it, don't we?"

Lexy pricked up her ears.

"There's no news, then?" Hope gave him an anxious glance.

Tristan looked grave. "We've searched everywhere. Tammy's frantic."

"I'll keep on asking people," said Hope. "Guy's been looking everywhere too – he's ever so upset about this, you know."

Tristan gave her an awkward look. "It was Tammy who got the idea about the dogs into her head, you know. Obviously, *I* don't seriously think they…"

"Well, I wish you'd convince her," Hope cut in.

Lexy watched Tristan with interest. Guy Ellenger had given her the impression that the Caradocs were united in thinking that his chihuahua collective had murdered their beloved moggy.

"I'll try, but you know what she's like when she gets a bee in her bonnet." Tristan flicked his chestnut hair again, and turned back to Lexy. "Are you sure you wouldn't like to come for that audition?"

"Quite sure, thanks," affirmed Lexy.

"Nothing I can do to persuade you? You'd make a perfect principal boy with that lovely little crop. *Dick Whittington* here we come, eh?"

"Oh, shut up, Tristan." Hope pushed herself up with a loud scrape of her chair.

Tristan shut up. He gave Lexy a quick shrug and a wry smile. "Nice to have met…"

"Excuse me." Kitty suddenly popped up like an aggrieved Judy in a puppet show. "Do you have an… animal with you?" The query, delivered with some force, was directed at Lexy.

"Only a very small one," said Lexy, apologetically, using her thumb and forefinger to indicate Kinky's size. "He's under the table."

"Oh, no he isn't." The manageress pointed.

Kinky was over by the cake trolley, awkwardly but determinedly wolfing down a cream horn. There was also a ravaged chocolate éclair beside him on the floor, and he had very clearly licked the side of a frosted carrot cake. The other customers in the café had started laughing and pointing.

"Oh, crap," said Lexy.

"That's not one of Guy's little bas…?" Tristan looked confused.

"No, it's mine. Kinky," Lexy breathed despairingly.

Tristan Caradoc instantly gave her an appreciative glance.

"Kinky, eh?" he murmured.

Lexy closed her eyes. She was going to have to give that dog a different name. She strode over to the chihuahua.

"Can't take him anywhere," she apologised to Kitty, grabbing him up. Globules of cream dropped from his funnel on to the oak floor.

"He's not supposed to be here in the first place," the manageress reminded her. "For reasons of hygiene."

"Yeah, I know – and I'm sorry about the cakes," said Lexy. "I'll… er… pay for them, of course." And how would she do that, exactly?

"No, it's all right, put it on my bill," said Hope.

"I couldn't let…"

"Now, now – allow me to sort this out, ladies." Tristan produced a wallet and peeled off a couple of ten pound notes. Ordinarily Lexy would have rather walked over hot coals than let strangers bail her out, but if they were actually going to argue over it…

She gave Tristan a quick smile of thanks.

"Ghost walk – ten o'clock, tonight," he murmured. "Special one, just for you." He thrust a small leaflet at her.

"Lovely." She nodded weakly, slipping it into her back pocket.

"Is he for real?" Lexy said a few moments later, outside the café.

"Oh, yes," said Hope. "In fact, that's the problem. He's been the archetypal ham for so long that he's actually started living it."

They grinned at each other, and by common consent set off along the high street towards the sea front. Ahead of them a heat haze sprang up from the road, making everything shimmer.

"Think he overheard much?"

Hope shook her head. "Even if he did, he won't remember. His only real interest is himself."

They walked on in silence for a while.

"So, will you do it?" Hope asked, looking straight ahead.

Lexy bit her lip. "Listen, I do really want to help you, but whoever wrote those letters must be pretty sick. If you don't tell the police, they might send something equally vile to someone else. Anything could happen."

Hope's shoulders slumped. "Just for a couple of weeks, then?" she pleaded. "Investigate for a fortnight, and if you don't find anything I'll hand the letters in to the police."

Lexy considered. It wouldn't hurt, she supposed, just to make some brief enquiries. "All right," she said, slowly.

Hope broke into a grateful smile and started thanking her profusely. Lexy waved her away. "Listen, it would help if I had a starting place. Are you quite sure you can't think of anyone here who might have a grudge against you?"

"No," said Hope. "I keep myself to myself. I don't think I've ever made an enemy of anyone." But her eyes were carefully blank, Lexy noted.

"Any indication that someone else you know might have got one of these letters?"

Hope shook her head. "If it was anything like mine, they probably wouldn't want to shout about it anyway, would they? That's the whole point."

61

"Guess so. OK, I'll try to think of another angle. But you have to show me those other two letters." The letters that would hold the clue to whatever Hope was hiding.

"I'll dig them out," Hope said, reluctantly. "By the way, how much do you…?"

Lexy steeled herself. Go on, say it. Say, Two hundred and fifty pounds, please, with a deposit of fifty pounds payable now.

"If I find out anything worth knowing, we can settle up then," she found herself saying, without quite knowing why. Talk about looking a gift horse in the mouth. She could almost hear Kinky's heavy sigh.

"Thank you. I can't tell you how much I appreciate this." Hope looked tearful again, but composed her face quickly to greet an elderly couple approaching from the other direction.

"I guess you know everyone around here," said Lexy, when the pair had passed on.

"Oh, yes. There's not many Clopwolders I wouldn't be able to name. That's why I don't want my past becoming public property again…"

They reached the promenade, and leaned on the pastel green railings. The small beach was beginning to fill with holiday-makers, staking out their patch of sand and shingle with towels, deckchairs, wind-breaks and other fortifications. The shrieks of children mingled with those of gulls.

"So why were you so upset yesterday morning?" Lexy enquired, with studied indifference. "Was it me?"

Hope looked sheepish. "Partly. I was tense anyway, because of these letters. Then one of our customers, Avril Todd, came in. She's such a bitch." Hope gripped the railing, making her knuckles stand out as white as shells. "She's been complaining about our complementary medicine. It's all so petty. We've been selling alternative remedies alongside our conventional medicine for ages now and whatever profit we make from them goes towards helping people on low incomes pay for treatment for their pets."

"Bit like Robin Hood?" Lexy suggested, remembering the freebie Guy had given her, and wondering if she looked that much like a charity case.

"Well, we don't exactly rob the rich, but we do make a point of suggesting to our well-heeled customers that their pekes and shi-tzus and Persian cats would benefit from something from our alternative range. Trouble is, Guy made the mistake of recommending the stuff to Avril Todd. She reckoned it didn't work, probably because she hadn't been using it properly, so she's trotting around the village broadcasting the fact, and now she's threatening to go to the Trading Standards people." Hope made a noise of disgust.

Lexy nodded. Enter Detective Inspector Peculiar. Sounded as if Avril Todd had made a little visit to the police, too.

"And it's not only that," went on Hope, her eyes sparking angrily. "When they moved here, she and her husband bought two beautiful little cottages in Windmill Hill and knocked them into one. Sacrilege! *And* they've put in PVC replacement doors and windows. They've ruined two homes which should have gone to local families instead, except the Todds paid an inflated price for them, of course."

Lexy opened her mouth to speak.

"And even worse," Hope continued, "Avril's joined the am-dram group. She came for an audition, and made a hell of a fuss when Maurice, that's the director, didn't select her. In the end he gave her a job helping out backstage, and the next thing we knew she was props manager. Then she did a couple of walk-on parts, and before we knew it, she'd joined the cast."

Hope shook her head disbelievingly. "She's one of those people who deliberately set out to make themselves indispensable. As well as the props and bit parts she does all the running around, gives us lifts when we're playing at other venues so people can have a drink after the show, bullies local businesses into giving sponsorships and God knows what else." She expelled a long breath, and Lexy managed to get a word in.

"What's her husband like?"

"Rod Todd? He's a wuss. A doormat. She's got him right under her thumb." No surprise there, then.

"And is Avril the flirtatious type?" Lexy quickly continued. She might as well take the opportunity to make some enquiries about her forthcoming surveillance job.

Hope regarded her in astonishment. "Good grief, no. She's Margaret Thatcher's evil twin." She paused. "You saw her."

True.

"Anyway," Hope continued, "I was already uptight when you turned up. Then as soon as I looked at you I thought you were a visitor from this holiday camp over at Marshlands. It attracts the sort of people who…" She paused, awkwardly.

"Have tattoos, ripped jeans and close crops?"

Hope looked apologetic. "Hence my request for the money up front."

"Bet you were surprised to see I had a chihuahua, instead of a pit bull."

"Yes, I really lost the plot at that point. Especially when you told me you'd moved to Clopwolde. I thought you must be some kind of inverted snob."

Lexy grinned. "If it's any comfort, all I own of Clopwolde is a decaying log cabin."

"Must be one of the last ones left up Cliff Lane," said Hope. "There used to be about ten of them up there – all built in the seventies, I think, by a local landowner hoping to make a few quid from the holiday trade."

"What happened to the others?" Lexy asked.

Hope shot her a quick look. "Haven't you been to this part of the world before?"

"Nah. All this happened in a bit of a hurry," Lexy explained. "But," she forged on, seeing a certain curiosity alight on Hope's face, "I'm probably only here for a short while. Have to see how it goes."

"Oh…" Hope looked poised to ask an awkward question.

Lexy straightened up. "Right, better go and… get some provisions," she said. If only. "I'll… er… be in touch later about the other business. Try not to worry too much."

Try not to worry too much? Who was she trying to kid?

7

Lexy made her way back to Otter's End through a heath splashed vibrant yellow with flowering gorse. But she barely noticed this pleasing display as she marched along, forehead corrugated.

Poison pen letter writers were the pits, she thought. Gutless, spiteful, ignorant… she remembered a letter that got pushed under the van door when she was a kid and her parents were trying to find a place to stay for a while. Near Rochester, it was.

Piss off gypos. No one wants you in this town. Your worse than shit.

Angelica Lomax had taken one look, crumpled it up, yanked open the van door and leapt out, shouting and railing, black hair tumbling like a thundercloud.

Her father, however, retrieved the piece of paper, flattened it out and looked at it for a moment.

"It's *You're* worse than shit, actually," he remarked, smiling at Lexy. "And of course, gyppos has two p's." He folded the letter and put it in his pocket. "If that's the level of education in his town, I'd say we're better off elsewhere."

They moved on, but there were similar letters. Some with threats too – usually to torch the van. But those letters had been from strangers, people with built-in prejudice and fear of the unknown. People who thought that, because Lexy and her family were travellers, it naturally followed that they were thieves and swindlers. The letters had been written in malice, to keep them moving on.

But the anonymous letter Hope Ellenger had received was from someone who knew her. Someone acquainted with her past. Someone who wanted to hurt her. Or perhaps someone who, for reasons of their own, wanted her father's death re-visited.

Her mind engaged on the matter, Lexy made and ate a sparse lunch back at the cabin. Afterwards, tucked in a shady corner of the bleached wood veranda, with Kinky at her side, she began to jot down a plan of action.

The obvious choice was to stake out the vet's surgery, and try to catch someone delivering a fourth letter. But Hope wasn't sure if there was any pattern to the timing of the deliveries. Lexy could be stuck outside there for days. No – that wouldn't do. Perhaps she could try to find out if anyone had spent a significant amount of time on local history research at Clopwolde library? Maybe get talking to the librarian. Or some of Clopwolde's elderly residents, see if anyone had been digging for past scandals. Perhaps…

Lexy suddenly laughed out loud at herself. For the first time in years she realised that her life had some purpose. She was wanted – needed. Busy. Even if she probably wasn't going to get anything out of it. Her face screwed into a wry grimace. What was that Jung thing her dad used to say? *The least of things with a meaning is worth more in life than the greatest of things without it.* He wasn't kidding. Pretty much her whole married life had been without meaning.

For years she had fooled herself that Gerard Warwick-Holmes was still the exciting, sophisticated, slightly dangerous man who had seduced and married her when she was still a teenager – even though it was blindingly obvious that he was actually a flaky, philandering shit who wouldn't hesitate to use his charm and good looks to rip off his own grandmother. Lexy chose to live in denial, just going with the empty, hedonistic lifestyle. She had a stubborn streak running through her like Brighton rock. But she was desperately unhappy inside. She just hadn't realised quite how unhappy until she stumbled across Gerard's master plan.

For the last six months her husband had been out of regular work, following the final demise of *Heirlooms*. He did the odd private valuation, but they had to tighten their belts. He hated that. Hitting forty-five and no longer being top dog had been a severe blow to Gerard's ego. Lexy tried to reassure him that another job offer was sure to come along soon, but she hadn't been fully convinced. She wasn't sure she even cared.

Then six weeks ago she'd seen the small, shiny black card tucked in the top pocket of his suit jacket as she handed it over to the dry cleaners. She initially assumed that it was from a producer or agent. Gerard had certainly been on some kind of high at breakfast that morning, as if something major had happened, but he went all coy when she asked. Perhaps, Lexy thought, he was planning to surprise her.

Well, he did that all right, but it wasn't the surprise she expected. In fact, it turned out to be the last straw.

She examined the card before stowing it in her handbag. The name *Nico Van Steene, Dealer in Fine Arts* was embossed on it, with a Knightsbridge address.

Lexy had never heard of Nico Van Steene – he wasn't one of Gerard's usual art contacts. Had he offered Gerard some work? Could be interesting. She took a secret trip to Nico Van Steene's, to check the place out. A note in the window of his studio cum art salon stated that all viewings were by appointment only. The single oil painting in the heavily protected window was priced at twenty-five thousand pounds.

Lexy returned home, deep in thought. Late the previous night she'd heard Gerard open his private wall safe, the one concealed behind his dressing room mirror. He usually only kept his will in there. For some time now, Lexy had known the combination, although her husband had never actually revealed it to her. It was easy enough to guess. 2210. Gerard's birthday. He'd never had much imagination.

She sneaked a look, trying to get another clue to what Gerard was up to. Had he got a contract to source some paintings for

Van Steene?

If he had, it was a hellish lucrative one. Inside the safe dozens of bundles of fifty-pound notes lay crammed together like so many illegal immigrants. Lexy reeled back. Her initial impulse was to call Gerard immediately to find out what was going on. She did a rough estimate of the cash, instinctively not touching it. The figure made her feel ill. She decided then that perhaps it would be better to let Gerard carry on thinking she didn't know about it. Until she had found out exactly where the cash had come from herself, that was.

Except she'd gone one step further than just finding out.

Above Otter's End a passing gull gave a sudden scream. Lexy jumped, automatically checking her watch. She pushed herself up from the veranda deck, and went back into the cabin. After a moment's hesitation she went through to the bedroom. Just to check that this wasn't all some mad dream. Leaning down, she pulled the battered suitcase from under the bed, flipped the rusty locks, and eased up the lid. Yup. They were still there, shoved in any old how, some bursting from their thin elastic bands. Ten thousand fifty pound notes. The sight of them still took her breath away. As did the unexpected call drifting in through the cabin.

"Coo-ee! Anyone home?" The voice was soft, almost feminine.

Lexy dropped the lid, and pushed the suitcase back under the bed, prickling with shock.

It's not Gerard, a small, sane part of her reasoned. Gerard wouldn't call 'Coo-ee' in that camp way if his life depended on it.

She tiptoed out of the bedroom, sneaked up the hall and peered around the corner of the living room. Kinky was back on the sofa again, sitting up alert, staring intently but not barking.

Lexy crept further into the living room. Through the open hatch she glimpsed a face at the kitchen window.

A long, tanned face, sporting a moustache.

Lexy exchanged a glance with Kinky, then made a decision. Crouching low to avoid being seen through the hatch, she nipped across to the front door, opened it and walked around the side of the veranda.

The man stooping at the kitchen window gave another call.

"Hello," said Lexy, loudly.

The stranger jumped with a small shriek and swung round to face her. He did a theatrical double-take.

"Ooh – now, you're not Glenda, are you?"

This could be awkward. Lexy had finally met someone who knew her alter-ego. And who didn't, by the sound of it, know that she was dead.

Lexy spoke cautiously. "You mean Glenda Doyle?"

"That's right," prompted the man, comfortably. "Where're you hiding the old bat?"

He was around fifty, well-maintained, exuding confidence. The heavy Rolex watch hanging loosely on his wrist looked like the real McCoy, as did the diamond pinkie ring.

Lexy sucked a long, awkward breath through her teeth. "Actually, I'm afraid she's… passed away."

"Passed away?" His round brown eyes goggled at her. "What? – you mean *died*? Not… not today?" He looked around wildly as if he expected to see an undertaker's van or something.

Lexy fought back an inane urge to giggle. "It was a few weeks ago, actually."

Her companion ran a neatly manicured hand through cropped brown hair. "I cannot believe this. I've been in the States. I mean, I literally just got back. I own the place along the way." He waved limply through the trees. "Are you a relative? Do you know what happened to her? Did she have an accident?"

Lexy chose the second question. "Apparently it was her heart."

70

"No!" he ejaculated. "I *told* her to take it easy. She was on tablets, you know. Well, no, you probably don't know."

"No – I didn't know Glenda," confirmed Lexy. "I'm not related or anything. I just moved here, actually."

"Moved here?" He looked taken aback.

"Look, do you want a cup of tea or something?" Although her new neighbour was a bit startling, she wasn't getting any life-threatening vibes from him, and Lexy thought he might even be able to fill in a few blanks for her. "My name's Lexy, by the way." She stuck her hand out.

Her companion grasped it, flashing the diamond ring.

"Edward." He suddenly smiled apologetically, revealing a set of impossibly perfect white teeth. Lexy was reminded of the vet. Was there something in the water round here? "Tea would be just the ticket, sweetie."

Once inside, Edward gazed around, his perfectly round brown eyes puzzled. "But it's exactly the same as it was before. This awful furniture and everything." He picked up a china police car bearing the legend *A Present from Hunstanton* from the mantel-piece and turned it over distastefully in his long, shapely hands.

"Yeah – I only moved in the night before last," explained Lexy, going through to the kitchen, switching on the kettle and dropping teabags into a pair of chipped mugs. "Haven't had much of a chance to do anything yet."

"So Glenda's nephew... what was his name? Oh, yes...Derek. He didn't even turn the place out when she died?"

Lexy spoke through the open hatch. "Guess not. I don't think there's much of value in here. I got the impression that he wanted to be rid of the whole shebang as quickly as possible. He had it for sale on the Internet about a week after Glenda died." She grimaced. "Well – he is a lawyer."

"And we all know what they're like, dear." Edward continued his inspection of the living room. "I only met Derek once, but I took an instant dislike. Shifty-eyed, bloated little toad."

"Yeah, he sounded like a shifty-eyed bloated toad on the phone. Still – it was handy for me having the place furnished."

"Even if it does look like a sitcom set from the nineteen-seventies."

They grinned at each other.

"Hey – who's the little pooch?"

"Name's Kinky."

"Cute. Been in the wars, has he?"

"Yeah, kind of – he tore his ear on some thorns outside."

Lexy wondered how Kinky would react at being referred to as cute. To her surprise, he allowed himself to be fussed over. He even managed to look as if he were enjoying it. Lexy felt a sudden stab of guilt. She was never one for cuddling.

"So what brought you here?" said Edward, looking up from his ministrations.

"Oh, just fancied a change of scene."

He gave her a keen glance. "From London, are you?"

"Yup," said Lexy, then abruptly changed the subject. "How long did you know Glenda for?"

She wanted to find out more about the woman whose work persona she had borrowed. Lexy wondered if Edward had any inkling that Glenda had been a private detective.

Edward sighed. "Oh – must be the best part of twenty years." He stared into the middle distance. "Let's see – she moved here in eighty-eight, I think it was. Took a while but we gradually got to know one another as neighbours. She was never one for mixing, Glenda, but she didn't seem to mind me. Otherwise, she pretty much kept to herself. Kept some funny hours, too." He gave a short laugh. "In fact, if she hadn't looked like Attila the Hun on a bad hair day, I'd have sworn she was on the game."

Lexy also laughed, rather too loudly. He didn't know, then.

"We often used to sit in that little kitchen and verbally dissect the villagers," Edward went on. "She knew quite a lot about them, too, for someone who was such a loner."

"That a fact?" murmured Lexy.

"To tell the truth, I think I was probably the closest thing she had to a friend. Sad, really. I wonder how many turned up for the funeral?"

Lexy shook her head. "No idea. I think her son said it took place in Chelmsford or somewhere. Where the rest of her family live. Here's your tea, by the way. I'm afraid I haven't got any milk – sorry." She passed it through the hatch.

Edward put Kinky down, and came over, taking the mug from the hatch.

"Marvellous – you're very sweet."

You haven't tasted it yet, she thought, heading into the living room to join him.

Edward gave her a sideways look as she came in. "And have you met any of the charming residents of Clopwolde since your arrival?"

She gave a hollow laugh. "A couple."

"Rum bunch, aren't they? I'm afraid you need to be a fifteenth generation Clopwolder to be accepted in this place."

"You an outsider too, then?"

Edward grinned, reminding Lexy of an irrepressible child.

"No – strangely enough I'm a fifteenth generation Clopwolder."

Lexy raised her eyebrows.

"Surname's de Glenville. I'm the last in a long line of Suffolk de Glenvilles. Annoys the hell out of the Village Institute, because I won't play the country squire role."

"Are you meant to be the country squire?" asked Lexy, with keen interest. She'd never met anyone who looked less like her idea of one.

"My father was," replied Edward, soberly. "Sir Lawrence Melvyn de Glenville." His round brown eyes rolled heavenwards.

"Chairman of the local Conservative Party, Chairman of the Clopwolde Village Committee, Patron of St Ethelred's – the local church, that is – tireless charity fundraiser, rabid local historian, organiser of the annual village fete, benefactor to the poor yah-dee, yahdee, yah."

"I sense that it's not your scene," observed Lexy.

"Nah. Anyway," he went on, "who have you met so far on your travels in this part of the world? I could give you the low-down on them."

This could be interesting. Lexy grinned, thinking back. Chronologically speaking, the first person she had met was Roderick Todd, but she decided to keep quiet about him for the time being.

"OK. First off I met a bad-tempered woman with a Yorkshire terrier."

"Isabella Crotch. Estate agent, local councillor, complete bitch," he replied, promptly.

"That fits," Lexy agreed, impressed. "Then I met Hope Ellenger, the vet's receptionist. Thanks to him." She indicated Kinky, who was schmoozing up to Edward in a very over-familiar way. She'd have to have a word with him later.

Edward blew out his cheeks. "Nice girl. Can be prickly, though." He rubbed his neat moustache reflectively. "She and her brother tend to keep themselves to themselves. I guess you met Guy, as well?" He peered at Kinky's ear. "This looks like his work."

"Yeah, he's a dab hand with the needle and thread," said Lexy.

"Gorgeous, too, isn't he?" said Edward, slyly.

To her annoyance, Lexy felt herself blushing. "He's all right," she said gruffly. "Er… he's not…?"

"Gay?" supplied Edward, brightly. "Unfortunately, no. Propositioned him once, when he was worming one of father's retrievers, and he made it quite clear he played for the home team." He frowned. "It's just that I've never seen him actually out on the field. Oh, well, naught as strange as folk, especially the folk around here."

"Do you know Avril Todd?" asked Lexy, in what she hoped was a light tone.

"Oh, gawd help us, you haven't run into her already, have you?" Edward snorted.

"She was at the vet's, too."

"Ah, now she is the archetypal bad incomer," said Edward. "Gives the rest of you a bad name. She and her old man moved here from wherever, bought a couple of the gorgeous little cottages on Windmill Hill that the villagers here don't stand a chance in hell of being able to afford, knocked them into one…" He stopped, then went on, "Lord knows how they got the planning permission for that. Anyway, now she's making a bid to take over the Clopwolde-on-Sea Players, our local am-dram group, having joined through the back door…" He stopped again. "Not sure how she did that either. At any rate, from my personal perspective as a longstanding member of said group, the woman is a monumental pain in the arse, if you'll forgive the expression." He grinned easily.

"Guess you know Tristan Caradoc, too?" Lexy asked. Might as well squeeze this one for all it was worth.

"Dreadful old ham," said Edward, at once. "Used to be a professional actor, as he won't tire of telling anybody who can stay awake long enough. Moved down here about ten years ago with his wife Tammy, and now they give us poor sad amateur actors the benefit of their experience and hog the leading parts every season. Or they did until Sheri-Anne Davis, the veterinary nurse, joined the company. Moody little cow off stage, but she's got a terrific voice, and she can act. She's been getting all the female lead roles recently, and that's put Tammy's nose right out of joint. She hasn't worn very well, our Tammy."

Lexy was silent, taking all this in.

Edward's angular face became pensive, and he wandered restlessly across the room. "Planning to stay in Clopwolde long?"

It was a good question. "Not sure. I'm going to see how it goes," Lexy replied truthfully.

Edward nodded as if he had expected this answer.

"So what were you doing in the States?" she asked.

"Visiting, mostly. I have lots of friends in San Francisco."

Lexy nodded. That figured.

"Been to the States yourself?" he asked.

"A couple of times," she admitted. "In a previous life." She tried not to sound bitter.

He gave her a sympathetic look. "And now you're on your own?"

"Just me and the dog," she said, gruffly, amazed to suddenly feel a lump forming in her throat.

"That's sometimes the best way." He sighed. "I split up with my long-term partner just before I went to 'Cisco. Trouble is, he lives in Clopwolde – owns the big 1930s memorabilia shop in the high street, in fact, so I'm going to keep running into him. I've been dreading coming back, truth to tell."

"Why'd you split?" asked Lexy. "If you don't mind me asking."

Edward gave a humourless laugh. "Usual story. Stuff going on behind my back, you know?"

"I know," Lexy agreed vehemently.

"Money issues. Clandestine meetings. There's nothing worse than trusting someone who's got secrets." Edward cradled his cup reflectively.

"I think we must have been married to the same bloke."

"I wouldn't put it past Peter." Edward drained his cup with polite relish and glanced down at his Rolex. "Guess I'd better go and see what's happened to the old shack in my absence.

Last spring, when I was away for a few weeks, I came back to discover I was housing the national squirrel collection in my roof. Little buggers had chewed through all the electrics."

"Blimey – hope they don't do that to mine." Lexy looked up at the wooden ceiling.

"You should be all right," he said. "My place is a bit older and more run down than this."

"Is that possible?"

"You'd be surprised. Anyway, it was good to meet you, sweetie. Sounds like you're in the same boat as me, and what with Glenda being… well, I guess we're neighbours now, so any time you want to bitch about the ex, or just put the world to rights, you just pop round. You'll always be welcome."

Again, Lexy felt the lump rise to her throat. "Sorry to have to be the one to break the news about Glenda."

"A real wake-up call," he said, soberly. "I'm going to get my cholesterol levels checked first thing tomorrow."

Lexy watched Edward walk off along a narrow path across the heath, his hands thrust in the pockets of his expensive linen trousers. So there were more cabins up here. She had thought there must be. She wondered what he was doing living, like her, on what was essentially a holiday site. He was obviously from an established Clopwolde family. Perhaps he was an eccentric. The cabin seemed suddenly very silent now that he had gone. She felt like popping next door to see him again already.

Pushing aside her unexpected loneliness, Lexy picked up the camera and squinted through the viewfinder. It felt very odd to be on the verge of what was essentially a spying mission. Astonishing what some people were prepared to do to save a marriage. She had no such tolerance where Gerard was concerned, not after she found out precisely how he came by all that money in his safe – and that had taken some detective work in itself.

She shut her eyes, suddenly exhausted, and sank on to the sofa.

"Must go to Windmill Hill for a recce," she murmured. Kinky's paw twitched. The sea sighed distantly.

Far out on the horizon, a single black cloud crouched like a bruise on the otherwise perfectly clear blue sky.

Lexy awoke with a jerk. She'd been dreaming about squirrels, dozens of them rampaging around Otter's End chomping on electrical cables.

Bemused, she stared around. The room was hot and stuffy, and dust still danced thickly in slanted shafts of fading sunlight.

Her eye caught the clock on the mantelpiece. Seven forty-five.

She gave a loud yell. Kinky skedaddled off the sofa.

Lexy tore around the cabin frantically. At exactly ten to eight she ran out, clutching the camera, notebook and pen. She yanked open the door of the Panda, threw everything in, ran back into the cabin to grab a confused Kinky, and in another minute the car was trundling down Cliff Lane belching clouds of smoke.

8

Lexy accelerated along Clopwolde high street scattering indignant tourists, and by the blunt strategy of heading straight for the windmill, located Windmill Hill. It was a cul-de-sac culminating in the grassy knoll upon which perched the gleaming white tower itself.

Number four was near the top, strangely at odds with its neighbours as it was twice the size with an integral garage. The property was surrounded by a freshly clipped low privet hedge. Even as Lexy arrived, a woman emerged from the white PVC front door wearing a tight-fitting blue skirt, twinned with a blue long-sleeved top that stretched across her ample chest. Rust-coloured hair, severe features – it was Avril Todd, large as life and twice as ugly.

Lexy drove swiftly down to the end of the cul-de-sac, turned around smartly and parked a couple of doors down from number four, slouching low in the driver's seat to avoid being seen.

Avril Todd was backing a dark blue Volvo out of the garage. She stopped at the end of the drive, got out of the car, strode back up and closed the garage doors. Then she settled back in the driver's seat, putting on her seatbelt with a certain amount of fussing, and drove off.

A rusty lime green Panda followed at a discreet distance.

The Volvo took a left at the bottom of the hill. It soon became obvious from the road signs that Avril was heading for the A12 using the back roads; clearly she didn't want to drive directly through the village centre.

On reaching the by-pass, which was unexpectedly busy, Avril found a gap, pulled out and drove off in the direction of Lowestoft. Lexy waited with growing impatience for another lull in the stream of vehicles, aware of the Volvo disappearing into the distance. She eventually accelerated out in front of a bus, causing a flurry of horn-blasting. Kinky's eyes widened even more than usual.

"There she is." Lexy pushed the Panda up to seventy-five and overtook a Porsche – probably the first time that had ever happened. Up ahead, the Volvo was about to cruise out of sight around a bend.

Lexy steamed along, keeping one eye out for speed cameras and police cars, the Panda's steering wheel vibrating so much that her teeth rattled.

They tore around the bend. Lexy gaped at the long, empty stretch of road in front of her, and pounded the steering wheel in frustration. The Volvo was completely out of sight. But that meant it must have been doing about a hundred and fifty, which was crazy. Then she saw it, in a side road on the left, winding between two fields. A small signpost proclaimed that the lane led to a place called Nudging.

Lexy slammed her foot on the brake and swerved into the inside lane, causing another fanfare of honking and gesticulations. Talk about covert surveillance. Somehow she managed to slow in time to make the turning. Kinky only kept his hold on the seat by digging his claws into the striped fabric cover. He glared at her.

"Sorry, mate," she said through gritted teeth. "Didn't realise it was going to be this mental."

The Panda squeaked and clanked along. The Volvo, still just visible ahead, seemed to be slowing. Lexy thankfully put her foot over the brake.

She watched as her quarry turned through an open five-barred farm gate with a public footpath sign to one side. It bumped along a rutted track lined on both sides by an over-grown hedge. Lexy drove slowly to the gate, pulled on to the verge alongside it, and stopped, letting the engine idle.

She wasn't going to follow. It would be too obvious. Anyway, the Panda wasn't built to go off-road. It could only just about deal with being on-road. Lexy watched the Volvo slowly disappear from view around a corner. It seemed to be drawing to a halt. She rolled down the window and strained her ears. She heard the engine cut, and a door slam. Hallelujah. She switched off her own engine. The Panda stopped with something suspiciously like a death rattle. But Lexy wasn't going to worry about that now; she was far more interested in finding out exactly what Avril Todd was up to. Could she really be meeting a lover? At her age? And with that hair?

She waited for two minutes, to give the woman a chance to start doing whatever she was doing, then turned to Kinky. "C'mon, we're going walkies."

Lexy walked cautiously up the farm track, camera swinging around her neck. The setting sun had tinted the path ahead gold and pink. She squinted. There was a public footpath sign positioned next to a stile in the high hedge up ahead, right on the corner. Lexy strolled towards it like an innocent dog walker. The Volvo would be in sight any moment. Whatever Avril was up to, a quick click and that would be it. Three hundred and fifty quid in the bag. It was all going to work to plan. She felt a smile of relief creep over her face.

Until she heard the shrieking, that was.

Lexy stood immobilised.

"I don't understand… what's happening? Are you mad?" It was Avril's voice, weak, but shrill, coming from the other side of the hedge.

"Oh-oh," said Lexy.

"W…what the hell is that?" Avril bleated.

Her question was followed by a high, chilling scream.

Moments later a car engine gunned. Lexy instinctively dashed to the protective cover of a nearby bush, shepherding Kinky with flapping arms. Avril would be turning the Volvo and coming back down the track any second. Something was clearly wrong.

It took Lexy a few more seconds to realise that the sound of the car engine was receding. It wasn't turning. It was carrying on up the track. She burst out of the vegetation and raced up to the corner. The Volvo was disappearing over the crest of a hill, dust billowing behind it like smoke.

"Bollocks," Lexy yelled. What was she meant to do now? It hadn't occurred to her that the track actually led somewhere. She would have to get the Panda and follow, off-road or not. She turned and started running back towards the gate. But what about that scream? It had come from the field. Perhaps she ought to take a quick look. She changed direction again. Kinky, who had been trying to follow her, gave up and sat on the verge, his back foot scratching uselessly at the plastic funnel on his head.

Breathing hard, Lexy clambered over the stile, and jumped down.

Then she almost screamed herself.

9

A figure lay flat out on the grass in front of her, blood dribbling from a messy head wound.

"Oh, sh…" Lexy bent reluctantly over the slumped form, with its glassy, lifeless eyes. The piled-up rust-coloured hair was unmistakable, although now it was sadly squashed out of shape, revealing itself to be a wig. The hair that escaped from under it was thin and grey, and the tight blue outfit was creased and disarrayed.

Kinky had finally managed to squeeze backwards through a gap under the stile, when Lexy went bounding back over it again.

"Quick – got to find a phone!"

She pelted down the track, trying to think straight.

Avril Todd dead? *That* wasn't meant to happen. Avril had come here to meet someone and, instead of sweeping her into the expected passionate embrace, that someone had cracked her head open and then driven off in her car. And Lexy hadn't even seen them go back over the stile. She frowned. So how…?

But now wasn't the time. She yanked open the door of her own long-suffering car, ushered in the panting chihuahua and jumped into the driver's seat.

"You'd better start," she yelled hysterically. It did, as soon as she remembered to turn the key.

She accelerated up the lane in the direction the Panda had already been pointing. She was bound to come across a farm-house or cottage soon where she could raise the alarm. A minute later there was very nearly a collision as the Panda whined around a particularly sharp bend. A white estate car coming the other way was forced to swerve into the hedge inches in front of them.

Lexy jerked the handbrake on and wrenched open her door. She raced across to the other driver. "Quickly – can you call the poli…"

The words died on her lips as she watched the tall, pale man unfold himself like an ironing board from the driver's seat.

DI Bernard Milo's expression was bleak. "Do you always drive like that?"

"No, of course not!" Lucky he hadn't seen her earlier. "But there's been an… an accident and…"

"I'm not surprised. What was it – a shunt?" He scrutinised her car.

"Not a car accident!" Lexy was almost dancing with frustration.

"What, then?"

"Someone's just been killed. Murdered!"

That concentrated his mind.

"Right. You see it happen?"

"No – I heard her scream, though. And I saw her after…" she faltered.

"Where did it happen?"

"In a field just down there." Lexy pointed wildly.

"You'd better show me." DI Milo jumped back into his driving seat. "Take your car and I'll follow."

Lexy threw herself back into the Panda and executed a ragged three-point turn that would have failed a driving test. Where the hell had Milo suddenly materialised from? Wasn't it was bad enough finding Avril Todd stone dead without him popping up like some morbid jack-in-a-box? Why couldn't it have been a nice, sensible plod?

In fact, Lexy had an overriding urge to floor the accelerator and make a break for it. If she'd been in anything but the Panda she would have done exactly that.

Kinky, gripping the seat cover with splayed claws, eyed her nervously.

"OK, Alexandra, get a grip," she said aloud, taking deep breaths as the car ground along. "You can deal with this."

But how, exactly, was she going deal with it? DI Milo was going to find it a mite strange that Lexy had just happened to stumble across a very recently murdered woman in the middle of nowhere. In fact, he might even wonder if she had something to do with it. Lexy went cold at the thought.

She turned distractedly through the five-barred gate.

She'd have to make up some story about why she had been there. The truth would be out of the question, of course. There was no way she was going into explanations about assuming the workload of dead private detectives, to say nothing of her real reason for being in Clopwolde-on-Sea.

She yanked on the handbrake and sat back, panic rising in her chest. Avril was dead, Lexy had no idea why, and nothing useful to tell the police. Except that her husband suspected she was having an affair. Well, Roderick Todd could tell them that himself. Lexy forced herself to breathe slowly. All she needed to say was that she had been driving around and lost her way. There. Simple. She just had to hold her nerve.

But as Lexy began to unwind slightly, she realised with dawning horror that after Roderick Todd had told the police he suspected Avril was having an affair, he would go on to tell them he had hired a private detective called Lexy Lomax to follow her.

"Oh, no," she moaned, clutching her head. It was all going to come out. She could already see the newspaper story the next day.

Mysterious Death of Clopwolde Woman

A resident of the Suffolk village of Clopwolde-on-Sea was found dead in a nearby field yesterday evening. No arrest has yet been made in connection with the incident , but in a bizarre twist, Alexandra Warwick-Holmes, 29, wife of TV's former 'Mr Heirloom', Gerard Warwick-Holmes, admitted to having followed Mrs Avril

Todd to the place of her murder while masquerading as a private detective. Mrs Warwick-Holmes, sporting a tattoo, ripped denims and a short crop, claimed to be 'taking some time out' from her marriage, and appears to be living in a ramshackle holiday cabin near the idyllic Suffolk seaside resort.

Gerard would be there like a shot.

At least he wouldn't get his money back, Lexy thought grimly, because the police would already have confiscated that when they searched Otter's End. After arresting her on suspicion of murder.

She forced herself to think for a minute. OK. There might be one very slim, very minute chance of wriggling out of this unscathed.

"Right, whatever I say, you back me up, pal," she muttered to Kinky.

But the chihuahua was staring beyond Lexy.

"Everything all right?" said a hollow voice, right in her ear.

Lexy jumped violently. She hadn't even realised she'd pulled up opposite the stile and stopped.

DI Milo was stooping beside her open window.

"Yeah, course. Just sorting out my…" She swallowed hard. She'd almost said 'alibi'. That would have been a good start.

She got out quickly, forcing the policeman to move out of the way.

A sweet smell of wild honeysuckle lingered on the damp evening breeze, as if to dilute the grisly reality of what lay ahead.

"So where's the body?"

"In that field." Lexy pointed uncertainly. It all looked different now dusk was falling.

He tackled the stile, stepping over it nimbly, on long, stork-like legs. Lexy followed more slowly, bizarrely expecting Avril Todd to be gone. Perhaps she had imagined the whole thing. It certainly felt like a dream. If only.

Milo had stopped short. He flipped open his phone. "Ambulance required urgently," he intoned. "Location – country lane to Nudging, just off the A12 on the Lowestoft side of Clopwolde. Up a farm track on the right, about a quarter of a mile along the lane. Middle-aged IC one woman with a head injury."

"Might be a bit late for an ambulance," Lexy mumbled.

But the detective was back on the phone, making an abrupt call for police assistance. "Yes – it's DI Milo," he snapped. "Haven't forgotten me already, have you, PC Spencer?" He flicked a button and shoved the phone back into his top pocket. It rang again immediately.

He checked it and cancelled the call, then took a pair of blue latex gloves from his pocket, snapped them and pulled them on. Turning to Lexy he said, "You arrived just after this happened, did you?" As he spoke he shrugged his arms out of his jacket, and dropped it on the ground.

"Yeah." Lexy wondered what he was doing.

"Did you see the attacker?" DI Milo was rolling up his sleeves.

"No. By the time I got here, he was driving off in the car that she must have got out of a couple of minutes earlier." She indicated Avril, trying to avoid looking at her head.

"Get the registration?"

Lexy told him. He put out a rapid call.

"How do you know it was a man driving?"

"Just assumed."

The policeman crouched over the dead woman, pulling something out of his shirt pocket. "What were you doing here, anyway?"

Here we go. Lexy took a deep breath. "I'd been driving around, lost my way. I saw the Volvo parked up this track. I just nipped up here to ask the way back to Clopwolde. I heard shouting and a scream as I walked up the track, then I saw the Volvo disappear in a cloud of dust." She paused. "I wasn't sure what to do at first, then I checked in the field."

"And you don't know this woman?" He turned, gave her a significant look.

"No." Well, she didn't *know* her.

DI Milo nodded grimly.

That was the first hurdle cleared.

"Right. I'm going to try resuscitation."

Lexy, still high on relief, thought the policeman was joking. But he had actually started the routine, alternatively pumping Avril's ample chest, then breathing through a filter into her slackened mouth.

She watched him, dumbfounded. It was blindingly obvious that Avril Todd had checked out. At least fifteen minutes had passed since Lexy found her, and she wasn't exactly a picture of health then.

Lexy suddenly felt her legs bend under her like hot candles, and she slumped down on the stile, trying to breathe evenly. If she wasn't careful she'd have DI Milo trying to resuscitate her next. At least reinforcements were on the way. She wouldn't be alone with him any more.

"Come on!" he shouted at the corpse. "Wake up!"

Lexy squirmed. The whole bizarre situation, the mad car chase, the unexpected scream, the murdered body, the policeman desperately trying to pump life back into it, all ran in front of her eyes like a film on a loop.

"Stop it," she burst out. "Can't you see she's dead?"

Milo ignored her. Lexy berated herself furiously. He was trying to save a woman's life, albeit a futile act. It was what she should have done the moment she found the body. The problem was that even then Avril Todd had looked utterly dead. Some instinct had told Lexy that the blow on the head must have killed her instantly. Lexy shivered. The question was – why? And by whom? Who had been waiting for Avril in the field?

Was it lover boy? Perhaps they'd had some kind of an argument, almost immediately after they had met. Lexy remembered Avril's voice, rather shrill and faint, but unmistakably hers. She looked back over the stile and down the path where she'd been walking when she'd heard the scream, trying to calculate the distance through the yellowish dusk.

What had Avril shouted? *I don't understand…what's happening? Are you mad?*

Lexy frowned. Was her lover trying to break it off? That would be the obvious conclusion, but somehow Avril's response didn't fit. *W…what the hell is that?* sounded more like she was just plain confused. Lexy rubbed her chin.

DI Milo, meanwhile, had fallen back on his heels, breathing heavily, his head bowed. He'd finally given up. Avril's head had flopped untidily back. Lexy felt a pitiable urge to go and straighten her wig.

She leant down to stroke Kinky, who was sitting at her heels. His bright eyes met hers through the dusk.

She heard DI Milo call his control, cancel the ambulance and request the police surgeon instead. When she looked over at him again he was going through Avril's jacket. He pulled out a white plastic card and squinted at it through the fading light. In a moment he was back on his mobile again.

"…found a library card on the deceased – from the photo it identifies the woman as Mrs Avril Geraldine Todd of 4 Windmill Hill, Clopwolde-on-Sea. There may be a husband or children – would you please send a DC to that address to make initial contact. Get whoever it is to call me when they arrive. And put me through to SOCO…"

Lexy tuned out the rest of the call. Alarm had enveloped her again. She hadn't been expecting Avril Todd to be identified so soon. That wasn't good. As she was only too well aware, there wouldn't be anyone at home when the police called at the Todds' address because Roderick was at his old boys' reunion in Lincoln. Probably on his second or third pint by now. But he might have his wife in the back of his mind, wondering how the surveillance was going.

What on earth was he going to say when he found out? Would he break down? He had, after all, seemed fond of his straying wife. Lexy hoped that they'd managed to say goodbye to each other before he'd left.

She sat on the stile, her heart banging in her chest.

DI Milo was hunched down beside the dead woman again, staring intently at the ugly wound on her head, using a small torch to illuminate it in the fading light. Lexy wondered how he could get so close without throwing up.

"Did you touch anything?" he barked, looking over at her.

"Of course not," said Lexy, witheringly. She hadn't been watching *The Bill* every week since 1990 for nothing.

He stood up and walked around the body, staring through the gloom, then went over to the hedge and prowled along it to the far corner of the field before slowly returning.

"There's a gap in this hedge," he said. "Did you notice it?"

"No – funnily enough I didn't," she snapped. "I saw a dead body and ran for help, like any normal person would."

He ignored this. "Looks like someone has recently gone through it."

Lexy was suddenly alert. "That's why I didn't see anybody climb over the stile after the murder. Whoever did it must have dodged through the hole in the fence and straight into Avril's car."

"Convinced she was dead, were you, when you found her?"

"Yeah. As a dodo. I could tell."

"Expert, are you?"

"No, but…"

"Ever seen a dead body?"

"Not until now."

In the distance, sirens were wailing.

"Did you hear what was being shouted as you approached the field?"

Lexy told him.

The detective retrieved his jacket, shook it and put it on, then began scribbling in his notebook, holding it up to the fading daylight to see.

Within minutes the dusk was suffused with blue flashing lights as three police cars bumped up the lane and stopped behind DI Milo's white estate. A four-by-four and a large van completed the cavalcade.

Uniformed officers spilled out of the first car, followed more sedately by plain-clothed policemen and a man carrying a black briefcase, whom Lexy assumed to be the police surgeon.

Milo left Lexy and went to meet a short, slight man with darting eyes and a sharp suit.

"Bernard," said the newcomer, briskly. "What the hell are you doing here?"

"On my way to another call, sir." DI Milo sounded as wooden as a Chippendale cabinet.

Lexy started. Another call? Bit of a coincidence.

But if it wasn't another call, what was he doing there? For a brief moment her mind freewheeled as she remembered his sombre grey eyes boring into hers and his question. "Did you see the attacker?"

But it was only a brief moment. DI Milo was driving his own car when they had almost collided minutes after the murder, not a blue Volvo. And he hadn't been spattered with blood.

She studied him, standing lanky but alert in front of his senior officer.

"Another call?" the other man snapped. "I thought you were…"

"I got flagged down by this lady, sir," Milo cut in, steadily. "*She* found the body." He jerked his head at Lexy.

The sharp-suited, sharp-eyed policeman turned and gave Lexy the once-over, clearly disliking what he saw. She could almost see his mind working: if anyone had cracked Avril over the head, this scruffy little itinerant had to be a front runner, probably to get money for drugs.

"DCI Andrew Jameson, Lowestoft CID," he said, tightly. "And you are?"

Lexy met his gaze. "Alexandra Lomax."

"Are you local?"

"I moved down here two days ago. And…"

"I see. Well, this is an unfortunate start to your stay. We'll need a statement from you. Wait there, please." He turned to DI Milo. "I assume you've done the preliminaries and secured the scene, Bernard, seeing as you appeared to be here first."

They began walking away from her. "I'll set up an incident room at Fenmere," she heard the DCI say. "I'll be based there for the duration of the investigation. Now, what the f…"

Lexy stared at the ground, trying to steady herself for what promised to be a long night ahead.

After a few minutes the man with the black briefcase left, speaking to another detective. Lexy overheard him as he passed.

"…initial impression is that death was caused by a blow to the left temple with a long, heavy object with a blunt edge – like a baseball bat…"

"Like a baseball bat…" Despite her state of nervous alarm, Lexy filed this piece of information away.

In the lane, the officers who had arrived in the van were pulling on blue coveralls, gloves, caps and large blue bootees. They looked like overgrown babies.

"This the witness?" one of them called, pointing at Lexy.

DI Milo turned. "Yes. This is Ms Lomax," he said.

"Did she go near the deceased?"

"Yeah, I did," said Lexy, before Milo could reply for her again.

"Need to take some samples from you then, love. Is that OK?"

The giant baby approached and grinned at Kinky, sitting at Lexy's feet. "Is that a dog, or a rat in a hat?"

Both Lexy and the chihuahua gave him a weary look.

He used a complicated camera to photograph the soles of Lexy's trainers, then bent over and twanged a couple of hairs out of her head.

"Just to eliminate you," he reassured her.

She'd eliminate him if he did that again, Lexy thought, rubbing her head.

"And you." He turned to Kinky and snipped his tweezers.

"He hasn't been near the body," Lexy said, quickly.

"Only joking, love. I'd be a bit surprised if Fang here went in for murder and mayhem."

He obviously hadn't met Kinky before.

"How long's she been here?" One of the other SOCO guys was squatting by Avril Todd's head. Two more were starting to put up a tent behind him.

Lexy squinted at her watch through the semi-darkness.

"About half an hour?" She looked at Milo, who was also submitting to the tweezers, for confirmation. He nodded. "I attempted resuss, by the way," he added, stonily.

"So the body's been disturbed?" The SOCO team exchanged frustrated glances.

"I wasn't just going to assume she was dead, although I realise now that was probably an inconvenience to you."

After a fist-clenching silence, Milo left Lexy abruptly and began conferring with DCI Jameson again, his pale face almost luminous in the dusk. Within minutes, there was a heated debate going on, although Lexy could only catch the odd word. "…fit enough…" "…got this far…" "patronising…" After a few minutes Milo wheeled away and returned to Lexy.

"The DCI would like you to give a statement down at the station," he said stiffly.

"Can't I do it here?" she said, alarmed.

"No."

"So am I under arrest?"

"Not if you co-operate." He glanced back at the DCI, who was bearing down on them.

"Bernard, you might as well escort Ms Lomax to Fenmere yourself. Then I want to see you there, in the incident room." He consulted his watch. "At twenty-two thirty hours. On the dot."

They went back into the lane, Lexy practically having to run to keep up with DI Milo's angry strides. He paused by one of the police cars, his bleak face turning blue sporadically in its silently rotating light. Officers were clambering back and forth over the stile, organising floodlights and scene of crime tape. In the field, the SOCO team moved stiffly around inside their illuminated tent like Egyptian mummies in an old horror film.

"Best if we go in your car," Milo said. "I'll get uniform to bring mine back."

He hailed one of the officers.

The man, breathing heavily with exertion, came over to them. "Sir?" He peered through the gloom. "DI Milo?"

"Correct, PC Cartwright. I have to escort a witness to Fenmere. Would someone kindly do the honours with my car?" He held up the keys.

"No problem, sir," said the officer. "Wasn't expecting to see you here, sir. Are you… back?"

"Looks like it, Rob."

Lexy listened to this exchange in some confusion. Perhaps DI

Milo hadn't been on duty when she'd run into him. But he said he was on another call. She rubbed her cropped hair and glanced helplessly down at Kinky. He gazed imploringly back at her; she knew this was only because he wanted his dinner, but told herself he was urging her to hold it together.

They walked towards the lime green Panda, and Lexy unlocked it wordlessly. DI Milo squashed himself into the passenger seat, his knees somewhere up near his nose.

"You can push it back," Lexy told him.

Kinky was relegated to the rear seat.

Lexy turned the ignition key and the Panda spluttered indignantly into life.

"It's going to be impossible to turn around with that lot blocking the way," said Milo abruptly, gesturing at the line of police vehicles. He had obviously remembered Lexy's earlier three-point turn. "We'd better carry on up the track."

Lexy let out the clutch. It would probably be curtains for the Panda's suspension, but that was the least of her worries.

10

From time to time Lexy eyed the fuel indicator as she negotiated a series of lanes, guided by the detective's muttered lefts and rights. Tonight's little escapade would take her down to less than a quarter of a tank.

Fenmere was a small, sleepy town, about three miles away from Nudging. The police station was original Victorian with a blue lamp over the door like something out of *Dixon of Dock Green*. Lights blazed in all the windows and police vehicles were parked haphazardly along the road. Murder was obviously a big deal in this neck of the woods. Lexy backed the Panda awkwardly into a corner of the small car park.

Dogs weren't allowed in, so Lexy had to leave Kinky in the car. "Won't be long," she lied to him through the window. Kinky stared incredulously at her through the funnel, clearly not believing she was going to leave him locked in the car in the dark, after the night he'd had.

DI Milo escorted Lexy through the reception area and ushered her into a small room with a table and two chairs. "Wait here and I'll get someone to come and take your statement."

"Why don't you do it?" Lexy asked.

"I'm off the case," said DI Milo.

"Why?"

"I think that's my business, don't you?"

He turned and left.

While she waited, Lexy studied the wall posters fretfully. Drugs, theft, guns, prostitution. Nice. Why was DI Milo off the case?

Her nemesis reappeared shortly with a uniformed police-woman in tow.

"This is WPC Lamb." The policewoman gave a thin smile.

"She'll take down your statement and read it back to you. If you're happy with it, sign it and then you can leave, although the investigating officers will probably need to speak to you again in the next day or so." A narrow flash of ice-grey. "You're not planning to leave your current address at present, are you?"

Lexy shook her head. With twenty pence to her name and a quarter of a tank of fuel? She'd be lucky.

The detective inspector left the room without a backward glance at her.

"Want anything to drink before we start?" WPC Lamb asked, unenthusiastically.

"Vodka and tonic, please."

She gave Lexy a jaded look.

"Perhaps just some water, then."

The WPC returned with two plastic cups, placed one in front of Lexy then pulled a lined form towards her and took a pen from her top pocket.

"Right, this will be your witness statement," she informed her, in the lifeless monotone of officialdom. "You now explain to me what happened in your own words, and I'll write it down. You read it over afterwards and sign it if it accurately reflects what you saw."

"I can write, you know," said Lexy.

"We have to do it this way," she said, unsmiling. "Ready?"

Lexy went over her fabrication again. She finished by explaining how she panicked after finding Avril and went on a mad dash for help. "Which was when I ran into DI Milo, just up the road from the field."

WPC Lamb looked up sharply.

"He was on another call, apparently."

The policewoman pursed her lips but bent over the witness statement again. Lexy continued with her monologue, listening to the soft scrape of the biro. What was lying to the police called? Oh, yes – perverting the course of justice.

WPC Lamb finished writing. "Please read your statement, and sign it if you agree that it is a true account of the events."

Lexy's eyes roved unseeingly along the neat rows of capitals.

She felt herself shaking, and wished that Kinky was there, under the table, leaning companionably against her foot.

She turned to the end, scribbled her name and passed the witness statement quickly back to WPC Lamb.

"Thanks." The police constable looked at her. "Are you all right?"

Lexy was aware that she was sweating, beads of the stuff standing out on her forehead. "Yeah. It's just been a bit of a shock."

"Is there anyone you can call? Someone who can come and meet you?"

Lexy shook her head. "No – I've got my car here, and my dog. I'll be fine. Er… wouldn't mind going to the loo before I go?"

"There's one just off reception. Follow me."

Lexy got up, aware of how scruffy and grimy she felt. The WPC in her neat uniform only made things worse.

Lexy was directed to a door marked Ladies. She splashed cold water on her burning face, took several deep breaths, then let herself out, slipping across the empty reception area towards the front door.

Except it wasn't completely empty.

"Do you know that it's an offence to give false information to an officer of the law?" said DI Milo, quietly.

He had been leaning against the far side of a central pillar, reading through the statement. He must have taken it from WPC Lamb as soon as she'd let Lexy out.

"What?" Lexy blustered.

"Lomax? What's all that about? Your surname's Warwick-

98

Holmes, isn't it?

Lexy let her hand fly to her mouth, gave him a look of contrition. "Oops, I completely forgot."

"Forgot?"

She forced herself to smile reasonably. "Lomax is my maiden name." She hated that patronising expression, but now was not a time for foibles. "I've been using it for a while now. For personal reasons. Guess I just got used to it."

His eyes were narrow slits of grey.

She thought for a moment. "How do you know my real surname, anyway?"

"I ran a check on your car index."

The DVLA. At least he hadn't recognised her from Gerard's witless antiques show.

"Will my real name have to be in the papers, if this gets reported?"

DI Milo appeared to consider the question. "Why don't you want it to be?"

He wasn't making this easy. "I've left my husband, if you must know. He doesn't know where I am, and I don't want him to find out."

"Why?"

DI Milo had obviously never watched *Heirlooms in Your Attic*. "Because he's not a very nice man." Lexy ground out the words. "I just want to live down here privately for a while until I decide what to do next. OK?"

"You picked the wrong place to take a scenic drive, then."

"Tell me about it."

"Your husband hasn't been violent towards you, or threatened you at all, has he?"

"Nope," said Lexy. He hadn't had a chance yet.

"And you haven't done anything illegal?"

"Nope," she said again, looking him firmly in the eye.

99

Apart from the odd five hundred grand she'd nicked. And a spot of perverting the course of justice.

He nodded. "All right. I think I can agree to keep your real name out of the press release."

"Thanks," said Lexy, quickly. That was easy.

"But there is a condition."

Lexy froze.

"I want you to come out to dinner with me," he went on. "Do you like Thai food?"

Lexy felt the colour rise in her cheeks. "Yes, I do like Thai food," she said woodenly.

"Good. I'll pick you up at eight o'clock on Sunday night."

She suppressed a retort. She was clocking up a lot of firsts tonight. First time she'd done a private investigation job, first time she'd seen a murder victim, first time she'd given false evidence to the police... not strictly true, she thought, remembering an incident with her dad, when they had to go to Somerset for a few months and not talk to anyone... But it was certainly the first time she'd been blackmailed by a policeman.

DI Milo watched her intently, until his mobile suddenly chirruped. He delved into his pocket. "Milo."

A faint yammering came from the phone.

The DI stiffened. "I see." His expression was unreadable.

The voice jabbered on.

Oh great, thought Lexy. They've tracked down Roderick Todd and he's told them everything.

"Right, thanks." Milo flipped the phone shut. "Just had a tip-off. Volvo's been found."

"What?"

"Abandoned in a ditch about two miles away from the crime scene. No one in it."

"So whoever it was just used the Volvo to get away, then drove it off the road and picked up their own car," said Lexy, slowly.

"Looks like it."

"Wonder if anyone saw the second car parked up?"

"What are you – a frustrated detective?"

"No – that's you, isn't it?" she said, pointedly.

At that moment the front door opened and a pair of plain-clothed policemen strode into the reception area. "Venus?" one of them said, sounding astonished. "You all right, mate?"

Venus? Lexy stared uncomprehendingly at the detective.

He gave his colleagues a bloodless smile. "I'm fine. Just a flying visit."

The newcomers carried on through the reception area, making hearty comments to Milo, but looking, Lexy thought, slightly embarrassed.

"Thought he'd been pulled off active duty after…" she overheard heard one mutter under his breath as they passed through the door.

"After *what*?" she wanted to yell after them.

Milo was holding the front door open, clearly wishing to escort her from the premises. Thoroughly disconcerted, Lexy followed him out to the police car park and unlocked the passenger door of the Panda. "Hi, Kinky," she said softly. The chihuahua wagged his tail to show that there were no hard feelings.

"The investigating officers will contact you if they need any further information," said the detective. "Oh – have you got a mobile phone?"

"No," said Lexy, heavily. "Not any more."

"You should get one," said DI Milo, seriously. "Especially if you're driving alone at night."

"Thanks for the advice," Lexy said.

"See you at eight on Sunday, then."

"Eh?" Oh, yeah, that. Lexy got in and fitted the key into the ignition. After a couple of turns, the engine spluttered into reluctant life.

She wound down her window. "By the way," she said, tapping her watch. "Didn't you have an appointment at twenty-two thirty hours? On the dot?"

DI Milo shot a look at his own watch and cursed under his breath.

Only when the police station was well out of sight did Lexy let out a long breath. "Well, pal," she said to Kinky with false brightness, "I hope the Case of the Missing Cat doesn't give us this much trouble."

She found herself gripped by a bout of hysterical giggling. Kinky's look turned to one of alarm.

It was half past midnight when Lexy drove back along Clopwolde high street towards Cliff Lane. A few people were still variously strolling or staggering around the village centre. The car wheezed and backfired a couple of times, making a group of teenage boys duck.

"Come on, Panda," Lexy pleaded. "Don't make me walk up the hill." But with a final apologetic shudder, it fell silent. Lexy coasted to the side of the road, and stopped under a streetlight. She felt like screaming.

She opened the door, got out, and hoisted the bonnet up. As she scanned the unfathomable, oily depths of the engine, Lexy became aware of approaching footsteps. She straightened up and looked around, composing her face into the best impression of a helpless woman she could muster: a kind of contorted smile that probably made her look more like a psychopath.

"Oho! Alexandra Lomax, as I live and breathe! Pray, what are you doing?"

It was Tristan Caradoc. Not exactly the knight in shining amour she had been hoping for. More like a pompous ass in a cloak and a top hat.

"I'm trying to find a dipstick." Funny, that.

"Oh – you ladies…" Tristan bent over the engine, fished out the oil gauge, wiped it on a handkerchief, re-inserted it and checked it again.

"Bit low, but not critical. What happened, anyway – did the engine cut out?"

She nodded.

"Well, that won't be your oil." He scanned the car's innards. "Bit of an old banger, isn't she? I should know – I'm married to one, ha-ha."

Charming. "Been all right until now."

"There's your problem." Tristan suddenly pointed. "Loose connection. Got a torch?"

"Thanks," Lexy said gruffly, when the engine was ticking over again.

"My pleasure."

Lexy was well aware that she now owed Tristan Caradoc two favours.

As if reading her thoughts, he threw her a mock-accusing glance. "And where were you earlier, madam, when I was waiting all alone in the graveyard, clutching my flaming brand?"

"I'm not with you."

"*That* was precisely my problem," he said. "Our ghost walk!" He produced another of his leaflets and held it out to her. "How could you have forgotten! On such a lovely, velvety black night, too," he added, huskily.

Might have been for you, mate, Lexy thought. She'd been having a real-life horror show, and pleasurable thrills hadn't exactly featured high on the menu.

She dutifully scanned the leaflet. At the top was a picture of a church and graveyard, backlit by a fork of lightning. Below this was written:

Explore Olde Clopwolde by night!
Listen to Tales that will Terrify!

An experienced actor, whom some of you might recognise(!), will show you a side of Clopwolde village that you could never imagine – in your worst nightmares! Lighting your way with a flaming brand, he will recount ancient legends of ghosts, ghouls, demons, witches and…the Drowned Sailor who Walks the Pier!

(Starts from St Ethelred's churchyard at 8pm and 10pm every Friday. Tours last approx 1½ hours and include a pub visit!)

"Were you really waiting for me?" she asked, half-guiltily.

Tristan smiled. "I kept an eye out, but I knew it would be a forlorn hope. Anyway – there were several very loud ladies from Philadelphia who had done the eight o'clock session, and liked it so much they were clamouring for it all over again." His copper eyes danced riotously. "Now then – I want a promise from you – ghost walk, next Friday night, ten o'clock."

"All right, all right," she said. As long as it would make them quits.

She waved Tristan off with a relieved smile, the ghost walk leaflet tucked behind the curled-up, fed-up form of Kinky on the front seat.

They pulled up at Otter's End a few minutes later.

"C'mon, pal," Lexy pushed open the car door. Her words seemed to be bitten up by the darkness. She turned her head sharply at the sound of a snapping twig, and peered blindly into the shadows, finding herself fumbling with the keys.

She pushed open the door and groped for the light switch. Kinky hopped in and made a beeline for the kitchen. Lexy shut the front door, locking it behind her. She yanked the curtains closed, and joined Kinky in the small kitchen. The dog was sitting pointedly in front of his empty food bowl.

Sighing, she took one of the dog biscuit samples from the cupboard, and emptied the contents into his bowl. She released Kinky from his ruff and watched him dive in.

"I'm tempted to join you down there, mate." Lexy put a small saucepan of water on to boil, and poured a measure of porridge oats into it.

She waited pensively for the gruel to cook, even managed to force some of it down straight out of the pan, then went into the living room and began pacing the floor, going over and over the unexpected and horrible events of the evening. Two particular questions plucked insistently at her mind.

Did the murderer see her? And, if so, did he recognise her?

Skin starting to crawl, Lexy crept to the bedroom, shed her clothes and got under the pink candlewick bedspread.

She heard Kinky patter down the hall, and felt him jump lightly on to the end of the bed, and curl up. Moments later there was a small snore.

Lexy lay awake.

Perhaps she should have come clean with the police. It had been a mad, risky thing to do, giving false witness like that. But she was already in deep water, what with the stolen cash under the bed. She didn't want to get busted before she'd managed to off-load it.

Lucky she had a card up her sleeve. Just the one. All she needed to do was play it right.

11

When Lexy came to the following morning, she lay blankly for a moment, struggling to remember where she was. When she did, she wished she had stuck with the amnesia.

Kinky was scratching urgently at the door. Lexy checked her watch. It was gone nine. Her stomach was frisking about like a nervous racehorse.

She got up, walked swiftly through the cabin and unbolted the back door. The view that met her was every bit as peaceful as it had been the previous day, but Lexy's nerves were unsoothed. A lot was going to depend on the next couple of hours.

Kinky, seeming to sense her apprehension, attended to his toilet quickly and returned to her side.

She gave him the last packet of Doggy Chomps. Somehow or other she had to get some cash that day.

Lexy went to the bathroom and quickly began to wash, her ear cocked for any sound. She had one remaining clean t-shirt. She put it on and stood in front of the bathroom mirror, staring unseeingly until she became aware that she was gripping her toothbrush so tightly she was in danger of snapping it in two.

The phone rang.

Kinky barked.

Lexy leapt out of the bathroom still half-dressed and snatched up the receiver, almost knocking her front teeth out.

"Yes?" she said breathlessly.

"Oh… er… is that Ms Lomax? It's Roderick Todd here."

Thank Christ. "Mr Todd…"

"Is everything all right?"

Lexy forced herself to keep her voice calm. "Where are you at the moment?" She had been rehearsing this conversation in her mind since yesterday evening at the murder scene, when she realised there was only one way out of this mess for her.

"In my hotel room. Why?"

"Are you on your own?"

"Yes, of course." He sounded indignant.

"Look. I'm afraid I've got some bad news."

"Oh?" She imagined his quick frown.

"Mr Todd, I'm really sorry. Your wife was killed last night."

"What?" His voice was suddenly faint. "Avril killed? My Avril? Oh, God – are you sure? Was… was it a car accident?" He obviously knew how she drove. She heard his breath start to quicken.

"No. She was… found murdered." This wasn't easy.

"Murdered? By… who?"

"The police don't know yet."

There was a silence. "Mr Todd?"

"I *knew* this would happen one day." His voice was hollow.

Lexy frowned. "You did?" Well, she wished he'd bloody well told her before she agreed to follow the woman.

"I told her back in Maida Vale that if she kept on doing this it would end in disaster. I *begged* her to get help. But she was addicted to it, you see."

Oh yeah. The sex thing again.

"Do… do you know… how… it happened?" he faltered.

"She was struck on the head," said Lexy. There was no way of delivering the news delicately. "The blow killed her outright. I was following her, as we arranged, but I arrived on the scene too late to see her killer. He'd just made his escape in her car," she added. "But he abandoned it not far away."

She heard a giant sniff. "Where was this?"

"In a field. A place called Nudging."

"A field?" Roderick Todd was clearly bewildered. "What was Avril doing in a field? She didn't even like the countryside."

Did Lexy have to spell it out? "Well, she was meeting some-one, of course. I was hoping you might know who that was?"

She crossed her fingers. As soon as Lexy had the answer to that question she was going to give an anonymous tip-off to the police. Salve her conscience for withholding evidence.

"*Meeting*?" The voice registered even more astonishment, but this time tinged with scorn. "She wouldn't have gone to *meet* any of them."

"Them? What do you mean – *them*?"

"You know. Her victims."

Victims? Rather a blunt way of putting it.

"You mean she had *more* than one lover?"

Roderick Todd spluttered. "Lover? Avril didn't have any lovers. I'm talking about her *blackmail* victims."

"Oh… my… God," said Lexy.

"Didn't I make that clear?"

"Not exactly."

"Sorry. I… I find it difficult to cope…"

There was a sob, then suddenly it all came out, a torrent of words, as if he was in a confessional.

"She promised me that she'd stopped doing it after last time, but I *knew* she was at it again. She gets a particular look in her eye. And she'd started spending hours in the library, of course. That's what happened last time. She looks through local news-paper archives and finds past scandals, makes connections, snoops around. She does it very subtly." He stopped to gulp noisily, then rushed on. "It always follows the same pattern – when she finds something she can use, she sends the person concerned a few anonymous letters, hinting that she knows about their secret. If they seem to be rattled, she suggests they might want to pay to keep it quiet. Keep it from being raked up again."

Lexy shut her eyes briefly. *Hope Ellenger.*

"Her 'clients' are almost always willing to pay to keep their dirty linen out of sight." He paused, and Lexy heard him trumpet into a handkerchief. At least she hoped it was a handkerchief. "As soon as I found out what she was doing last time, back in Maida Vale, I faced her with it and she became very contrite. Straight away she agreed to our moving. We came here, and I encouraged her to throw herself into house and garden design."

Lexy gave a mirthless smile, remembering Hope and Edward's comments about the Todds' renovations.

"It's not as if we were short of money," went on Mr Todd. "In fact, I couldn't understand why Avril was sending these horrible letters, and she didn't seem able to explain it herself. I thought perhaps it was some event in her childhood."

That would have been a nice irony, thought Lexy.

"You should have got her some help, Mr Todd," she said, pointedly.

"I know, you don't have to tell me – but after last time…we had such a huge showdown. She promised me sincerely that she would never do it again."

Lexy tried to imagine the well-nourished Avril Todd tearfully making this pact with her small, insignificant husband.

"Anyway," he sighed, "over the last year, I gradually realised that she was… at it again. I asked her outright, once or twice, but she denied it. She covered her tracks very carefully. I looked everywhere for some sort of evidence, you know, envelopes, magazines with letters cut out, but she never seemed to leave anything around. The only real thing I had to go on was her mysterious weekly nights out, the ones that she told me she spent attending am-dram committee meetings. When I found out that wasn't the case, I suspected she might be using the time to distribute her… letters. You know, under cover of darkness. I felt I needed some evidence to confront her with, which is when I decided to call your number. I thought if I got a photograph of

109

her leaving letters, I would be able to have it out with her." He paused. "But surely she wouldn't have gone to meet one of her victims in person?"

"Do you have any idea who she might have been sending the letters to?" Lexy asked urgently. Other than Hope Ellenger.

"Oh, it would almost certainly have been the members of the Clopwolde Amateur Dramatics Society," he said, promptly. "If she's running true to type. It was an am-dram group in Maida Vale, too. And in Reigate."

Reigate? He hadn't mentioned Reigate.

"They were the group of people with whom she was most involved in the village." He paused. "She didn't really socialise with anyone else. Oh, my poor, stupid Avril."

Lexy was stunned by Mr Todd's news. But she had to steel herself for a bit longer, because having broken it to him that his beloved wife had been killed, now was the time for the really tricky part.

"Mr Todd?"

"Yes?"

"Obviously the police don't know we're having this conversation."

His voice was cautious. "No?"

"No. They will probably be waiting to break this news to you when you return home, as they don't know where you are at present."

"Right." He drew the word out.

Lexy squeezed her crossed fingers. "You see, when I gave my witness statement I didn't actually mention that I was on a sur-veillance job, following your wife. I said I was just driving around, and I'd got lost. I said I saw her car parked up a lane, so I just stopped to ask her the way."

Roderick Todd cottoned on quickly.

"So what you're saying is the police don't know I hired a

private eye to follow my wife?"

"No," said Lexy, gently.

"And they don't know that Avril was involved in sending out these letters?"

"Not from me," said Lexy. "I didn't realise that myself until you told me."

He became very calm. "So all I need to tell them is that I had no idea what Avril was doing or who she was meeting last night?"

"That's about the long and short of it."

There was a brief pause.

"And if it is proven that she was... murdered because she was trying to blackmail someone, I can say I had no idea what she was up to? So that it doesn't look as if Avril had been doing this with my knowledge?"

"Yup," confirmed Lexy. Everyone had a price – that's what she was relying on.

"And it will help you out too?"

"More than you know."

"Then I agree."

Lexy sank weakly to her knees, still holding the phone. That had been a close one.

"You'll have to act as if Avril's death is a terrible shock to you when you see the police this afternoon," she reminded him, respectfully.

"I won't need to act."

"No... of course not."

"In spite of this arrangement between us, I still consider it imperative her murderer is found, of course," Mr Todd continued. "I won't be able to rest. I can rely on you in this respect, can't I?"

"Sorry?"

"To find Avril's killer, I mean. You're in a unique position to do so."

No, no, no. Definitely no. Lexy gave a forced laugh. "Listen, Mr Todd, when the killer made his getaway in your wife's car, he would have left his DNA and prints all over it," she told him. "As soon as the forensic evidence comes back from the police lab, they can nail him. They won't need this evidence we're… keeping private."

"Well – if you're sure?"

As eggs is eggs. Lexy replaced the receiver and walked slowly back into the bathroom to put on her jeans.

Avril Todd a writer of poison pen letters. A blackmailer. And all the time Lexy had thought she was some kind of man-eater. She thought back to the morning two days ago when she had met Roderick Todd.

It's not who she's meeting so much as what's she's doing.

Lexy gave a grim smile. When she did the next surveillance job, she'd make damned sure that she and the client were both playing in the same rock and roll band.

When she did the next surveillance job? Lexy punched the rim of the bath. What was she thinking? There would be no more surveillance jobs, or anything else that even smacked of the words *private* and *investigations* in the same sentence.

And as for her existing work – well, Hope Ellenger's blackmail letter problem had just solved itself, to put it brutally. She certainly wouldn't be getting any more. And as for Guy Ellenger – well, he could *cherchez la chatte grotesque* himself. She would tell him that this afternoon, when she went round there.

Lexy nursed her hand. She could feel Kinky's eyes on her from where he stood in the bathroom doorway.

A sudden, sharp rap at the front door made them both jump.

Lexy struggled to do up her jeans as she went to answer.

Hopefully it would be Edward. It would be good to see a friendly face.

She pulled open the door.

A man and a woman stood expressionless on the veranda.

Oh, crap.

"Alexandra Lomax?"

She nodded silently.

They held up warrant cards, and the man stepped forward.

"I'm DI Tony Malik and this is DS Maggie Caine. It's about the murder of Mrs Avril Todd last night. Is it convenient if we come in?"

Lexy ushered them through, relaxing slightly. They hadn't arrested her on the spot. That was promising. And DI Milo must have kept shtum over her assumed name, which was big of him. She ought to feel grateful. But she guessed there would be plenty of time for that over dinner on Sunday night.

She extracted that thought from her mind with some difficulty.

"Have you arrested anyone?"

"It's a bit early yet," said DI Malik. Lexy saw perspiration running down his neck. "The forensics team is on to it, but these things take time."

How long did it take to scrape a bit of DNA off a car seat and analyse it? In the meantime a murderer was running around free. Lexy pursed her lips. With what she knew, she probably *could* suss out who it was quicker than the police. After all, she'd met most of the suspects, if Roderick Todd was right in assuming that Avril's blackmail victims were confined to members of the Clopwolde am-dram. She grappled with her conscience. If she and Mr Todd had decided, for reasons of their own, to withhold certain information from the police, the least she could do would be to follow some of the leads herself and point the boys in blue in the right direction. She liked Avril Todd even less now she knew how low the woman had sunk, but it wasn't right that her killer should stay free. Especially if he'd happened to spot Lexy in his rear view mirror as he drove away from the scene.

The policewoman's eyes flickered with practised ease around the living room.

"We'd like to go through your statement again with you, Ms Lomax."

Lexy tried to look relaxed. "Sure. Can't offer you tea or coffee or anything, I'm afraid, I'm a bit disorganised here. Only just moved in, actually. I can't believe I got caught up in all this."

Now that was a true statement if she'd ever made one.

"Was there any particular reason that you chose to drive towards Nudging last night?" asked DI Malik.

"None whatsoever," replied Lexy, airily. "It was a nice evening, and I was just following the country roads, taking in the scenery, trying to get familiar with the area."

"OK." The questioning went on. The three of them sat perspiring for twenty minutes. Lexy resolutely stuck to her story, secure now in the knowledge that Roderick Todd wasn't going to blow her cover. She was almost starting to believe it herself.

"Right," said DS Caine, eventually. "I think that covers everything. We shouldn't have to bother you too much again."

"Good," said Lexy. "I mean…"

But the officers smiled understandingly. They all stood up.

"Oh, yes – one more thing… have the press been on to you at all?" asked the policewoman.

"No." Lexy stared at her, alarmed. "DI Milo said he'd keep my name out of the press statement."

"Oh – OK." She gave Lexy a quizzical look. "We haven't released anything officially yet, because we haven't been able to trace any of the relatives, but sometimes these things get leaked out. So, let us know if you see anyone hanging around. And because we haven't released anything yet it's imperative you don't tell *anyone* about what happened last night, for obvious reasons."

"Course not." As if she'd do that.

"We're trying to track down the husband at the moment," the policewoman went on. "We believe he was away overnight."

"Poor bloke." Lexy gave her a bland smile.

The detective inspector's phone burst into life. He answered it briskly, then turned to his colleague.

"Maggie – we have to go."

"Thank you for your time," she said to Lexy. Call us on this number if you think of anything else that could help us." She handed her a card, and they left.

Lexy closed the front door with exaggerated care.

"And to think we came here to get away from it all," she said to Kinky.

12

The more Lexy thought about the notion of trying to identify Avril's killer herself, the more she liked it. It would be an atonement, a way of getting rid of her guilt. Because she did feel guilty. She could make a start by carrying out some low-key enquiries in the village about where the various members of the Clopwolde am-dram society had spent the previous evening.

She went through to the kitchen, reheated the porridge she'd left from the night before and made herself a cup of black tea. She found herself still dwelling on the thought of having dinner with DI Milo the following evening, not so much now because the idea offended her moral sensibilities, more that she was looking forward to eating a meal that tasted of something.

After breakfast Lexy collected up her remaining money. It consisted of five pence left from the two pounds that Hope Ellenger had given her on Thursday, ten pence that she'd found down the back of the sofa, and a handful of coppers. She might just about be able to get a can of the cheapest dog food going. She didn't tell Kinky.

Her thoughts strayed to the fifty-pound notes crammed into the battered suitcase. It was so tempting just to borrow one of them. Get some proper provisions in. See herself and the dog through until she got a job. If she'd done that in the first place she wouldn't be involved in any of this sorry farrago now.

But then she reminded herself how Gerard had got the money. Lexy was well aware that her husband wasn't exactly an angel when it came to valuations, or anything else, for that matter. But you had to know where to draw the line. The Gillespie affair went beyond it. Way beyond. She felt a familiar stab of fury.

Kinky gave a small whine, and Lexy put out a hand to him.

"We're not going to touch a single note of that money," she vowed. "A single note. We'll get by."

She locked the cabin door and was shortly negotiating the wooden steps set into the cliff face, Kinky hopping neatly down after her.

Lexy had decided to walk into Clopwolde along the beach, and keep an eye out on the way for small change that might have dropped where people had been sitting. And perhaps a discarded sandwich or two. That reheated porridge and water mixture hadn't really hit the spot.

The tide was out, leaving a broad strip of shingle. A scattering of people were sunbathing, strolling, or just gazing out to sea.

They set out in the direction of Clopwolde, to the hypnotic soundtrack of waves on shingle.

After just a few minutes Lexy was damp with perspiration and her nose was burning. She started to wish she had worn her baseball cap – it was somewhere in the jumble of underclothes back at the cabin. And no one appeared to have left a single penny.

A party of gulls shrieked and wheeled noisily at the water's edge.

"It's all right for them," Lexy said morosely to Kinky, as she scanned the ground. "They're not coping with life's grisly realities. All they have to do is cruise up and down the beach, planning their next bit of fun."

"I'll drink to that." The amused voice behind her made Lexy twist around sharply.

"It's all right – only me." It was Edward de Glenville, wearing a loose white shirt, long khaki shorts, leather sandals and a disarming smile.

Kinky wagged his tail, and Edward squatted down and stroked him.

"You look exhausted, sweetheart," he observed, giving Lexy a sidelong glance.

"Yeah, I feel it. I had rather a… hectic time after you left yesterday."

"You too, huh?" Edward sat down heavily, wincing as the pebbles shifted under him.

He gave a theatrical sigh. Lexy sat next to him. "Care to tell me about it?" She could see he was dying to.

"I decided to go and see the ex."

Lexy raised her eyebrows. "At the memorabilia shop?"

"Yes," Edward went on blithely. "Thought I'd face up to the situation instead of skulking about the village trying to avoid him, which is ridiculous. I mean, we're both in the am-dram for starters. And we're meant to be rehearsing *South* bloody *Pacific* today."

"What…" began Lexy.

"Not the Nellie Forbush role, if that's what you're thinking," he interrupted, reprovingly. "No – Sheri-Anne Davis beat both me and Tammy Caradoc to that one. Can't think why. But I'm Stewpot – which is almost as good. I get to wear a sailor suit and sing *There Is Nothing Like a Dame*. He demonstrated, ringingly.

A few people looked around the sides of their windbreakers.

Lexy cut him off. "So what happened at the shop?"

Edward sighed. "Well, let's just say that Peter has a few less items of memorabilia than he started with yesterday morning."

"You mean you nicked them?"

"No," said Edward indignantly. "I smashed 'em. Then I got arrested and driven off to Lowestoft police station."

"Seriously? You know, I was…"

"But Peter agreed not to press charges." Edward smiled complacently.

Lexy eyed him. "So… everything is sorted between you?"

"Well – we're talking, even if it is only in expletives. Should make for an interesting rehearsal." Edward picked up a pebble and turned it over in his hand. "Anyway, I've been down the shop this morning, cleaning up. It's open for business again now." He gave her a lopsided smile. "And I think Peter and I are too."

So that's two members of the am-dram lot to cross off the list of suspects, mused Lexy. If Edward and Peter were having a gay calamity at Gentler Times yesterday evening, they couldn't have been murdering Avril Todd.

Edward squinted at Lexy. "Are you all right, sweetie?"

Lexy drew a deep breath. She couldn't keep this thing to herself any more. "I had to go to the police station last night as well."

Edward gazed at her in sudden interest. "You did? Why? What on earth can you have been up to? You only just got here!"

Lexy hesitated. "I was out with Kinky yesterday evening and I… well, I stumbled across a corpse."

Edward stared at her in astonishment, and then gave a peal of laughter. "A corpse? What, just lying there?"

"It certainly wasn't strolling around admiring the view." Lexy began to laugh herself.

"Did you actually fall over it?" Edward snorted.

"No. I climbed over a stile, and there she was." Lexy's laugh faded. "With her head smashed in. Murdered."

Edward's smile snapped off. "You poor girl."

"It had just happened. The killer was driving off when I got there."

"That's… that's terrible." Edward had gone grey. "Did you see…?"

"No. I called the police," she fibbed, wanting to skirt over the DI Milo detail, "and suddenly the place was crawling with uniforms, and I was bundled down to a local nick to give a statement."

"Did you find out who it was? The victim I mean?"

Lexy hesitated.

"You did, didn't you? Was it someone from the village?"

Edward was looking at her like an expectant baby seal.

Lexy guessed there was no real harm in telling him. In confidence, of course. "Yeah. It was Avril Todd."

Edward gave a high-pitched shriek. More faces looked around striped wind-breakers.

Lexy made urgent shushing movements.

"No!" Edward shook his head, his round brown eyes enormous. "Avril? Dead? Murdered? I can't believe it! I just cannot believe it. I mean, I spoke to her only yesterday afternoon at the village hall. She was ordering someone around, as usual. She was an insufferable old cow, of course, but that's no reason to kill her." A look of delicious anticipation suddenly passed across his face. "Just wait until I tell the rest of the cast about this!"

"Ah, no – you can't," said Lexy at once. "It hasn't been made public yet."

"Please don't tell me I have to keep this secret," implored Edward. "I shall implode."

"Look – R… her husband doesn't even know yet," said Lexy, urgently. "If you give one hint that you know what's happened to her, I shall get into serious trouble with the boys in blue. They'll hang me out to dry."

"Here – you're not a suspect, are you?" Edward looked mouth-wateringly scandalised at the thought.

"Probably," said Lexy. "But only because I was in the wrong place at the wrong time."

"Grief, darling – wouldn't it be absolutely awful if it got pinned on you?"

"Yes," said Lexy. "But that won't happen, because I didn't do it."

"Where did it happen, out of interest?"

"In a field off the A12. Near a place called Nudging."

"What was Avril doing over there?"

"No idea."

"What were you doing over there?"

Lexy groaned. "You sound like Inspector Morse. I just fancied going for a drive, checking out the scenery. I lost my way. Saw her car parked and went up to ask her for directions."

"You need sat-nav, lovie."

"Now he tells me."

Edward put his head on one side, observed Lexy sympathetically for a moment, then pushed himself up and held out a hand.

"Come on – I'm taking you to my place for a drinky-poo. I know I need one after hearing all this. It's just over there – no excuses, now."

"Yes, but…" Lexy allowed herself to be pulled upright, with only slight resistance. After all, there might be something to eat with the drinky-poo, even it was only an olive.

Edward headed purposefully for a ramshackle set of steps leading up the cliff side, nothing like the sturdy ones that Lexy had recently descended. A single metal bar wound with barbed wire hung across the bottom step, bearing a sign which read DANGER – KEEP OUT.

He ducked airily under it taking care not to snag his shirt, and held out a hand to Lexy.

"You sure?" she said. "They're not going to collapse or anything?"

"Of course not, sweetie. I've been using them for years. They're a short-cut to my place." He grinned impishly, as if concealing a secret joke.

Lexy slid under the bar and stared up at the rotting steps.

"It's much safer than it looks." Edward started upwards, two steps at a time. Kinky scampered ahead of him, his eel-like tail whipping from side to side.

Lexy shrugged and followed, squinting up into the glaring sun.

High above them a dark oblong shape protruded over the crumbling cliff edge like a single rotten tooth. As they approached it, Lexy thought she could make out marks on its flat surface.

"What the hell's that?"

"Great-uncle Cornelius's tombstone," replied Edward, promptly, as if he had been waiting for her to ask. "And I'm expecting the old bugger to appear any day now."

"You what?" Lexy threw him a startled look, but Edward didn't look in the grip of denial. He was inspecting the cliff face dispassionately.

Lexy clambered up the last steps, feeling faint with hunger and trepidation, and found herself looking at a further dozen tombstones, overgrown and crooked, surrounded by a tumble-down wall.

Edward smiled sadly. "And to think that a hundred years ago this graveyard was half a mile back from the sea. Not any more, as you see. The last remains of the old church fell into the sea fifty years ago. And since then, in really high tides, we sometimes get a skeleton or two from this graveyard washed down on to the beach. Or a skull appearing in the cliff face."

Lexy felt herself shudder. Even on a guileless, sun-filled day like this, the ivy-covered graveyard looked dank and menacing, as if the dead were awake and waiting silently for this last indignity.

"So what do you think?" Edward was saying, his impish grin suddenly back.

"About what?" asked Lexy, confused. "Great-uncle Cornelius?"

"No. About my humble abode." Edward had turned away from the graveyard and adopted a pose reminiscent of a magician's glamorous assistant. "Ta-da!"

Lexy turned round. "Bloody hell."

Set back in the trees, in a golden hollow, lay a small mansion. It was built of honey-coloured stone, with Dutch gables, mullioned windows and a long portico supported by slim columns.

"So – you don't live in a log cabin, then?"

"No," he admitted. "Although I thought I might have to eventually." He grinned. "My father, God bless him, wasn't exactly keen to leave the de Glenville ancestral home to such an unsuitable son. There was a nasty moment when I thought it might go to my cousin George, but he turned out to be even worse than me. Member of the Labour Party, for a start. Come on," he added, "don't be shy."

Finding it hard to believe her eyes, Lexy followed Edward across a lawn, already yellowing in the heat, to a large, studded front door. It opened with an atmospheric creak into a shadowy entrance hall. Kinky's claws clicked loudly on the marble floor as he trotted in.

A huge Victorian coatstand stood in one corner, overhung by a set of enormous stag antlers and complemented by a grotesque elephant's foot umbrella stand. In the other corners, ghost-like figures stood in various affected poses.

"It has statues," said Lexy, gazing around in awe.

"Oh, yes. Statues and busts galore. I talk to them." Edward patted the alabaster head of the Emperor Claudius affectionately.

He gave a sudden small squeal. "Post! I completely forgot to check the letterbox when I got home yesterday. Must have been the jet-lag."

He let himself out of the front door, and reappeared moments later with a big sheaf of letters and plastic-wrapped magazines.

"Ruddy National Trust," he snorted. "I keep telling them father's dead. Come through to the kitchen and I'll organise a couple of large G and Ts."

The kitchen was as big as a barn, and very clean and tidy. On the walls were framed photographs of Edward through the years, in various poses with dogs and horses and cars. A smiling woman with a maternal air appeared in many of them. Over the huge butler sink was a long black and white photograph of an assembly

123

of bowler-hatted men sitting in three ordered rows, leaning on canes and smoking curly pipes. "Clopwolde village committee 1953" said Edward, seeing her eyeing it. "That's father bang in the middle. Big moustache." He gave her a knowing grin. "Not something he'd want to be wearing in this day and age."

Lexy peered at the stern-faced figure. Edward had inherited his mother's features.

She sat at a vast oak table, scarred and bowed by what looked like centuries of use.

Kinky wandered over to a long, well-chewed stick propped up in the corner and sniffed at it appreciatively.

"Have you got a dog?" Lexy asked. Edward followed the direction of her gaze. "Not any more, sweetie. The stick used to belong to Nimrod, my father's retriever. I keep it for old times' sake."

Lexy watched him flip through his post.

"Do any other de Glenvilles live here?" she asked, curiously.

"Nope, I'm the last, except for Cousin George," Edward replied cheerfully. "After Dad popped off last year."

He gave a sudden exclamation. "Not another one of these!"

It was an oddly familiar-looking plain white envelope. He ripped it open, and gave a sudden shout of delighted laughter.

"Can you believe this?" he grinned, sliding it over to Lexy, whose expression had frozen.

It contained a statement made from a combination of letters cut from a newspaper.

HE WAS PUSHED, WASN'T HE?

"*Two* poison pen letters! Now I really know I've arrived!"

Lexy felt her heart quicken. Avril had been quite busy recently, by the looks of it, and she obviously had a bit of a theme going. "Any idea who might have sent this?"

"Nope."

"What does it mean?"

He snorted. "I can only assume that someone thinks my old man was pushed when he had his accident last year. Ridiculous."

"Accident?"

"He had a fall. From the cliff. Rather unpleasant."

"Are you going to do anything about the letter?"

"Like go to the police?" Edward shook his head. "I'm going to completely ignore it. Whoever's sending them will get bored eventually. It'll be someone with a sad little life and a chip on their shoulder, whose only kick is trying to bring down people who are happier than they are. Why give them the satisfaction?"

"What did the other one say?" asked Lexy.

"The first one? It just said, *I know who killed your father.*"

"Did you keep it?" Lexy asked, quickly.

"Yeah – I framed it and hung it up in my living room." Edward giggled at her expression. "No – of course not, sweetie. I tore it up and binned it. It was weeks ago, before I went to the States."

He glanced down at the letter he had just opened. "Don't know why they're banging on about this – the old man wasn't killed. He just fell." Edward's face became serious for an instant, and he picked up the letter, tore it into pieces and dropped the resultant confetti carelessly into a bin. "I can't wait to see what the next one's going to say! The de Glenville family had so many skeletons in their closet – and a few out of it, dear – that your friendly local poison pen writer could keep himself amused for years."

Lexy sensed that Edward was more rattled than he let on, and was glad he wouldn't be receiving any more, although she couldn't tell him that.

"Right – time for refreshments." She watched him open an enormous fridge and take out a litre bottle of gin, twisting the lid as he did so. He poured generous measures into two tall glasses and delved back to get tonic water and ice. Lexy caught a glimpse of a pie with a latticed pastry top. She came very close to drooling. Kinky's nose twitched compulsively.

"*Voila!* Get on the outside of that!" Edward handed her the glass, pushing the fridge door shut with his hip.

Lexy gazed at the drink. She'd rather get on the outside of that pie. Should she ask Edward for something to eat? She cringed. No – she just couldn't. It would be too embarrassing for words. She sipped her drink gingerly.

Edward sat opposite her and cupped his chin in his hands, gazing at her. "Now – what's the matter, sweetheart?"

"What do you mean?" she asked.

"You have a pensive quality."

Lexy gave him a wan smile. "Sorry. I'm a bit preoccupied today. To be honest, I need to get a job."

Edward raised his eyebrows, surprised.

Lexy pressed on quickly. "I don't care what I do – bar work, cleaning, shop assistant, deckchair assistant… Any ideas?"

He blew his cheeks out. "What – in Clopwolde? Tricky. There's not even enough work for the locals." He registered Lexy's crestfallen expression. "Tell you what – I'll make some enquiries."

"Thanks," said Lexy fervently. "I guess you must know a lot of people."

"Everyone who's anyone in this place, darling."

Lexy gave Edward a significant look. "I'm specifically after a cash-in-hand deal, if you know what I mean."

"Want to remain incognito, do we?"

"Exactly that," replied Lexy.

Edward looked around. "I'd offer you cleaning work here, if you'd stoop to it, but I already have…"

He put a hand to his mouth and gave a sudden singing exclamation. "Time!"

Lexy looked up at the clock. It was half past eleven.

"I need to be at the rehearsal."

"When?"

"Fifteen minutes ago. Not a full rehearsal, it's just Sheri-Anne, Tristan, Peter and me running through a couple of numbers." Edward stood up and drained his gin and tonic. "Want a lift down to the village?" he asked, swinging a car key.

"Thanks, I will." Lexy stood up too, and rounded up Kinky, who was still sniffing around the chewed stick with great interest.

"It's going to be a pretty strange old afternoon, what with everyone wondering where Avril is, and me trying to join in the general surprise at her absence," Edward remarked as he led the way through a back door.

"Look on it as a test for your acting talents," she said, firmly, shooing Kinky away from the stick, which he was clearly intent on dragging out with him.

"Couldn't I just…"

"No. Not if you want to keep me out of trouble."

"OK, OK. I'll do my astounded 'Where on earth can she have got to?' routine."

Lexy just hoped he'd be able to keep the news to himself better than she had.

A sleek maroon Jaguar stood in the shade of a lilac tree in the back drive. A minute later they were bumping gently down a dusty track, the engine a muted purr. Lexy leaned back in the soft, squashy leather seat, feeling so comfortable that she found herself wishing they were setting off on a long drive, instead of the short hop to Clopwolde. A long drive with no particular destination. Driving away from all her problems and…

"Here we are."

Her eyes snapped open. The car was parked just outside the village hall.

Sheri-Anne Davis was outside, a cigarette in one hand. She was writing on a large chalkboard propped up on a windowsill. It said:

Important – All Cast Members – Full Rehearsal, Sunday at 10.00!

She wore a pair of microscopic shorts and a cropped top which showed off her tanned midriff and glittering belly-button jewel a treat. A cutesy little handbag dangled from her shoulder.

"Ooh, dear, look at her," said Edward. "I thought we were doing *South Pacific*, not South Pole Dancing. Allow me." He jumped out of the car, and came round to open Lexy's door.

"Thanks again," Lexy said, awkwardly. How embarrassing was that, to fall asleep when he was doing her a favour?

"It was a pleasure, darling. Bye-ee."

She watched as Edward flounced up to Sheri-Anne open-armed and air-kissed her on each cheek, before disappearing into the building.

Lexy nodded to Sheri-Anne, who was grinding out her cigarette with a killer heel. "You look amazing. Did you get that tan in Clopwolde?"

Sheri-Anne gave her a condescending look. "No – from a spray. Sunbathing's bad for you."

Lexy glanced down at the squashed cigarette butt, then quickly back to Sheri-Anne. Now wasn't the time.

"Well, it doesn't look in the least orange," she lied.

Sheri-Anne looked gratified.

Lexy gazed meditatively down the high street. "So… what's the nightlife like around here?"

The girl laughed scornfully. "It's like, totally awesome – if you like pub quizzes."

"No music venues, raves, anything in the area?"

"No, it's crap. There's a couple of clubs in Ipswich." Sheri-Anne gave her a superior look. "Personally I prefer going out to dinner, that kind of stuff?"

"Oh, right," said Lexy. She tried to imagine Sheri-Anne at a dinner party, discussing literature and the arts.

"Were you out last night?" She tried to make it sound chatty.

"No. I was working late." Interesting.

"Going out tonight, then?"

"Yeah."

"Anywhere nice?"

"Well…" Sheri-Anne clearly didn't want to tell Lexy, but she couldn't resist bragging. "Bellington's. In Norwich. It's a bistro." Sheri-Anne said the word with relish, as though it were an exotic concept.

Lexy arranged her features to convey that she was impressed. The other girl snapped open her little handbag and pulled out a glossy card, handing it to Lexy. "This is it."

"Cool – I might try it."

Sheri-Anne gave her a once over. "They've got, like, a dress code." She turned and pushed open the heavy front door to the village hall. "Bye then."

A couple of men walking past stopped dead.

"Yeah, all right – put your eyeballs back," muttered Lexy. To think that only a few days ago men were ogling *her* like that! How demeaning.

Irritably straightening her t-shirt, she continued along the road. That was Sheri-Anne accounted for anyway, working in the surgery late last night, although Lexy thought it unlikely that the girl was the type to go around thwacking people over the head. She wouldn't want to break her nails.

Something about their exchange was bothering her, all the same. Lexy walked thoughtfully down the high street, keeping a weather eye on Kinky. Before long she found herself at the bottom of Windmill Hill. She registered the road name, and stepped back instinctively in the shade of a hedge, wondering if Roderick Todd had returned from Lincoln yet. She craned her head round and up the road. There was a police car parked half-way up, with two uniformed officers in it. They must be waiting for him. In fact, he might drive past at any moment and it wouldn't do for her to be loitering on…

"*What* a dinky little doggy!" Lexy spun round, to be greeted by the sight of Kinky lying on his back on the pavement, being caressed by a grey-haired old lady. They both looked up at Lexy. "Isn't he adorable?"

Lexy gave her a wan smile.

"Is he yours?"

"Yup."

"What's his name?"

"K... Keith." Probably best.

"Aw, isn't that sweet? Hello, Keith."

Kinky gave a brave grin.

"I think those police are there about the Todds," said the old woman, straightening up with a groan. "At number four. At least it's number four now. It used to be number three and four, till they knocked them into one. Terrible thing to do, that was."

"Is something wrong then?" Lexy asked, wide-eyed.

"Eh? Oh, yes. We think it must be to do with Mrs Todd. Avril. The police have been round asking when we last saw her, and if she was with anyone. I wonder if there's been an accident." The old lady thought for a moment.

Kinky took the opportunity to right himself, having done his duty.

"You see, her husband, he's away at some do. He went off yesterday afternoon. Told Reg at number two that he was going to Leicester or somewhere."

Lexy just stopped herself from saying 'Lincoln.'

"The police broke into their house," added the old lady. "Don't know what Avril's going to say when she gets back." She gave a wheezing laugh. "That fancy glass door of hers is all shattered."

Lexy winced.

"...Horace was in there on his own, so they asked if Reg next door would have him until Mr Todd gets back, but Reg isn't very happy about it because he's allergic."

Lexy remembered the mewing cat basket that Avril had been holding when she first encountered her at the vet's.

"Did anyone see Mrs Todd yesterday?" she asked.

"Well, it's funny really," confided the old lady, "but I saw her myself at half past seven yesterday evening. Striding up this hill like the clappers she was. Clack, clack, clack, lugging that big tapestry bag of hers." She gave another wheezy smirk, then her unkempt eyebrows descended in a frown. "But my young neighbour Dorothy at number fourteen, she reckons it was quarter past seven that Avril came up here. And I could see the police believed her, not me, on account of that clock of hers. But I know what I saw, and when I saw it. *Coronation Street* was just starting." Her whiskered chin shook indignantly. "Anyway, I'd better be on my way, love, or my old man won't get his dinner. Bye-bye, Keith."

Kinky wagged his tail politely.

13

Lexy retraced her steps to the high street. She couldn't see that it would matter much whether it had been a quarter past seven or half past that Avril had come striding up the hill. It was clearly an issue of pride to the old lady, though.

As she moved further into the village centre, Lexy noticed something different about Clopwolde. On every lamp-post and standing structure there was a poster with vivid black and yellow lettering.

LOST CAT

LARGE REWARD FOR RETURN.

YOUNG FEMALE CAT ANSWERING TO

PRINCESS NOO-NOO, WITH CREAM-COLOURED,

SHORT CURLY COAT. MISSING SINCE WED 3RD.

PLEASE CALL TRISTAN OR TAMMY

IF YOU THINK YOU MIGHT HAVE SEEN HER.

Underneath was a mobile telephone number and a muzzy photograph of the cat, Princess Noo-Noo, lying down. She looked, Lexy thought, almost like a normal cat. Nothing like as deformed as Guy Ellenger had described her. He was obviously given to exaggeration. Not entirely perfect, then.

She groaned inwardly. She wasn't exactly looking forward to telling the vet that she had decided against trying to find the creature, but the sooner she did, the sooner she could start looking for a sensible job.

She walked past the side alley where the vet's surgery was situated, wondering if it opened on Saturdays. She might be able to tell him there and then, get it over and done with. She swung abruptly into the narrow lane, at the same time as a laden figure approaching from the opposite direction. They just managed to avoid colliding.

It was a large, plump woman, heavily made-up. She had a large bag in one hand, from which a number of long, rolled canvases protruded, together with a sheaf of the brightly coloured missing cat posters Lexy had just been studying.

"Sorry," said Lexy.

The woman gave her an irritated look. "That isn't one of Guy Ellenger's chihuahuas running loose, is it?"

"No, he's mine," said Lexy. "Come here, Kinky."

The chihuahua had started sniffing at the woman's bag, and Lexy hoped he wasn't about to cock his leg over it. The woman obviously had the same idea, as she heaved the bag into her other hand.

"I do know Guy, though," said Lexy. "We met the other day. I've just moved here actually. My name's Lexy Lomax." She stuck out a hand.

"Tammy Caradoc," said the woman guardedly.

That would explain why she was toting the missing cat posters – she'd obviously just been plastering them all over the village. Lexy felt another stab of guilt.

She studied the woman. Tammy Caradoc was clearly in her fifties, a few years older than her husband, and she looked it. She must have been beautiful once, and she was trying to keep up the illusion, but the thick make-up couldn't disguise the lines. In fact, it accentuated them. She had flicked-back blonde hair with grey showing through, and wore skin-tight jeans and a blue paisley smock top that must have been twenty years out of date. It made her look a good ten years older than she should have done. She also looked unhappy.

"You're an actress, aren't you?"

That brightened her. "Yes. Did you recognise me?"

"Of course," said Lexy, thinking back to what Tristan had said in the tea shop. "You were in *Bergerac*, weren't you?"

133

Tammy's smile widened. "That, and a few others. My husband Tristan is a well-known actor too."

Lexy made a noise of polite interest. He was certainly good at acting like he wasn't married.

"You do know the vet's is closed?" Tammy started walking down towards the surgery.

Lexy followed her. "I just wondered if Guy might be at the surgery anyway, doing paperwork or something."

"He doesn't work on Saturdays," said Tammy, "except for emergencies." They had reached the door.

"Looks like Hope's not there either," Lexy name-dropped as they peered into the unlit reception. "Or Sheri-Anne." As soon as she spoke, Lexy remembered that Sheri-Anne was at the am-dram rehearsal.

So did Tammy, by the look of jealous rage that flashed in her eye. She mopped her forehead. "I'm dropping off some canvases for Hope, as a matter of fact, if your dog hasn't…"

"Kinky!" Lexy glared at the dog. "Er… does Hope paint?"

"She does the stage backdrops. She's going to start them this weekend, but she likes to do them in rough first."

Tammy hoisted the bag of canvases on to her hip, produced a bunch of keys, selected one and unlocked the door. "It's all right," she said, clocking Lexy's expression. "Hope does allow me into her inner sanctum."

Lexy walked thoughtfully back to the high street, stopping outside the newsagent's.

Looked like the plant nursery job was gone; the card wasn't there any more. Typical. She went in, hoping to sneak a quick look through the local newspaper's job section. But the man behind the counter kept his eye firmly on her, and after a few minutes she had to give up and leave.

She and Kinky threaded their way through crowds of sunburnt tourists. Even somewhere as dignified as Clopwolde-on-Sea couldn't escape the type of holidaymakers who thought it was a good idea to put their rolls of blubber on parade. It was like negotiating a pack of rutting elephant seals. With some relief Lexy found a quiet bench to sit on in a public garden. Kinky found a discarded half-saveloy by a bin. Lexy watched him scoff it down. Poor little blighter.

The vision of dinner with DI Milo the following night rose unbidden again in her mind's eye, and she let it. Green curry, red curry, fragrant rice, tempura, stir-fried noodles… she almost moaned out loud.

The only problem was what might be for dessert.

Gritting her teeth, Lexy took out her notebook.

A number of things about Avril's death had been bothering her, especially since speaking to Roderick Todd that morning.

Why had Avril driven out to a remote field last night if not to meet someone? She began to jot.

Avril had clearly known exactly where the field was, and when she arrived, had probably got into it through the gap in the hedge, as Lexy hadn't noticed her climb over the stile. Perhaps she got whoever she was blackmailing to drop the money somewhere in the field, and she'd gone to collect it. Might even be her usual *modus operandi*.

But someone had either followed Avril through the gap or was already waiting in the field.

The killer had breached the etiquette of the game. But why had Avril invited trouble by choosing such a remote location for the drop? Not advisable if you were a lone female blackmailer, albeit a large, meaty one.

Lexy wished she'd had the presence of mind to ask Mr Todd how Avril had picked up her payments in the past, if indeed he had known. She looked at her watch. He must have arrived home by now, and might even be on his way to Fenmere police station to make a statement. She felt a little surge of anxiety at the thought, and swiftly turned her mind to another peculiarity of the previous night.

What had Avril meant by her cry of "W... *what the hell is that?*" just before she uttered her final scream? Had she seen something she didn't understand? Something that didn't make sense?

Or could she have been referring to the murder weapon?

A long, heavy object.

That's what the police surgeon had said yesterday. His initial impression of the cause of death was 'a blow to the left temple with a long, heavy object, probably blunt-edged, like a baseball bat'.

Lexy imagined the scene. Avril, believing herself to be alone, heading straight to the hidey-hole where she expected to find her money. Then, perhaps hearing a movement, turning around and finding herself face to face with her armed killer. Her initial reaction would be surprise and indignation, hence the weak, slightly querulous cry.

"I don't understand...what's happening? Are you mad?"

She thought for a moment. She could understand the cry being querulous, but why weak? From what she'd gathered about Avril, Lexy thought she'd be letting out a strident holler at that point.

Then Avril had seen the murder weapon, raised.

Lexy realised she had been living this scenario so deeply in her imagination that she had taken the part of the murderer; her right arm was raised threateningly above Kinky, her expression one of violent rage.

A family of four had come to a halt nearby and were watching her silently. Lexy hastily lowered her hand to pat Kinky's head, and simpered at the onlookers.

But the exercise had taught her something valuable. The killer would probably be right-handed, if he'd given Avril a blow to the left temple.

And, as Mr Todd had confirmed that morning, the killer was likely to be a member of the Clopwolde Amateur Dramatics Society.

While these were all probabilities, rather than certainties, they at least gave Lexy something to go on.

So far, she had established that at least two members of the society, Hope Ellenger and Edward de Glenville, had received poison pen letters. Both, she mused, were right-handed. She remembered how Edward had stood as he twisted the lid from the gin bottle, and how Hope had held her coffee cup. But Edward had an alibi – she'd already established that, although it needed checking. Frankly, it was hard to imagine either him or Hope in the role of murderer, but she couldn't afford to rule anyone out because she instinctively liked them. Which brought her neatly to her next visit of the day.

Kittiwake was, as Guy Ellenger had described, halfway along a meandering lane called Gorse Rise, facing out over the vibrant purple heathland that surrounded Clopwolde. It was an old-style green and cream bungalow, rather in need of a coat of paint, like the vet's surgery. It was made to look even shabbier by the pristine bungalow next door, called Amalfi, which was brilliant white, painful to look at in the burning sun.

Lexy pushed open the wooden gate to Kittiwake. Two black and white cats, one sleek and slim, one fat and fluffy, were sunning themselves on the tiled porch. They blinked up benignly at Lexy's approach, until a snorting bark from Kinky sent them scattering.

He gave her an insouciant look.

"Right, that's your last warning," she snapped, picking him up and gripping him tightly.

She pressed the doorbell. Immediately she heard a familiar sound. The bark of a chihuahua, magnified fourfold.

She glared down at Kinky, daring him to bare his teeth. The last thing she needed was for Guy Ellenger to have to spend the afternoon carrying out surgery on his own dogs.

But he was quiet, his bat ears pricked and his large dark eyes full of interest.

Lexy heard a muffled voice and the door opened.

A turbulent confusion of small dogs hurtled out.

"Hi," said Guy Ellenger, giving her his wholesome smile.

"Hello," said Lexy, wobbling slightly in the maelstrom.

"How's the ear?"

"Eh? Oh – *his* ear." She looked at Kinky. "Yeah. It's er… getting better." She realised she had forgotten to put Kinky's plastic funnel on.

Guy Ellenger was inspecting his stitching. "That healing cream's pretty good, isn't it?" he said. "Expensive, but worth it. And don't let anyone tell you otherwise."

Lexy gave him a sharp look. Avril's threat to his Robin Hood act had obviously got to him. Not that he needed to worry about that any more.

"It does work really well. Thanks for donating it to me," she said quietly.

"Well, you know – he's a deserving cause," said Guy, ruffling Kinky's head. "It's all right, you can put him down to play with the others," he added.

Lexy grasped Kinky even more firmly. Play?

"Go on – it's fine. They'll be gentle with him."

He had no idea.

Gingerly, Lexy unloosed her grip on Kinky, and lowered him into the swirl of tiny dogs, her eyes tightly shut in prayer.

But the expected frenzy of snarling, snapping and flying fur didn't happen. When Lexy opened her eyes the chihuahuas were doing the unseemly sniffing thing that dogs always feel the need to do. Then, compulsory greeting over, they scampered into the house like kids at a birthday party, and disappeared from sight.

"Blimey," she said.

"Chihuahuas always like their own kind," remarked Guy. Lexy wished he'd shared this little gem of information earlier.

"Fancy a cuppa?"

She nodded fervently. He led her through to a homely-looking kitchen, crammed with the apparatus of cooking – a multitude of pots and pans, jars, bottles, utensils, recipe books. Her eyes locked on what looked and smelt like a freshly baked malt loaf, sitting on a rack.

"I expect you've had lunch," he said, organising two mugs, and switching on a red electric kettle.

"No!" she stated with some force. She wasn't going to let this chance pass her by.

He looked slightly taken aback. "Oh, well – in that case, let's christen this." He picked up a bread knife, and placed the loaf on a wooden cutting board. "Don't mind it still warm, do you?"

In a voice hoarse with emotion, Lexy made some kind of incoherent affirmative.

She watched him cut several generous slices, subconsciously noting that he was right-handed. "Did you cook it yourself?" There just had to be a wife or girlfriend somewhere in the equation.

"Yup. Made the dough earlier this morning with fresh yeast. Rises really well in this weather."

Carrying a laden plate, and wearing a reverential look, Lexy followed the vet through to a shaded patio that gave out on to an overgrown lawn. Chihuahua tails were visible now and again.

"I don't garden too well though," he admitted, apologetically. "But I do try."

"You should see mine." Lexy settled herself in a rusting wrought iron chair and took a bite out of the malt loaf. It tasted like a moist piece of heaven. She savoured it, eyes closed.

Right. She needed to tell him she couldn't do the lost cat

thing. Strike while the iron was hot.

"Um… this cat…"

Inside the bungalow a phone rang.

Guy Ellenger rolled his eyes. "Won't be a moment."

Lexy helped herself to another slice of the loaf, and idly watched the dogs tumble on to the patio, one by one, and flop down in the shade of a large pot. Kinky peeled off from the crowd to sit next to her. At least she thought it was Kinky – he was almost indistinguishable from the others. She drummed her fingers quietly on the table.

Guy Ellenger reappeared. "Man about a dog. Not urgent, luckily." He glanced at the table. "Malt loaf OK?"

"Best I've ever tasted," Lexy assured him truthfully, popping another piece into her mouth.

"Excellent." He settled down beside her. It was now or never.

"So, this cat…" she mumbled.

"Oh, yes – this cat," snorted the vet. He threw a dark look in the direction of the immaculate bungalow next door. "Unbelievable that they've accused my lot of savaging it! As if they'd do a thing like that. They're chihuahuas, not Rottweilers, for heaven's sake…"

Lexy gave him a feeble smile.

"…anyway, they're used to cats, I've got two of my own, and they've never so much as touched them. But," he added, "If by some unfortunate misunderstanding they had attacked Princess, there would be some kind of evidence, wouldn't there? Or are they seriously suggesting that the dogs ate the thing whole?"

"Do you think they can hear us?" asked Lexy.

"What, the dogs?"

"No, the neighbours."

Guy Ellenger shook his head. "They've gone out. There's a mini-rehearsal in Clopwolde village hall. Am-dram stuff."

Lexy nodded. Not for Tammy there wasn't, now Sheri-Anne

Davis had taken over the lead role.

"I mean, aside from anything else," Guy continued, returning abruptly to the subject in hand, "can you imagine what it would do to my business if these allegations about the cat got out?" He frowned. "Things are difficult enough at the moment."

"The thing is…" said Lexy.

"Nothing I can't handle, of course. Just some local woman causing trouble. First of all she made a song and dance about our complementary medicines. Got my sister in a right state. In fact, I've never seen her so… anyway… would you believe this, the other night this bloody woman dropped an anonymous letter through the surgery door."

Lexy swallowed the remains of the slice and coughed, spraying crumbs across the table.

"Very unpleasant it was too," he continued, passing her a paper napkin. "She'd somehow found out about something that happened in our past, years ago."

"Really?" It was hard to know what to say.

He gave her a defiant look. "Fact is, my father died from a fall, and then my mother drowned herself."

"I'm sorry," murmured Lexy, trying to look suitably shocked.

"But it was almost as if she was taunting us with it," he went on. "Asking us *why* our mother had drowned herself." A dark shadow passed over his face. "Well, I say us; I wouldn't dream of showing this letter to Hope. The way she is at the moment, it would send her right over the edge."

"D… did you go to the police?" Lexy managed to ask.

He frowned. "No, I went over to her house yesterday afternoon and had it out with the woman. She won't be doing that sort of thing again in a hurry."

Lexy closed her eyes briefly. "We're talking about Avril Todd, aren't we?"

"Yes." He stared at her. "How do you know?"

141

"She's sent letters to other people."

"What? Like some kind of serial poison pen writer? Lucky I caught her at it. Perhaps now I've had it out with her she'll stop plaguing other poor…"

"She's been murdered," blurted Lexy.

"What?"

"Avril Todd. Last night." Lexy couldn't believe she was telling Guy Ellenger this. DI Milo would crucify her.

"Murdered? How do you…?"

"I found her body. Soon after it happened."

His eyes flicked uncertainly. "Where was this?"

"In a field. Near a place called Nudging. Off the A12. I just happened to be driving around there yesterday evening. It's nice countryside." At least, it had been nice until she got over the stile.

"In a field? Avril?" He looked confused. "What was she doing?"

"Your guess is as good as mine."

"What sort of time was this?"

"Some time after eight."

She could almost see his thoughts falling over one another. "So – I take it someone else got an anonymous letter and decided to take more drastic action than I did?"

"It's looking that way."

"I suppose you called the police?"

"Yeah, course. That's how I know who Avril was." She gave him a half-smile. "I was there what seemed like half the night giving a statement. I was lucky they didn't try to pin the thing on me."

But the vet didn't smile back. "How did it happen?"

"She was hit on the head."

They sat in silence for a few moments. Guy Ellenger stared into the middle distance, a rose-red bloom suffusing each of his smooth cheeks.

He'd picked the wrong day to confront Avril about a poison pen letter, thought Lexy. And he knew it.

"It's all right," she said. "You went to see her in the afternoon. No one's going to think you did it."

"Of course not," he said, sharply.

"How do you think Avril found out about this thing in your past?" Lexy asked.

The vet shook his head. "Who knows? I imagine she either came across it in a back edition of a local paper, or someone who remembered told her. It was all over the village at the time."

"Must have been tough," said Lexy.

"Yes, well – long time ago. If the police want to see me about yesterday afternoon, they know where I am. I haven't got anything to hide – Avril was fine when I left her, if a little shaken, because she'd been rumbled." He cleared his throat. "Right. I suppose we should get on with the matter in hand."

She glanced at him blankly.

"This cat," he reminded her, a pale version of his sincere smile back again.

Blimey, he could multi-task too. From murder to missing moggies in one fell swoop.

"Oh, yes." Now was the time to let him know. Lexy gave him an apologetic shrug. "The trouble is I'm not sure I can…"

"I think someone stole it," he interrupted. "Not sure why. I'm just hoping it wasn't for any nefarious purpose."

"How do you mean?"

"Sometimes domestic cats get nicked by people who run dog fights. Travellers, usually. Something to warm up the pit bulls with."

Lexy felt as if someone was pumping her with red hot steam. "Not all travellers," she said slowly, through clenched teeth.

"No, of course not," he said, looking at her in sudden alarm, and perhaps dawning realisation.

"But the ones who do should be castrated," Lexy stated. "Without anaesthetic."

"Yes, quite. And I would be more than happy to oblige, should that be the case." He sounded like he meant it, too. "But, anyway, let's not jump to conclusions. That was a worst-case scenario. There are other reasons why cats are taken." He drew a deep breath. "Now, the fact is I did see someone hanging around here on the night Princess disappeared. It was dark, of course, so I couldn't see clearly."

"What did they look like?" asked Lexy.

The vet shrugged. "A kid, in his teens, ordinary – about five eight, thin, wearing a dark jacket with the hood pulled up over the head and face, like they all do." He spoke quickly, as if he wanted to get the conversation over with.

"Where was he?" asked Lexy.

"Well, when I first saw him, which was when I opened my front door to let in my own cats, he was outside the Caradocs' bungalow, leaning against the dividing wall. I didn't really think much of it. A couple of the bungalows down here are rented out to families in the summer and I assumed he had come from one of them." He paused. "I thought he looked vaguely familiar, though. Anyway, I went inside, and a couple of minutes later there was… the thing is, the dogs were making a godawful racket out in the garden, at about the time the damned cat went missing. They must have smelt a fox, or something. The Caradocs obviously heard the row, and, when they discovered Princess was gone, they put two and two together and made five. See my problem?"

Lexy nodded grimly.

"I rushed out to the back garden and looked over the fence to see if there was a fox legging it up the lane. And who should I see instead but the kid with the hoodie, heading towards the village.

Holding a bag."

Lexy studied the clean, set curve of his jaw. So he thought this kid had somehow stolen Princess Noo-Noo, and made off with her in a bag? She ran a hand through her cropped hair. Why Princess? If someone was going to swipe a pet cat, why would they choose one that was kept under lock and key, when any number of moggies were wandering around loose? The kid could have had one of Guy Ellenger's, for a start.

So what? The vet was lying? Because somehow the cat had got out, and the dogs had it before Guy could stop them? Found himself having to make up a cover story, and dragged her into it?

"It's possible, isn't it?" Guy had turned to look at her. "That this kid stole her?"

Lexy gave him a searching look. "Don't you think the cat might have been struggling and yowling?"

The vet shook his head. "Not necessarily. Once an animal is enclosed in darkness, they often stay quiet."

Lexy looked at him dubiously. "Have you told the Caradocs about this bloke?"

Guy gave an embarrassed laugh. "They're refusing to talk to me at the moment. I can't imagine what they're saying around the village."

According to Tristan, thought Lexy, it's only Tammy who's doing the slandering.

"It's unlucky that your dogs started kicking off the moment the cat disappeared," she said, slowly. "Although they might have been barking because they heard this kid breaking in next door."

Guy's head jerked up. "Yes," he said. "That's it! Why the hell didn't I think of that? They would have kicked up a storm if they heard someone trying to break in… or at any comings and goings whatsoever, for that matter."

145

The dogs chose that moment to illustrate this statement by belting around the corner of the house as one, Kinky giving tongue as loudly and piercingly as the others. Lexy winced. He'd better not try that at home.

"Very good guard dogs," said Guy, his voice raised above the hullabaloo. "But try telling that to Tristan and Ta…"

He was interrupted by the sound of a car turning abruptly into the drive of Amalfi. Doors slammed.

"Damn, that *is* them – they're back early." The vet jumped up like a guilty teenager. "Won't be a minute – I'll just go and sort the dogs out."

He disappeared around the corner of the bungalow in the direction of the barks.

Lexy stood up too, and walked distractedly around the patio. So Guy Ellenger had also, unbeknown to his sister, received a poison pen letter, although he had the advantage of knowing who delivered it. Hope had said that it would 'devastate' Guy if he found out that someone was threatening to rake up the past.

He does a good impression of a grounded human being, but he's really a mass of neuroses.

Seemed that Hope didn't know her brother as well as she thought she did. Far from throwing a wobbly when he got the letter, he'd simply gone and had it out with Avril. But what if the visit hadn't gone quite the way he'd said? Not that he could have killed her there and then. But perhaps later…

Lexy needed time to think. She could really do without this cat caper, but the vet had taken her by surprise with his rapid change of subject from Avril to Princess Noo-Noo, and somehow she'd managed to get herself talked into looking for the blasted thing again.

"The Caradocs are back," he confirmed.

"I could drop round there later," Lexy said. "Say I've heard they lost the cat, and tell them that I was walking along Gorse

Rise on Wednesday night and I saw this guy outside their place about ten, and a few minutes later, I saw him striding off back towards the high street with a bag. Exactly what you saw, in fact."

"Would you do that?"

She nodded.

"I've already met them, which might make it a bit tricky. They'll wonder why I didn't mention this about Princess Noo-Noo before. I'll have to think of something. And I'll do a bit of probing, while I'm there, too. See if there's any other reason for the cat's disappearance. In the meantime," she suggested, "you could try to remember whether, and where, you've seen the kid before, if you thought he looked familiar."

"Yes – I'll rack my brains," said Guy. "Er... would you like some more malt loaf?"

Lexy looked at the empty plate. She realised that she didn't recall having seen Guy eat any.

"Perhaps I should just go next door and get on with it?" While she could still move unassisted.

"One last cup of tea," he insisted. He gathered up the plates, and disappeared into the kitchen. Lexy leaned back in her chair, fighting a sudden urge to fall asleep with her mouth open.

She eyed Guy blearily through the kitchen window as he put the kettle on. Watched as he picked up a telephone receiver, jabbed a couple of numbers and started talking into it.

Lexy struggled up. Damn – bet he was telling someone about Avril. She should have told him not to broadcast it, but she would have thought he'd have the sense not to.

She made her way across to the kitchen door. He was still on the phone.

"...bound to be asking awkward questions. It's not as if I hid my dislike. Look, I haven't got much time. Can I ask a favour? A really huge one? Yes? Let me tell you what it is first. You know

147

you were at the surgery yesterday evening? What? Yes – the surgery, like you said you… Listen. If anyone asks, I want you to say that we were there together. All evening. Do you understand what I'm saying? What? Yes, I'm really, really grateful. You know I am. You're an angel. Bye-bye for now."

Lexy moved slowly back to her chair, stunned. Guy Ellenger had just set up an alibi for himself.

Lexy watched him through the kitchen window, carefully pouring hot water into a teapot. Despite the cloying heat, she felt goose pimples break out over her arms like miniature pink mole hills. Was she looking at Avril's killer?

She rubbed at her arms fiercely. Get real, woman. Guy wouldn't have told her about the anonymous letter and his visit to Avril yesterday afternoon if he'd then gone on to murder the woman later. Not unless he liked to live really dangerously.

No – he'd set the alibi up because he had clearly been alone yesterday evening, and was worried that he might be in the frame, bearing in mind his visit to Avril that afternoon. It was understandable, really. But who was he sweet-talking into covering for him? Lexy's lips twisted. She thought she might just know the answer to that. Someone who had legs up to her armpits and held his stethoscope every day. She sighed inwardly.

"Here we are." The vet appeared in the doorway with two more cups of tea.

They sat sipping in silence for a while.

"This business with Avril being murdered." Lexy placed her cup precisely on its saucer. "It hasn't been made public yet. You won't say anything to anyone, will you?"

"Of course not," the vet replied smoothly.

14

Lexy stood up, giving Guy Ellenger a tight smile.

"Right – I'll go next door, then. Would you look after Kinky while I'm there? They probably don't want a chihuahua in the house at the moment."

"Yes, of course." Guy Ellenger eyed her uneasily, obviously wondering what had brought about her sudden coldness. As well he might. "Well, good luck."

She refrained from snorting.

She trudged around the side of the bungalow and let herself out of the wooden gate. She was *really* in the mood for doing this now. How could someone with eyes like a good-natured labrador be so insincere? It was Gerard all over again.

Lexy walked next door to the Caradocs' wrought iron gate, pushed it open and crunched angrily up the neat gravel drive.

Raised voices were coming from inside the bungalow. She hesitated. Good timing. Sounded like they were right in the middle of a blazing row.

"Well, how else could it have happened?" A woman's voice, high and out of control. "You're the one who always has the bathroom window open."

"Only when I'm in there with the door shut." She recognised the aggrieved baritone as Tristan's. "Do you really think I'm stupid enough to leave it open when I'm finished? Anyway, what about the time you left the kitchen window open?"

"There was a bloody bee in the kitchen," came the over-wrought retort. "I wanted it out. I'm allergic to bees, in case you've forgotten."

"How *could* I forget, the number of times you bang on about it! Anyway, Princess was out of the window like a shot

149

that day, wasn't she?"

I can't say I blame her, thought Lexy. She pressed the doorbell.

There was an instant silence. Moments later the front door was flung open.

"Yes? Oh, it's you."

Tammy's face was red and swollen, and two tear tracks had streaked through her eyeliner and pancake foundation. Lexy felt a pang of sympathy.

"It's about your cat," she said, tentatively.

The woman's face changed in an instant from misery to wild hope.

"Have you found her? Have you found my Noo-Noo?"

"No," Lexy cut in, urgently. "Not found. I just think I saw something that might help you."

"What?" The woman had practically grasped Lexy by the shoulders. "Tristan! Come here!" she yelled.

Lexy was starting to feel shabby. Tristan's voice sounded in the hall.

"What now?"

Tammy swung round to her husband, revealing Lexy. "This lady thinks she saw something that can help us find Noo-Noo."

"Hello," said Lexy.

Tristan's expression instantly changed to one of wariness.

"It's… erm… Alexandra, isn't it?"

Not so cocky now, are you, chum? Not now the other half's cramping your style.

Tammy looked from one to the other of them, her eyes slightly narrowing.

"That's right," Lexy confirmed. "Hope Ellenger introduced me to Tristan in a café the other day," she said to Tammy, one eye noting Tristan's features relax. "Only I didn't realise you were looking for a cat then. Even when I saw the posters in the village it didn't exactly click. It was just when I was speaking to your neighbour Guy earlier that…"

"So what exactly did you see?" Tristan interrupted, pushing his flowing hair back.

Lexy started trotting out her story. "I just happened to be walking up Gorse Rise the other night, Wednesday it was, some-time after ten. I saw someone hanging around outside your place. A young bloke, medium height, thin, wearing a hoodie. A few minutes afterwards I saw him walking up towards the high street. He… er… had a bag."

Tammy Caradoc turned urgently to her husband, who had gone grey. "Oh, my God, Triss, I told you. She was stolen." She put her hand to her mouth. "I told you it was nothing to do with those chihuahuas next door."

Lexy raised her eyebrows at Tristan.

Tristan looked heavenwards. "I'm sorry, darling, I'm not being rude, but who the hell would want to steal Princess? I know she's a perfectly adorable cat, and I love her to bits," he added hastily as Tammy gave a stifled sob, "but she isn't exactly… anyway, how would they have got her? No one had broken in." He stared haplessly at Lexy.

"Do you know that for sure?" she enquired mildly.

"Of course I know," he rasped. "We were here all evening. I think we might have noticed if someone smashed a window and stole our own cat from right under our noses."

Lexy rubbed her chin thoughtfully. "Was Princess actually in the same room as you all evening? Until she went missing, of course."

"Absolutely," confirmed Tristan, tossing back his mane of hair again. "Well… pretty much."

"Triss and I were both in the lounge," explained Tammy. "I was watching TV and Tristan was sitting in the corner, sewing."

"Theatre costumes," he clarified, coldly.

"Noo-Noo did what she usually does," Tammy went on. "She

151

sat down for a bit, then wandered off for a bit, then…"

"Scratched hell out of the new kitchen wallpaper," supplied Tristan.

"…then wandered back in. In and out, in and out. It's a cat thing." Tammy's lower lip began to tremble.

"Can you remember what time it was when you noticed she was completely gone?" asked Lexy.

"Not exactly, but it was around the time she usually gets her bedtime biscuits. A quarter past ten. But we both definitely saw her about ten minutes before that." Tammy gave another great sniff. "She came into the lounge to remind me she was hungry. But I was watching that stupid hospital drama thing, which didn't end until half ten. So when I ignored her she went stalking out again, with her funny little tail held up high." Her voice broke down, and she began to sob. "That was the… last… time we saw her."

"Yes – and a couple of minutes later those stinking little dogs next door started barking their heads off," interjected Tristan, putting a comforting arm around his wife. "We even heard them over the telly."

"Oh, stop going on about that," Tammy wept. "She's been stolen and you know it."

"How? Why?" Tristan's expression was irate. "No – she must have crept out somewhere and…"

"But are you certain no one could have got in?" Lexy cut in. "Was your back door unlocked, for instance?"

"No – we always keep it locked," said Tristan, tightly.

"Listen," said Tammy, blotting her tears with a paper hanky, her voice firmer. "Why don't you come and see for yourself?"

"Thanks." Lexy stepped into the hallway, noticing Tristan glare at his wife.

"What are you with all the questions, anyway," he said, turning to Lexy. "Some kind of freelance detective?"

Lexy gave a bark of embarrassed laughter. The Caradocs were obviously not the only ham actors around here.

"No, no – just sympathetic. I … er… actually had a cat stolen myself once," she ad-libbed recklessly. "I know how distressing it is."

"Did you get it back?" asked Tammy, at once.

There was a pause. Tammy and Tristan regarded her, she in agony, he with growing suspicion.

"Yeah, of course," said Lexy, with a relaxed grin. "He was tracked down after a few days."

"Gyppos, I suppose?" said Tammy.

Lexy smiled dangerously. "No – actually it was a middle-class housewife who craved a child-substitute."

Tammy blinked. "Goodness. How… peculiar."

"Ye-es," her husband agreed, standing aside to allow Lexy to follow Tammy past a small alcove containing coats, jackets, walking boots and umbrellas.

The hall carpet looked as if it had been threshed. Clumps of wool lay everywhere, and there were long tracks of baldness right along its length. The light wooden panelling along the wall bore deep, criss-crossed gouges, two or three feet up, as if a dwarf had taken a knife to it.

"Are you sure it's not a Bengal tiger we're looking for?" Lexy asked.

Tammy gave her a watery smile. "She's always been a bit of a handful – very playful. That's why we never let her out. She'd be straight up a tree or on to a roof."

Lexy glanced further up the hall wall. Beyond the reach of the cat's claws were rows of stills from plays and television shows, all featuring the Caradocs. Tammy clasping the arm of a young-looking John Nettles, apparently wearing the same outfit she had on now; Tristan as a pantomime dame, wearing a massive pink frilly petticoat and an absurdly coquettish expression;

Tammy laughing uproariously with Ian McShane, this time wearing a floaty red smock; Tristan as some kind of tramp, slumped on a bench.

"*Waiting for Godot*, Edinburgh Festival '91," Tristan murmured behind her.

"Not now, Tristan," snapped Tammy.

Lexy felt a flash of sympathy for the man. Age had favoured him, just as it had been unkind to his wife. He'd ended up looking like her gigolo.

It was extremely stuffy in the bungalow. All the windows were double-glazed and locked.

"Sorry about this." Tammy fanned herself with her hand. Lexy wondered if it had occurred to her that she could open a few windows now. She decided not to suggest it.

They did a tour of the place, Tammy forcing Lexy to examine every nook and cranny. The Caradocs were right about security. How Princess Noo-Noo could ever have got out was becoming increasingly mystifying.

Like the hall, the rest of the bungalow was dominated by theatre and film memorabilia.

There was also a photo of Princess Noo-Noo. Just the one, but it was a big one.

Lexy realised with a shock that Guy Ellenger hadn't been exaggerating. This was no normal-looking cat. The muzzy image on the posters in the village failed to show the skin-tight curly astrakhan coat, the outsize comic ears, and the huge, placidly astonished golden eyes. She posed with one paw raised, long, naked-looking tail curled like a music clef. But her small, egg-shaped face, once you got used to it, had a kind of clownish humour. A cat in lamb's clothing.

"I know she looks like an experiment gone wrong," said Tammy, coming to look at the photo with Lexy. "But she's beautiful to me. And she understands everything I say."

Lexy nodded. She knew where Tammy was coming from. She glanced at the photo again. Was there something vaguely familiar about Princess Noo-Noo?

"Where did you say you got her?"

"It was near Mellowsham Farm, out on the heath." Tammy waved vaguely at the view from the living room window. "She was born in a litter of farm cats, but the farmer could see she wasn't right, so he just dumped her in a ditch, the bastard. Luckily Triss and I happened to be walking past that day."

Lexy turned this over in her mind as she followed the Caradocs through to the final room on the bungalow excursion, a back lobby. They stopped under a montage of black and white pictures showing Tristan and Tammy at least twenty years earlier, as Antony and Cleopatra. "Our salad days," said Tristan, solemnly. "When we were green in judgement. And much better looking."

"Don't be silly, darling. You're every bit as handsome now as you were then."

Tristan gave Tammy a quick, thin smile, and turned to Lexy. "So, you see, our security is as tight as a drum."

"Have you got a loft?" she enquired, looking through a half-open door at a natty little spiral staircase.

"Well… yes." Tristan faltered, glancing up the staircase then at his wife. "But that door's always locked."

"You might have left it open," said Tammy, sounding rather awkward.

"What do you mean, me?"

"You went up there for something on Wednesday night," she said. "Don't you remember?"

"I would *not* have left it unlocked," replied Tristan. "Let alone wide open."

"Better have a look, anyway." Lexy, feeling as if she had taken charge nicely of the situation, began to climb.

"Er… I'm not sure that's a…" said Tammy, mounting the

staircase behind her.

"It'll only take a moment." The key was in the lock, and Lexy turned it, and pushed the door open. But as the room came into view, she began to understand the Caradocs' reluctance. It was a room designed for a specific purpose. A large bed stood in the middle, adorned with rumpled black silk sheets. Various outfits in leather and lace adorned the walls, together with a selection of oil paintings that were frankly Rabelaisian. A long, thick bull-whip hung from a hook beside the bed.

Lexy, Tristan and Tammy refrained from speech as they made their way to the window. Lexy, in an effort to drag her mind away from the images that threatened to shoulder their way in, studied the window minutely. Unlike the others in the house, this one lacked double-glazing. It was split into two sections, the lower part plain glazed and the upper hinged to open outwards. It was currently open just a crack, the catch fixed on the first hole.

The window directly overlooked Guy Ellenger's back garden, although his patio, tucked around the corner of Kittiwake, was out of sight. Maybe four or five feet below the window she could see the top of the high dividing wall between the two bungalows.

Lexy squinted at the window lock.

"Recognise these?" Taking care not to touch the frame, she pulled a couple of short, curly cream hairs from the fitting.

The Caradocs both gazed at the hairs as if hypnotised.

"You do have sharp eyesight," Tristan remarked.

"For what it's worth," Lexy said, "I think someone climbed up on the dividing wall below, and opened this window wide. It would be quite easy to do from the outside. They could have coaxed Princess out, especially if she was hungry, then closed the window back down to its normal position and made off with her. The dogs next door might have seen or heard something going on – that would explain the sudden rumpus."

Tammy Caradoc looked down at the wall, then at her husband.

"Tristan, I think she's right. You must have left the door open, after all."

Tristan stared at the window. "Stupid," he fumed.

"I'm calling the police right now," said Tammy. "They might be able to get prints."

"Right, well, I've taken up enough of your time," said Lexy, turning abruptly towards the wrought iron steps. The last person she wanted to run into on the doorstep was Detective Inspector Milo.

Tammy and Tristan led the way through the house to the front door.

"I really hope you find her," said Lexy.

"Thank you so much," gushed Tammy. She suddenly leant forward and unexpectedly kissed Lexy on the cheek, enveloping her in a brief wave of Opium. "You've given us hope." She turned to her husband. "I suppose you should go next door, and tell him you made a mistake. I mean, even though he's a pain with those damned chihuahuas, he is the only vet for miles around, and if we get Noo-Noo back she's bound to need something for her nerves."

"I think we all will. But let's leave it until we're sure," murmured Tristan.

Lexy headed through the hall to the front door. "If there's anything else I can do, let me know."

The door shut and she watched the two figures turn away up the hall, grotesquely altered through the opaque glass pane.

Lexy walked back to Kittiwake. At the gate she was nearly knocked flying by Kinky and his new amigos. The vet was still sitting on the patio where she'd left him, his head cupped in his hands, looking preoccupied.

He raised an eyebrow. "How'd it go?"

"Fine," said Lexy. "They're even planning an apology visit to you."

"Result!" He sat up straight.

"Let's not count our chihuahuas," she replied, tartly. "They bought the theory about someone climbing up to the window, but they've decided to call the police."

Guy suddenly looked guarded.

"...so I guess it will be out of my hands," Lexy went on. "But I'm still going to have a look around – I've got a couple of ideas of my own. I'll get back to you in a day or two."

She gave him a curt nod and turned to go.

"Great. I... er... very much look forward to seeing you then." He still hadn't worked out why she had adopted the icy pose.

As she left, snapping her fingers at Kinky, she heard Guy clear his throat. "About the other business."

She turned back.

"With Avril Todd. Listen – thanks for tipping me off. Awful thing. I'm still reeling from the shock, actually."

Lexy regarded him coolly. Not enough to prevent you setting up an alibi for yourself.

"I expect the police will want to talk to me," he soldiered on, "seeing as I was with her earlier yesterday afternoon. I'm... er... just wondering whether or not to tell them about that letter? I mean, it might become public knowledge. And also it puts me in a very difficult position – gives me a motive, you see. What would you do?"

Lexy gave him a crooked smile. "I'm probably not the best person to ask." She turned to walk away. "Just do what your conscience tells you."

His reply was tinged with resignation and unexpected sadness. "Yes. Perhaps I should."

Lexy walked slowly down Gorse Rise towards the village, Kinky at her side. What had Guy Ellenger meant by that last comment? It had been almost unnerving.

She turned into the high street, her eyes on the pavement, subconsciously scanning for dropped coins. She was becoming more and more uncomfortably aware that Kinky had only had a small packet of dog biscuits and half a saveloy all day. She needed to get the poor little mutt something for dinner, but the paltry amount of change in her pocket wasn't enough for even the smallest can of dog food. She went into the public telephones by the church and checked the coin return slots. All empty, of course. She mooched around outside the Post Office, hoping someone would inadvertently leave their change in one of the stamp machines. They didn't. She even sat by the wishing well in the village square for half an hour, waiting for some fumbling kid to drop a penny or two while chucking coins in. But even the toddlers were tight in Clopwolde.

Lexy gave a gusty sigh and began to stump towards Otter's End. Like her, Kinky was going to have to eat rice tonight.

But as she turned the corner to Cliff Lane, Lexy saw someone she recognised coming out of the small grocery store on the corner. Someone who might lend her a quid, if she was lucky.

Hope Ellenger looked flushed. She regarded Lexy owlishly.

"Hiya… I was jusht getting something for dinner." The carrier bag she was holding clinked perfidiously. She took an exaggerated look up and down the street and bent towards Lexy. "You find out who it was yet?"

Lexy reeled back from a blast of gin fumes.

The girl was macerated. And it was only half six. She had to look twice to believe her eyes. "Who what was?" she said, confused.

"The letter writer, of coursh," said Hope. "It's doing my head in at the moment."

No – that was the drink. Lexy hesitated. At least Hope wouldn't be getting any more letters. Not that Lexy was in any position to tell her. Or that Hope was in any position to remember the following morning.

"Well, I…"

"Oh! I forgot," interrupted the other woman. "I'm meant to show you my other 'nonymous letters." She clapped her hand to her mouth. "Oops! Shush! I know – come with me – I'll show you now."

"It's OK," said Lexy. "I can manage with just the one. The others are the same, anyway, aren't they? Er, you haven't got any change on you, have you, Hope? I need to get some dog chow and …"

"Not *completely* the same," interrupted Hope. Her voice rose. "Come on, I *want* you to shee them."

Now it was Lexy's turn to look up and down the street. So the other letters were different? Hadn't she suspected as much? Perhaps she ought to take a quick look, to see if they threw any light on Guy Ellenger's parting comment.

"OK, OK," she said soothingly. "I'll come. Where do you live?"

"Jus' up here." Hope swayed off.

They walked a short distance along the road that led out of Clopwolde, and turned into an attractive courtyard of six terraced houses.

"Here'sh mine. Number three." Hope pointed to a set of steps leading up to a wooden door. She began a wobbling ascent.

"Shall I take that for you?" Lexy indicated the clinking carrier bag, which was swinging recklessly.

"No. S'all right." Hope and the bag got to the top and she fumbled in her handbag for the key. Lexy took a covert look at numbers two and four, to see whether any net curtains were twitching. They were. Both of them. This was obviously a regular source of entertainment. She couldn't resist giving the nosy bastards the finger.

Inside the house was modern, with wood flooring and tasteful rugs and furnishings. But, like Hope, it looked a bit dishevelled. The recycling boxes in the open area under the staircase were overflowing with newspapers, and, not surprisingly, bottles. Gin and vodka mainly.

Lexy wondered if the drinking spree dated back to when Hope opened the first anonymous letter.

She glimpsed a pile of dirty plates in a small kitchen.

"I'm sorry, it's such a messh," said Hope. "I've been *sooo* tired recently. Jus' been getting home and crashing…" She smiled beatifically, tottering sideways into the kitchen. "Go on, go through," she said, waving her free hand.

Lexy and Kinky continued along the hall to a front room full of early evening sun. It contained a well-sprung sofa with a rumpled cover that looked as if it had been much slept on. Television and DVD player in one corner; in the other a circular dinner table bearing a tall, wooden candelabra streaked with magenta candle wax. Next to this was a bunch of decaying tiger lilies in a vase, spilling orange pollen across the table like powdered paint.

A bookcase contained a collection of popular classics, and framed prints from the Tate hung on the wall. There were no photographs on the mantelpiece, or clues to Hope's hobbies or interests, unless you counted the collection of wine rings on the elegant coffee table.

Lexy watched Kinky undertake a detailed inspection of the skirting board.

A crash from the kitchen made them both jump. "You all right?" Lexy called. She went swiftly through.

Hope was perched on a stool, leaning heavily sideways, hair hanging over her face. She had broken a glass and the shards were scattered across the tiled floor. An open bottle of sapphire blue gin stood in front of her.

Lexy shut the kitchen door on Kinky, propped Hope up, found a dustpan and brush, and started to sweep up.

"Sorry 'bout thish." Hope watched her dolefully.

"Don't worry about it. Now, do you know where those letters

are?" Lexy flipped open the bin and emptied the pieces of glass into it.

"In my bedroom drawer. Under my underwear." Hope giggled.

Lexy closed her eyes briefly. "Would you like me to get them?"

"Yesh. And I'll pour us both a drink while you're gone." Hope turned to the bottle again.

"I'll have a coffee," said Lexy. "Perhaps you should, too?" She filled a jug kettle. Hope watched her with exaggerated interest. Lexy took two mugs from a wooden mug tree.

She made Hope an extremely strong black coffee, then went to get the letters. Hope's bedroom was as featureless as her living room. So was her underwear.

Lexy went back to the kitchen, placed the envelopes on the counter next to Hope, and pulled up a stool.

"All right if I have a look?" Lexy asked.

Hope stared at the envelopes and nodded.

Lexy withdrew a sheet from one of them. The letters were pasted on in the same style as the one she had seen previously.

I KNOW WHO PUSHED HIM

Lexy gave Hope a quick glance. "Was that was the second letter?"

Hope thought for a while, eyes shut, and then nodded.

"Same theme, then," Lexy commented. She opened the remaining one.

WHY DID MUMMY KILL HERSELF?

Lexy winced. "She doesn't beat about the bush, does she?"

"She?" said Hope.

"Or he," Lexy amended. "I read somewhere that poison pen letters tend to be a woman thing." Christ, what a slip-up. Hope was meant to be the inebriated one.

"I read that, too," the receptionist said, unexpectedly. "I bought a book on it. *The Pshy... Psychology of Anonymous Letter Writing.* I read it in bed last night. That's how sad I am."

"Nothing sad about reading up on the subject."

"Know your enemy," Hope's voice was harsh.

"So you were here last night?" Lexy asked. No harm in checking.

Hope became very still. She screwed her face up as if trying to think hard. "Ye…es," she said. "I was here all night on my own." She nodded emphatically.

Lexy mentally filed this away. Hope alone on night of murder. Almost certainly drunk. She could check this with the curtain twitching neighbours. She found herself regretting she'd given them the finger earlier.

"Do you know what this third letter means?" Lexy asked.

Hope looked at the words for what seemed like an age. Kinky, sitting at their feet, gave an impatient whine.

"Yes. I do know what it means." She knocked the rest of the coffee back. She sounded like she was sobering up fast. "It means that this person knows what really happened that night. So we're stuffed."

"Who's stuffed?" Lexy tried to keep her voice even.

"Me and Guy, of course." She sounded almost petulant.

"Do *you* know what really happened?"

"I was there, wasn't I?"

"Yes, but you said you were on the phone when your father… fell down the stairs. You had your back to him."

"No. That was a lie. I was *facing* him," said Hope, her voice rising to an uncontrolled shout. "I saw it *all.*"

"So you saw your mother do it? Push him, I mean?"

"Not my mother." Hope Ellenger gave her a pitying look. "My brother."

Lexy felt the blood drain from her face as effectively as if someone had turned a tap under her chin.

"Yes – *Guy* shoved my father down the stairs." Hope gave Lexy

163

a twisted smile. "That's why Mummy killed herself."

Lexy watched the seconds ticking away on a stainless steel kitchen wall clock in front of her.

"We don't speak about it, me and Guy." Hope's words were coming fast now. "It's like it never happened, but at the same time it's always there. It means we can't move on, not like other people. We can't have relationships or be normal."

Lexy didn't trust herself to speak. She didn't know what to say, anyway.

"But we got used to it," Hope ploughed on. "We threw ourselves into the veterinary practice, and we're doing the am-dram. It's like – we're… happy. At least I was until these letters started coming." Her eyes shone with a sudden dark lustre. "I knew our sins would eventually catch up with us."

"Not your sin," Lexy croaked. "*You* didn't do it."

"We're as guilty as one another." Hope toyed with her coffee mug. "Anyway, I've told someone now. Broken the link. So what are you going to do?"

Lexy shook her head. "Right now, I don't know. I'm going to have to go and think." She stood up, rubbed her forehead.

"What about these?" Hope indicated the letters. "What's the next one going to say?" Her voice had risen again. Lexy hoped the kitchen wall wasn't too thin.

She stood in front of the receptionist, took hold of her shoulders, looked into her eyes. "There aren't going to be any more letters."

"What? How…?"

"You'll have to trust me on this."

"You've found out who it was." It was a statement, not a question.

"Yes. And there won't be any more letters. OK?"

"OK." Hope's eyelids fluttered. Lexy heaved her off the stool, half-carried her into the living room. After re-capping the gin, hiding it from sight and putting the letters back in Hope's bed-room, she left her sleeping on the sofa.

Lexy strode back up Cliff Lane, but she couldn't keep up with Kinky. He ran all the way back, and was waiting on the front step when she arrived.

As soon as the door was open he rushed into the kitchen and stood in front of his empty bowl. He had been getting pretty fond of those Doggy Chomps. Lexy swore under her breath. She'd forgotten to ask Hope again for some bloody change for bloody dog food before she left. For some reason it had gone right out of her mind. Perhaps it was hearing the news that her brother was a murderer. Yeah, that would have done it.

She put a pan of brown rice on to boil. Kinky gave a couple of light, joshing barks. She hadn't overlooked something, had she?

He continued to issue increasingly shrill reminders during the forty minutes the rice took to cook, until Lexy almost lost her temper.

When she eventually forked a small pile of the stuff into his bowl Kinky sniffed at it and threw her a filthy look, then retired to the living room and lay on the sofa with his face turned into a cushion.

In this oppressive atmosphere, Lexy tried to come to terms with Hope Ellenger's revelation about her brother. Talk about a curve ball. Lexy wished she'd never spotted the woman now, and gone through that whole grisly scene. But she had to know, didn't she? As soon as she heard Guy Ellenger agree that perhaps he should do what his conscience told him, she had felt a strange compulsion to discover what that meant. He hadn't killed Avril Todd, Lexy was sure of that. But it did sound as if he was on the verge of confessing to a murder he had carried out twenty-four years earlier.

15

The following morning Kinky remained cool with Lexy, especially when he found out what was for breakfast. He sat in a corner of the kitchen wearing a look that would have had people reaching straight for their cheque books if it featured on an RSPCA poster.

Lexy regarded him disagreeably. "Well, what do you want me to do? Go out there and bag you a couple of squirrels?"

She saw his ears prick up.

"Dream on."

As she spooned down the remainder of the brown rice, Lexy peered out at the unkempt garden through one of the open windows. Ever since she got up that morning, she'd had an inexplicable feeling she was being watched.

A sudden disturbance made her stiffen.

But it was just a bird, a small pearl-grey one that fluttered out of the gorse and landed on a hawthorn tree near to the cabin. Lexy flipped through her mental list of species, but somehow she couldn't get a fix on this one.

Curious despite herself, she dropped to all fours and crept through the kitchen, out of the back door, and around the veranda, in order to get closer without frightening it away.

Kinky accompanied her expectantly.

"No – I haven't changed my mind about the squirrels." Lexy hooked a finger in his collar.

The bird was still there, its back to her. She could now see its markings in more detail, a strikingly marbled grey and white effect. "What on earth are you?" she whispered to herself.

As if in answer to her question, it opened its beak and let forth a beautiful, confused babble of notes.

Ah – warbler. She listened with pleasure.

That was until Kinky wrenched himself from her grip and raced towards it, barking dementedly.

The bird dived into the undergrowth in a terrified blur of grey.

Lexy leapt up, shot through with rage. She was about to give the dog the biggest earful of his life when she saw the man.

He was crouching behind a clump of young birch trees just outside the garden. Kinky raced towards him with kamikaze abandon.

Lexy gave a piercing whistle instead of her intended barrage of expletives. The intruder scrambled up and backed away through the gorse and heather. Kinky slowed and turned back, short hair bristling, angry barks still escaping from him.

Lexy ushered him in and slammed the door, almost breaking it in two.

Storming through the cabin, she rifled through the pockets of Thursday's jeans, left in a crumpled heap in the bathroom. She pulled out the now limp business card DI Milo had given her outside the vet's surgery, then pounced on the telephone to punch out the number of his mobile.

"Milo."

The voice sounded tired and irritated. Good. "It's Alexandra Lomax."

"Yes. Is something the matter?"

"Something the matter?" Her voice rose hysterically. "Listen – I've got some bastard reporter outside my cabin taking pictures of me. And you gave me your *word* you'd keep my name out of this business. I'll tell you what – you can stick your dinner tonight. I don't owe you anything now."

There was a pause, then DI Milo's voice, sounding both dignified and aggrieved. "I can assure you I've kept your name out of this, Ms… Lomax." He emphasised *Lomax*. "I've got no idea how the press tracked you down. There hasn't even been a press release yet. I'm very sorry if…"

"Yeah, well, it's a bit late for apologies now," she snarled, slamming the phone down.

Kinky watched her from the kitchen door as she stalked up and down the room. That was that, then. If the press were on to her already, she might as well go straight down to the local nick, find a proper policeman and own up to stealing Gerard's ill-gotten gains. At least she'd have the satisfaction of landing him in prison, too, by going public on his little…

There was a knock at the door.

Lexy jerked the curtain back. An earnest-looking girl stood outside, dark hair tied back in a ponytail, camera around her neck. Behind her, on the veranda, stood three other people, carrying recording equipment. A camera crew, no less.

"Right, here we go." Lexy strode to the long-suffering cabin door and yanked it open.

The earnest-looking girl began to speak in hushed tones.

"Er, sorry, but would you mind…"

"Yes – well done!" yelled Lexy. "It's me, Alexandra Warwick-Holmes, twenty-nine years old, thief, conspirator, perverter of justice, separated, disguised, in hiding and now you've found me – congratulations, have a cigar!"

"Erm," said the girl, looking apprehensively at the camera crew behind her. "It's just that we wanted to take some pictures of the Costello's warbler, but I think it's flown off now."

"Uh?" said Lexy.

"It's just that it's the first time it's been seen in this part of Britain for sixty years. It's seriously endangered, because of habitat erosion." The girl had a lisp.

Lexy swallowed. "Grey, is it?" she asked, weakly. "About yea big?" She opened her hands several inches. "With a marbled back?"

The newcomer nodded encouragingly. "It's got a mate here, too," she added. "It might even be nest-building, which would be brilliant."

Oh, yeah. That would be just dandy. An extremely rare, endangered bird deciding to build its nest in her back garden. She'd have every twitcher in the country camped outside for… but Lexy was so insanely relieved that her new visitors weren't reporters that even this prospect was bearable.

"So is it OK if we…?"

Lexy waved limply towards the garden. "Help yourselves. Just forget the stuff I said earlier, OK?"

"What stuff?" asked the girl, distractedly. She wasn't joking. The other bird-botherers had surged forward on her signal. Two disappeared behind gorse bushes and the one Kinky had seen off earlier crouched behind the same birch trees, now shouldering a telescope as large as a highland caber.

"What we're really hoping is that they'll breed on our bird sanctuary," the girl breathed, her cerulean eyes shining. "It's lowland heath, like you've got here – one of Europe's rarest landscapes, constantly under threat." A shadow passed across her face. "If we want to ensure the warblers breed and survive, we need to raise the funds to buy much more land like this."

Lexy stared at the girl. "Bird sanctuary?" she said, slowly.

The girl fished out a leaflet from her khaki jacket. "It's just the other side of Clopwolde. Why don't you come and visit us? I'm Gillian, by the way. Ask for me and I'll show you around."

"I will, Gillian. I promise I'll do just that. Must go now, but I'll definitely be there."

Lexy ducked inside and closed the door, sliding her back down it until she was sitting. She and Kinky exchanged a glance.

"So that's what it was," she said. "A Costello's warbler. I'm glad we've established that, because, you know, I thought I didn't recognise it. Oh, Kinky." She ruffled the dog's head, light-headed with relief. "Thanks for being a hero back there, mate." Kinky wrinkled his nose modestly. "Lucky you didn't catch him, though. I reckon I'm in enough trouble already without getting GBH to a twitcher added to my rap sheet."

She grabbed her bag. "Right, pal, you and I are going to visit Edward de Glenville now, and I'm going to swallow my pride and ask him to lend me twenty quid. Then we'll go and get you some more of those dog biscuits you like so much. And something nice for me, too." Seeing as the dinner she had been relying on that night was reduced to a smouldering pile of ashes following her call to DI Milo.

Lexy and Kinky left by the steps going down to the beach to avoid disturbing the bird paparazzi and, after a hot trudge across the shingle, up the rickety private steps, through the graveyard and across the parched lawn, Lexy finally hauled on the rope outside the iron-studded front door. But the bells jangled in vain, and the large door remained firmly shut.

She walked around to the back of the building. No maroon Jaguar, or any other sign of Edward. Damnation. She had assumed that as it was Sunday morning he would be lounging around at home, drinking coffee and reading the papers.

Then she remembered Sheri-Anne, writing on the chalk board outside the village hall the day before. There was a full rehearsal for *South Pacific* today, starting at ten. She looked at her watch. It was a quarter to eleven. Even Edward would be there by now.

She led Kinky, tail drooping, back down the steps to the beach.

As she scrunched along the firmer line of shingle left by the receding tide, she brooded over the previous evening's unexpected encounter with Hope Ellenger, wondering how the poor woman had felt when she came to. Would she remember what had taken place? Probably – she had been fairly coherent before she'd passed out – but would she be relieved or mortified to realise that she'd finally broken her silence on her father's death? A silence that had protected her brother for twenty-four years.

Small wonder she and Guy hadn't been able to move on emotionally. It certainly explained why Hope had become so distraught when she started to receive the anonymous letters. How sinister to discover that someone else knew their secret.

And how did Guy really feel when he opened Avril's last delivery to the surgery, the one that asked why his mother drowned herself? Did Guy think Avril knew the truth? If so, he had a very strong motive for wanting her out of the way permanently. But despite this, Lexy was still convinced he wasn't her killer. He hadn't panicked, as Hope did. He *knew* that only two people living were aware of the truth – himself and his sister.

So, where did that put Avril? Did she just make a lucky stab in the dark?

Lexy came to an involuntary stop. That could be it!

Kinky, a few feet behind her, started dragging a very dead flounder from the shallows.

Lexy thought rapidly. She now knew, thanks to Roderick Todd, that his wife had done most of her research by going back through the local papers and talking to people who had lived in an area all their lives.

What if she then took a guess that there was more to a death or suicide than met the eye? After all, a lot of families had secrets.

Take Edward. Avril had obviously found out that de Glenville senior had fallen off the cliff last year and died. She could have read about it in any local paper at the time. Then a few months later, she sent Edward a single-line letter:

I KNOW WHO KILLED YOUR FATHER.

The single line conveyed a lot. If Edward did have something to hide, it would be downright threatening. Even if he didn't,

171

it would be frighteningly suggestive.

Then to ram the point home, a few weeks later Avril sent a second one.

HE WAS PUSHED, WASN'T HE?

It implied much the same as the first letter. Lexy thought back to Edward's reaction when he opened it. Without any perceptible hesitation he had laughed aloud about it, carelessly handed it to her to read, made light of it. But Lexy remembered the way he'd torn it up and binned it. Avril might have twitched his chain a bit more than he let on.

Had she not been cut off in her prime, she might have sent another letter, before moving in for the final thrust – blackmail. That would be the test of Edward's guilt.

She'd used the same technique with the Ellengers, Lexy thought with growing conviction. All she really needed were the bare facts. Their father died falling down the stairs during a family argument, and their mother committed suicide soon afterwards. She could, as Guy had said, have easily discovered that from local newspapers in the library. Even without the supplementary whispers of scandal that Lexy was sure some local people had been willing to supply, Avril had made a leap of faith and landed on a safe ledge. Hope, with her longstanding burden of guilt, had obligingly read more into the statements than even Avril could have dreamed of.

Guy must have done the same, although he kept his head and confronted her. But what exactly had he said to Avril that Friday afternoon? And why had he really set up that alibi for himself for the evening she'd been killed?

Lexy stared out at the dove-grey ocean, her mind running up and down little corridors of possibilities. She screwed up her nose a couple of times, subconsciously noting a humdinger of a smell coming from somewhere.

There was a way to check what the vet had been up to that

evening, but she'd have to box clever. She didn't want to get on the wrong side of Guy Ellenger. He'd protected his secret for a very long time, and she wasn't sure which way he might jump if he learned it was out. She needed to make sure he didn't jump on her. Not in the hobnailed boot sense, at any rate.

Lexy glanced down at a familiar sound, to find that she was hemmed in on all sides by chihuahuas, one of them reeking of the dead flounder he had just rolled in.

"Morning," said Guy Ellenger, looking grave, and reaching into his inside pocket. "Hoped I'd run into you. I meant to give you this yesterday."

Lexy flinched, but instead of the imagined gun, Guy withdrew several ten-pound notes and handed them to her. She stared down at the money, her heart in her throat.

"But I can't…"

"Listen, if you find that cat it will be worth a lot more to me than the cost of Kinky's treatment. Look on this as expenses. I'm sorry – I've got to rush because I'm meant to be at an am-dram rehearsal – Maurice is going to kill me – *and* I need to get some stuff from the chemist for my sister. By the looks of it, she's not going to be well enough to make the rehearsal at all. Anyway, I'll see you soon."

He sniffed the air, grimacing. "Beach is a bit whiffy today, isn't it?"

"Yeah. Must be that rotting… oh great…" Lexy began dragging Kinky towards the sea. "Is Hope all right, by the way?"

He turned back. "Fine. Just a headache."

Yeah, I'll bet it's a real mother, too, thought Lexy, watching the vet and his leaping carousel of chihuahuas disappear out of sight between two beach huts. After she had sluiced the indignant Kinky down, she counted the money Guy Ellenger had given her.

"Fifty pounds," she said, incredulously. "Here, Kinks, you don't think this is hush money, do you? Perhaps Hope told him what happened last night. Told him that I know his secret."

Kinky was too busy shaking himself dry to offer an opinion.

"No," she reasoned, "if he was going to bribe us to keep shtum, he would have given us a lot more than fifty quid."

Having cleared up that point, Lexy and Kinky went straight to the fish and chip shop in the village.

They ate in the church square, Lexy munching chips in silent appreciation, while Kinky tackled a sausage longer than he was.

Lexy compiled a mental shopping list that didn't include brown rice. And, she reminded herself, noticing a sign for a 'nearly new' sale in the church hall, now she was above water again, she could get something to wear that would be suitable for a job interview. Nothing too dressy, just one grade up from ripped jeans and an old t-shirt. She grinned. Last time she went shopping for clothes it was in Harrods.

The church clock struck twelve-thirty.

"Come on, pal. We've got things to do." Lexy stood up and fished Kinky out of a flower bed.

They went into the church hall sale, and minutes later Lexy came out with a carrier bag. A pair of serviceable black jeans and a couple of decent tops. Perfect. They headed into the village centre. Lexy tied the chihuahua up outside the small Internet café. Time to start earning her expenses.

When Lexy emerged fifteen minutes later, she wore a self-satisfied smile.

"Thought so," she said to Kinky. "But I'll need to make a few calls when we get home. Let's head for the newsagent and get a paper."

Unfortunately, Kinky was intent on heading in the opposite direction, straight for a burly, unsuspecting English bull terrier. By the time Lexy caught up with him and subdued the other dog's owner, she found she was right outside the village hall. The heavy door was slightly open, and piano music and raucous singing drifted through it.

The song was instantly recognisable.

Lexy slipped in. A handful of people were singing on stage, Edward among them. He spotted her and did a theatrical double take, then gave an exaggerated wave as he proceeded to inform everyone that Bloody Mary was the girl he loved. In the background, Lexy saw Guy Ellenger and Sheri-Anne huddled together, heads close. She frowned.

After the number there was a loud hand clap.

"Super. Super, Edward – all of you, in fact. Let's leave it there. Stop on a high note," shouted a slim, dapper man. "Debrief in ten, so don't go away."

Lexy watched the actors disperse into small groups. She saw Sheri-Anne Davis, dressed in a short blue sarong and little else, jump gracefully from the stage, and pull a packet of Marlboro from some mysterious place on her person.

Edward also made his way across the stage, leaping down in front of Lexy.

Raising his expressive eyebrows, he leant towards her, lowering his voice and intoning, somewhat inaccurately, "It's been handbags at dawn today and no mistake! Tammy Caradoc left the stage well before cue earlier. Right in the middle of a scene, actually. I know she's overwrought about that precious lost moggy, but I…"

"Princess Noo-Noo," supplied Lexy, craning her neck slightly to watch Guy Ellenger operate a lever at the back of the stage.

Edward gave her a surprised look. "Yes – that's the one. Fancy you knowing that. You get around a bit, don't you, dear?"

"Their Missing Cat posters are stuck on every vertical surface in the village," said Lexy smoothly. "What do you think happened to the thing?"

Edward shrugged. "No idea, sweetie. If it had any sense it probably went off in search of a new home, although I don't know who'd give it one, poor creature. It's certainly not something I'd want gurning at guests in my humble abode."

"Humble abode," snorted Lexy.

He grinned at her irrepressibly. "Anyway, to continue, *I* think that Tammy C was more upset by the fact that she had to surrender her accustomed lead role to madam." He jerked his head at the athletic form of Sheri-Anne, who was now irritably tapping out a message on her mobile. A well-built young man in a rugby shirt hovered nearby with uneasy longing. Sheri-Anne glanced up and noticed both Edward and Lexy looking over at her. She gave them an impertinent stare back.

"Especially as Tristan is still the leading man," Edward was saying. "Sheri-Anne doesn't help, little mare. She's positively basking in the fact that the ageing company stud gets to canoodle up against her while his wife watches with slitted eyes from the sidelines. And to make it even more exciting, Sheri-Anne's latest beau, Lance – the lad over there with the six-pack who does a couple of walk-ons – is also pacing up and down the set, clocking Tristan's every move, and cracking his knuckles like a rabid gorilla. It's more entertaining than the bloody production."

Lexy fixed her gaze on the hapless Lance. So he was Sheri-Anne's boyfriend. He only looked about seventeen. Unlikely to be affluent enough to take her to swanky bistros. "What does he do?" she asked Edward.

"Student – agricultural college, I think. His dad's a farmer."

Lexy gave a mute nod, wondering if Lance had an inkling that Sheri-Anne's taste might also run to someone more mature. With eyes like melting toffee. Speaking of which, the vet was descending the steps at the side of the stage. He gave her a surprised wave and a flash of the healthy white teeth.

She forced her attention back to Edward, who was happily continuing his monologue. "Mind you, even Sheri's a bit off-colour today. Not her usual smouldering self."

She certainly looked tense, Lexy thought. The girl had stepped outside the stage door into a side alley, and was smoking a cigarette in quick, anxious draws. She snapped something at the still hovering Lance.

"Anyway, Tammy and Tristan retired home early." Edward was still prattling on. "Straight after Triss's love scene with Sheri-Anne. Odd, that. But Maurice is in an unexpectedly good mood today, even though Guy turned up late, and Hope didn't turn up at all, so he waved them graciously away."

"Which one's Maurice?" asked Lexy.

Edward indicated the slim, dapper man, who was heading towards them.

"And, of course, Avril didn't turn up again." Edward gave Lexy an inane smile. "Can't imagine what's happened to her."

She glowered at him.

"Neither can I," said Maurice, arriving at their side. "Still, it made for a nice bit of peace and quiet. Apart from the Caradoc histrionics, of course. I mean, what was that was all about?"

Edward opened his mouth to explain.

"Perhaps Avril's ill?" A slight, serious man with a 1930s hair style, who had been singing next to Edward on the stage, joined them. His face lit up when he saw Kinky.

Edward gave Lexy a significant look. Lexy furiously ignored him, and turned to the man, who had bent down to fuss Kinky.

"Hello – I'm Peter," he said, offering her a hand.

Edward's on-off-on-again lover. Lexy introduced herself.

"Must go and grab a coffee," said Edward. "I'm simply gagging. I'll get you both one, too."

Peter frowned up at him. "Don't bother, I'll get my own."

"Nonsense." Edward rolled his eyes and marched off, Maurice at his side. "Now then," Lexy heard him say, "Tammy and Tristan – therein lies a…"

177

Lexy caught Peter's look of affectionate exasperation.

"How's the rehearsal going?" she asked him.

"Apart from the off-stage dramas?" He gave her a wry look. "Not bad on the whole." He stroked Kinky's ears. "It's a change from The Scottish Play, at any rate."

"So you go in for the heavyweight stuff, as well?"

Peter grimaced, nodding. "Maurice decided to do Shakespeare at Easter. Naturally, he had to pick on the most unremitting one."

"Oh, I don't know – he could have chosen *King Lear*."

"Or *Titus Andronicus*." He grinned. "Perhaps we got off lightly after all. Anyway, we all insisted on *South Pacific* for the summer run. Aren't you gorgeous, eh?" he added.

"Huh?" said Lexy.

"Aren't you a darling little doggie?"

Lexy, relieved, smiled at Kinky. "Oh – yeah, he's really cute." When he isn't trying to kill things.

She studied Peter covertly, trying to equate this congenial man with the less flattering picture Edward had painted of him as secretive and duplicitous. Appearances could be deceptive, as she was now well aware.

When Lexy looked up again, a cloud still on her brow, Sheri-Anne Davis was stalking artfully across the foyer, her little designer handbag dangling from her shoulder.

"Would you mind watching Kinky a moment?" Lexy asked Peter, quickly. As he was already clasping the chihuahua to his chest, she didn't think he'd have a problem with it. Kinky gave her a long-suffering look.

Lexy walked into the foyer. Sheri-Anne was just disappearing through the door to the Ladies. Beside it was another door, marked CLOPWOLDE AMATEUR DRAMATICS – PRIVATE. Lexy approached this second one, pressed her ear against it and, after a quick look round, tried the handle. The door opened, and she slipped in. Inside was a row of lockers, some bearing the names of the cast, including Avril Todd. Various props stood around, among them a large fake palm tree and a pile of coconuts.

Lexy ran her eyes swiftly over the lockers. Looked simple enough. She approached Avril's, digging in her bag for a hairpin that had never been used for its original purpose.

In a few moments she had released the catch, and the grey metal door swung open. Just a hobby she used to have.

It was empty inside, apart from something that looked like a huge Hawaiian shirt. Lexy swallowed. Must be Avril's *South Pacific* costume. She wouldn't be wearing that again, unless she had asked to be buried in it.

Disappointed, Lexy closed the locker door, and moved to the one marked *Sheri-Anne Davis*. Unlikely to have anything of interest in it, but it was worth a shot. The catch dropped in the same obliging way, and Lexy found herself gazing at a selection of flimsy garments. She shuffled through them, not knowing what she was looking for. A plastic bag with what looked like a brick in it lay on the floor. She heard a toilet flush next door, and hastily withdrew. She was about to pull the locker door shut when a small, gold powder compact caught her eye. She grasped it, and flipped it open.

Inside was no powder, but a tightly folded sheet of paper. She drew it out, looked at it quickly, then replaced it, shutting the locker just as Sheri-Anne Davis walked in.

"Hi, Sheri-Anne," Lexy breezed.

The girl jumped. Up close, her pretty, leonine face was white and drawn.

"What are you doing in here? It's private." Her eye flicked to her locker.

Lexy kept her own eyes firmly on Sheri-Anne. "Just fetching something for Edward," she said, patting her pocket. "See you in a bit."

She ducked out of the locker room and into the toilets next door, locked herself in a cubicle, and only then allowed herself a shaky exhalation.

The message was made up in a familiar way, of letters cut out of a magazine.

LEAVE £10,000 IN TWENTY POUND NOTES IN THE PALM TREE AFTER THE REHEARSAL ON SUNDAY OR I TALK

Lexy blew her spiky fringe upwards. Well, hello. This was Avril Todd going for the jackpot. She must have found out something very juicy about Sheri-Anne. And if she had run true to form she had probably played cat and mouse with her for a while – then, seeing the letters were hitting home, she'd gone for the kill.

Only trouble was, so had someone else.

Lexy unlocked the cubicle and let herself out. She heard the locker room door shut and, peering out of the Ladies, she saw Sheri-Anne pass through the foyer and through the double doors into the rehearsal hall. No wonder she looked so haggard and jumpy. What had she been up to that would be worth ten grand for Avril Todd to keep quiet? How would she pay that kind of money? She was an eighteen-year-old trainee veterinary nurse. She'd be on a pittance.

Or a scam.

Looking around intently, Lexy slid back into the locker room, seized an old smock from a hook and wrapped it around her hand. She approached the fake palm tree and parted its floppy green plastic leaves. The top of the trunk was hollow, forming a cavity that dropped down about eight inches. Her ears straining for the sound of someone coming out of the hall, Lexy stuck her hand into it and felt around. Her fingers almost immediately closed around something. She drew it up. It was the brick-shaped parcel inside a plastic bag that she had just noticed in Sheri-Anne's locker. The girl must have transferred it to the palm tree. Lexy took a peek, then, heart thudding, she dropped the package back into the palm, flung the smock into a corner and slipped back out of the door.

Well, that was Sheri-Anne off the suspect list. She'd just made the cash drop, which meant she didn't know her blackmailer was dead.

Moments later, Lexy was back in the hall. The small cast was huddled around Maurice on the stage. Peter was still clutching Kinky, who was by now looking positively martyred.

The group hug was broken up by the warble of a mobile phone. It was Maurice's. He looked at the phone's display screen, frowned, withdrew apologetically and took the call. Lexy watched his face slowly pale as he listened, shaking his head, making little sounds of shocked disbelief.

Peter, Sheri-Anne, Lance, Guy and finally Edward fell silent one by one, as if each were hushed by an invisible finger.

Maurice finished the call and looked down at his polished black slip-ons.

"Listen up, everyone. I've just had a call from Roderick Todd. It's… er… very bad news, I'm afraid."

Lexy gave an anguished look at Guy Ellenger. His eyes met hers briefly. Edward glanced significantly at Lexy, and she mouthed back both at him and Guy. *Act surprised.*

"I'm sorry to have to tell you that Avril died on Friday night," said Maurice in a sepulchral voice.

There was a gasp of shock from the assembled players. Edward's was a little over the top.

Lexy watched Sheri-Anne's reaction. Her bland face registered surprise, but not concern.

"How did she die?" Peter was asking "Where? Was there an accident?"

Maurice held up his hands. "I don't know any details. All he said was Avril was dead." He shook his head. "That's knocked me for six. I think we'd better wrap up. If I find out any more I'll keep you posted."

The cast filed down the steps. Lexy saw Guy disappear through a side door.

"Dead? Avril? I can't believe it!" Edward expostulated.

"I heard there was a pile-up on the A12 yesterday," Lance supplied.

"How awful. Avril wasn't exactly a cautious driver, was she?"

Sheri-Anne Davis went straight through the foyer and outside, flipping open her mobile phone. Lexy stood just inside the large double door pretending to study the village hall meeting schedule. She heard the click of a cigarette lighter and smelt a wisp of acrid smoke. Then Sheri-Anne began speaking quietly.

"It's me. I've done it. Hope the bastard's happy now. No, I'm not hanging around, I don't give a toss who it is. We're out of here next week – that's all I care about. You, me, and our passports to Paradiso Beach." She gave a throaty giggle. Lexy frowned. Was Sheri-Anne speaking to the vet? "Speaking of which, it went really well at the barn on Friday evening... things got... you know... pretty hot..." Lexy stiffened. Friday evening? Sheri-Anne had been at the surgery on Friday evening. She'd agreed to give Guy Ellenger an alibi.

Lexy thought back to the call Guy had made. *Look, I haven't got much time. Can I ask a favour? A really huge one? Yes? Let me tell you what it is first. You know you were at the surgery yesterday evening? What? Yes – the surgery, like you said you...*

Lexy gave a short, scornful exhalation. Sheri-Anne hadn't been at the surgery at all. She'd been up to business of her own, and Lexy had a pretty shrewd idea what that might have been. But Sheri-Anne was obviously a very quick thinker, and after a momentary pause for thought, she'd gone along with Guy's request to provide him with an alibi, even though she hadn't been at the surgery either. Because Sheri-Anne Davis had realised that it would provide a perfect alibi for whatever she had been up to, too. Not so dumb after all. But who was Sheri-Anne's partner-in-crime? And where had Guy really been? He'd already killed once. Would he do it again?

Lexy hauled her mind back to the phone conversation she was eavesdropping on.

"...and, oh yeah," Sheri-Anne continued, "listen to this – we've just been told that Avril Todd's kicked the bucket."

There was a silence. Lexy screwed up her whole face in an effort to overhear the call.

"...didn't say how. Maurice told us, her husband rang him a few minutes ago. Just said she'd died. Perhaps she had a heart attack – whatever. Anyway, meet you tomorrow night at nine and we'll do the test, just to make sure. Love you, bye-ee."

Lexy walked slowly back into the hall, her head in a whirl. She rescued Kinky from Peter, who seemed set to take him home. The chihuahua gave her a chilling look.

"Do you want a lift back, sweetie?" asked Edward, who had been waiting with Peter.

"No, I won't, thanks. Still got some stuff to do."

"Sure?"

"Uh-huh – but thanks again."

"Well, see you soon. Come round whenever you like. Don't be a stranger."

"Thanks. Likewise. Er... you don't happen to know where Sheri-Anne lives, do you? She left her purse in the Ladies and she's gone home." She was getting far too good at lying.

Edward shook his head.

"Bartholomew Lane," said Peter. "It's over the back of the high street; second turning after the Post Office. Not sure what number, but anyone'd tell you up there."

"Great, thanks. I'll find it. Bye." Lexy launched herself hastily through the front doors before Edward offered to take her there, too.

16

An hour later found Lexy lounging on the grubby chintz sofa in Otter's End, knocking back a bottle of cold lager.

She checked her watch. Excellent. Her take-away would be arriving in just under half an hour. Seeing as she had spent much of the last two days anticipating a Thai meal, Lexy had decided to treat herself to one anyway. And it would be all the more pleasant for not having to sit opposite DI Creepster Milo.

She glanced with satisfaction through the open hatch into the kitchen, where cupboards were now stocked with numerous cans and packets. From the same kitchen came the heartening sound of a small dog crunching his way through a double helping of Doggy Chomps, which had been on introductory offer in the Co-op.

Lexy stretched luxuriously and took another glug of beer.

Then she spotted her notebook, where she'd scribbled a couple of telephone numbers when she had been at the Internet café earlier. Checking her watch again, she reached for the telephone, and dialled a number in Cornwall.

"Hello – is that Mrs Bullen? Sorry to call you on a Sunday, but I've got some information that might interest you. Yes – about a cat."

Lexy made a lot of notes during her telephone call, and when she rang off, she tapped her pen thoughtfully against her teeth. She was on to something here. Looked like her hunch about Princess Noo-Noo had been spot on.

It meant that the cat had almost certainly been abducted, and if Lexy's theory about the identity of the thief was correct, there was a very good reason why Guy Ellenger thought the kid in the hoodie had seemed familiar.

But she needed proof, and for that she would have to be

patient until the following evening.

She looked up eagerly at a knock on the door, grabbing a handful of notes and coins.

She would allow herself a leisurely meal, and then afterwards try to make sense of the other peculiar events of the last couple of days – the ones concerning Avril Todd.

She pulled open the door.

"Miss Lomax? One Thai red curry, one fragrant rice, one vegetable tempura, one crispy noodles," gabbled the grinning delivery man.

But Lexy's returning grin had stuck on her face. Beyond him stood an ominous presence.

Resignedly, Lexy paid for her meal, and the delivery man was replaced on the doorstep by DI Milo. His eyes were as sombre as a winter lake.

"Can we talk?" Unlike the previous occasions they had met he was dressed casually, in faded jeans and an open-necked shirt, but he still managed to look official.

"I've given you my statement," Lexy growled. "What else do you want?"

He gave her a complicated look. "Just let me come in."

Reluctantly, she pushed the door open wider and stood back.

"By the way, did you know about…?" He jerked his head behind him to where a group of men in combat gear were crouching at the far end of her garden, telescopes trained on a hawthorn tree.

"Yeah. Long story."

"I see." Looking around curiously, Milo settled himself on an easy chair with an orange and brown striped velour cover.

"Have a seat, why don't you?" Lexy dumped the bag of food on the coffee table.

"So – you decided on Thai tonight after all," he observed, ignoring her jibe.

"They didn't make you a detective inspector for nothing."

"Funny you should say that."

If he wanted her to ask why, she wasn't going to give him the satisfaction.

Kinky walked in, jumped on to the sofa and perched on the arm.

They all sat facing each other over the aromatic bag.

"Don't let me stop you eating," said the detective.

"I wasn't intending to." Lexy delved into the bag and began laying the dishes out with more defiance than she felt.

Milo's mouth twisted briefly. "So – that reporter who turned up earlier – did you manage to send him packing without him getting anything on you?"

"Yeah, thanks." Lexy spooned rice on to her plate, not looking up.

"I'm amazed that anyone from the press would quit so easily," he went on, shrugging his shoulders. "They usually set up camp."

She remained silent, spearing a battered cauliflower floret. OK, so he'd sussed out her misunderstanding over the twitchers. What did he want – an apology? In your dreams, copper.

"Anyway," he continued, "the official release went out this lunchtime, so it'll appear in the dailies tomorrow, but I'm guessing that Avril Todd's husband has probably told his friends and family by now, so most of the village will know already."

Lexy acknowledged this grudgingly. "He called the director of the am-dram group this afternoon while I was there. Um… did the press release go out without my name in it, by the way?"

"Your assumed name or your real one?"

"Either," she said tightly.

"Don't worry. You were just a passing dog walker. And hopefully it won't cause much national interest, anyway." He paused. "Does *anyone* know you're here? From your previous life, I mean?"

Lexy shook her head, chewing.

"Not even your friends or relatives?"

"Nope."

No one to tell. Lexy's dad was dead, her mother hadn't been in contact since she went off crusading, Lexy hadn't seen her grandmother for years and as for her friends...Friends? She hadn't really got any. Just Gerard's TV show hangers-on and a bunch of regulars in the local wine bar who were impressed by his minor celebrity status. She was a real Billy-no-mates.

"I felt a bit bad after you left the police station on Friday night," DI Milo said, in his matter-of-fact way.

Lexy stared at him, a battered mushroom half-way to her mouth.

"I think... well, obviously, I realise now, after our phone call this morning, that it might have looked like I was trying to coerce you into coming out for dinner with me tonight."

"You were," Lexy pointed out.

"I didn't mean it in the way you must have thought. Not in the man, woman way, that is." Did he give her a slightly pitying look? "I needed to get you somewhere where we could talk. I... just kind of made it difficult for you to refuse. I'm sorry."

Lexy popped the mushroom into her mouth and chewed it slowly. So he hadn't been planning on having her for dessert. Fine. "Talk about what?" she said, indistinctly.

"The murder, of course. You obviously knew more about it than you were saying. But I couldn't ask you officially."

Lexy didn't like the sound of this. Why was it obvious?

"I'm not part of the investigation, for a start," he continued. "I should never have got involved in the first place, actually – I'm meant to be convalescing from an... accident..." Lexy just caught the stricken look in his eyes. "As my DCI took great pains to point out to me on Friday, after you'd gone. While he confiscated my warrant card."

"Confiscated your ...?"

"Yes. He's a tetchy little sod."

"So you're not here on duty?" Lexy was beginning to feel alarmed.

"Nope. In fact, I've been suspended. Long story." He gave her an ironic smile. "But let's just say I'm not expecting a bonus this year."

"So, if you're suspended," she said slowly, "what *are* you doing here?"

Milo leaned back in the stripy chair, as if this was the question he'd wanted to answer all along. "That's easy. Right from the time I ran into you at the vet's, I had a feeling – call it a policeman's instinct – that you were up to something, and…"

"Up to something? Just because I've got a tattoo and…"

He shook his head firmly. "Nothing to do with your appearance, so forget that. Anyway, I thought I'd keep tabs on you."

Lexy bit her lip. He'd been following her. Her eyes flicked to Kinky. He gave her a sidelong glance.

"What were you doing at the vet's anyway?" she said, playing for time.

"What did it look like? Taking my niece's rabbit for a check-up while she was at school. Her mother – my sister, that is – thought it would give me something to do."

Lexy frowned. Somehow, she hadn't expected the policeman to have a family. A niece with a rabbit. "What was that stuff about investigating the vet, then?"

"I made that up. I wanted to get your details."

She felt outmanoeuvred at every turn. "Isn't that illegal? Anyway, you've been suspended, now. Why do you care what I'm up to?"

"As I said, I think you know more about this Avril Todd thing than you're letting on."

"And if I do?"

He sat up. "I might be suspended from the Force, but that

doesn't mean I don't want track down whoever brutally killed a woman on Friday evening. If you're sitting on information that will lead me to this murderer, I want to hear it about it. Off the record." A flash of fire in the grey ice.

It was a better answer. It hinted at a compromise that allowed Avril's killer to be netted, but let Lexy slip through the fine mesh.

"OK. What makes you think I'm holding out on you?" Might as well get him to spit out what he knew.

"I tailed you to that field on Friday night," he said, quietly. "I know you were following Avril Todd."

Ah.

"I *need* to know everything that you can tell me about this."

"Definitely off the record?"

"I've just had my warrant card confiscated and I'm suspended from duty. And my notebook's at home. I just want information."

"What will you do with it?"

"Give my colleagues in the Force an anonymous tip-off."

Lexy raised her eyebrows. "*I* was going to do that."

Did he look briefly impressed? Relieved? What had he thought she was going to do – find the murderer and tackle him herself?

"Let's trade information, then," he said. "The more we can give them, the sooner they can nail this scumbag."

Lexy felt herself relax slightly. "So you're going to tell me what you know, too?" she asked.

He nodded impatiently. "Yes, of course. OK – why were you following her?"

Lexy hesitated.

"Right," said Milo, "let me make this easy for you. You're a private dick, aren't you?"

Lexy choked on a noodle.

The policeman remained silent, waiting for her to recover.

"Not intentionally," she rasped, trying to get her breath.

"Go on then, tell me. You might as well."

Lexy sighed. He asked for it. "All right, from the beginning," she said. "I was broke. Still am. I'd just moved here and I was wondering what I was going to do, and suddenly I had this guy on the phone leaving a message that he wanted… well, there was a bit of confusion about what he wanted, but I called him back, and it turned out he wanted his wife followed. He was, er, offering quite a bit of money. He seemed to think he was talking to a private detective and I put two and two together and guessed that the person who owned the place before me must have been one, at which point it occurred to me that it probably wouldn't be too difficult to pretend that I was her, and to agree to follow this guy's wife about for one night. So I said OK."

So much for her agreement with Roderick Todd.

"I know it was wrong," she gabbled on, "but I was really desperate for cash and the dog needed…"

Milo raised a finger. "So you bought this place from Glenda Doyle?"

Lexy stared at him. "Not directly from her, obviously."

"Why obviously?"

"I'd have had to dig her up first."

"She's dead?"

"Knew her well, did you?" Clearly not, if he didn't know that Glenda had bought the farm six weeks ago. At least Edward had had an excuse.

"Our paths crossed from time to time. What happened to her?"

"Heart attack."

"Oh. I see."

He thought for a moment, then suddenly turned on Lexy. "So you thought you'd just step into her shoes, did you?"

"Well… yeah…"

"That was an incredibly stupid thing to do."

"You don't have to tell me." Lexy felt her temper rise. "It was a spur of the moment thing. A mistake. Haven't you ever made one? If I'd have known it was going to be like that – Avril getting her head caved in and everything…"

"Welcome to my world."

"You are."

"And in answer to your question, yes, I have made mistakes. Plural," Milo added.

They sat wordlessly for a moment.

Milo started again. "So you say that you were following Avril Todd because you thought her husband thought she was having an affair?"

Lexy nodded.

"But I'm getting from this that he wanted you to follow her for a different reason?"

"Yeah. Not that he told me at the time – idiot. It turns out that she was a… oh crap… she was a poison pen writer, OK? And a blackmailer."

Milo digested this information. "Gives us a slightly clearer reason why someone might want her out of the way."

"All right," said Lexy. "Your turn. What have the police found out?"

"Well, being off the case, I haven't been able to glean much. A friend of mine in forensics told me, on the quiet, that they've had some initial tests back on Avril Todd's stomach contents sampled at the post mortem."

Great. Lexy put a battered baby sweetcorn back on the plate.

"It seems she'd taken a strong sedative shortly before she was killed. It was surprising she was able to drive, actually. She must have had a death wish." He paused. "That is…"

Lexy nodded understanding.

"Now," he went on, "I followed you to Windmill Hill that evening and parked down the bottom, waiting for you."

"Oh, did you?" Sneaky git.

"You see Avril Todd get into her car?"

Lexy nodded.

"Did she seem unsteady or faltering?"

"Like she was on drugs?" Lexy thought back to that evening. Avril slamming her front door shut as she had driven past. Nothing faltering about that. By the time Lexy had turned the Panda around and arrived back opposite the house, Avril had been backing her Volvo out of the garage. She had then got out, marched up to close the garage doors, and got back into the car again.

Lexy shrugged. "I didn't notice her swaying about or anything." She pondered. "Although she did take a couple of minutes fussing about with her seatbelt."

Milo nodded and glanced down at the crispy noodles. "You didn't notice Avril eating or drinking anything when she was driving along?"

"You're joking, aren't you? Most of the time I only just had her car in sight. Are you sure she was on sedatives? It was more like she'd taken a humungous snort of coke."

"True," he agreed, reflectively.

"Oh, yeah. You were right behind me." She couldn't believe she hadn't even noticed him following her.

"Until you both took a sudden turn up the Nudging lane," went on Milo. "That's when I lost you. I took the next turn, intending to head you off. Which I did."

He glanced down at the crispy noodles again.

Lexy thrust a spare fork at him.

"Thanks." He almost smiled, but didn't quite make it.

"So, this sedative?" said Lexy, finally eating her sweetcorn. "Can they tell when she took it? I mean, couldn't she have taken it when she got there?"

Milo shook his head. "It had been in her system for at least twenty minutes before death. At least. That's the really baffling thing."

"Did she die straight away? As soon as she was hit on the head?"

"Yes. Death was instantaneous. Single blow to the left temple. Brain haemorrhage."

They contemplated the red curry.

"So any effort to revive her…"

"Would have been futile."

Lexy felt guiltily relieved at this, as she had made no such effort, although Milo had certainly made up for it. She glanced at him. That look of pain was back in his eyes again.

"Any idea what the murder weapon was?"

"No. But from what I saw myself, the impact wound was about six millimetres deep. Made with something hard and rounded at the end, like a walking stick."

Lexy couldn't stop her eyes darting around the room, trying to remember where Glenda Doyle's knobbly walking stick had been left.

"Bit of a mystery, in fact," he continued.

There was something in his voice.

Lexy froze. All that stuff about being suspended from the police force was bollocks. He'd been stringing her along, coaxing information out of her, and now he'd finished off her crispy noodles he was going to arrest her. Bastard.

"Really?" she said, coldly.

"Yup." He paused. "They've found a trace of DNA in the head wound that doesn't belong to the victim."

Lexy narrowed her eyes. "Therefore it belongs to the attacker?"

"As it turned out, it was dog DNA."

There was a heavy silence as they turned to Kinky. He blinked benignly.

"So – you going to arrest my dog?" said Lexy.

Milo gave a faint smile. "They reckon it came from a large dog. Labrador or something. Not that that would have made it any more capable of hitting Avril."

"So the attacker could be someone who owns a big mutt?" Lexy felt herself relax again.

"You've got it." Milo rubbed his clean-shaven chin. "Anyway, they're awaiting further tests on that." He shifted. "By the way, what do you know about these poison pen letters?"

After a moment's internal deliberation, Lexy told him about the two letters Edward had received and the four delivered to the Ellengers' surgery. She didn't divulge Hope's dark revelations on the Ellenger family history; she wasn't going to spill every last bean in the pot till she knew for sure that this cop, or ex-cop or whatever, was on the level with her.

"All the letters seem to be on the same theme," she said. "I think Avril was just digging, you know, making stabs in the dark. And when she hit a really sensitive spot she composed a blackmail letter. Like the one she sent Sheri-Anne Davis."

Lexy described the letter in the gold compact in Sheri-Anne's locker, and how the girl had left the package in the palm tree. She didn't mention that she thought she now knew why Sheri-Anne was being blackmailed. Not until she was sure...

"So, as far as you're aware, the package is still there, in the palm tree?" Milo gave her a keen look.

She shrugged. "Guess it must be."

"I ought to get it picked up for safe-keeping. Some other bugger might find it and have it away." He thought for a moment. "I'll get uniform to pick it up tomorrow – just say I got a tip-off about a robbery. My informants don't know I'm suspended, do they?"

Lexy regarded him with narrowed eyes. He still couldn't stop playing the policeman. That's what worried her.

Milo started stacking the empty foil containers into a neat pile.

"Right, so what do we know? We've got a murdered woman. We think the most likely reason she's been murdered is she's been writing obnoxious anonymous letters to certain members of the Clopwolde am-dram society and possibly blackmailing them. This is something she has history of. You got some paper?"

Lexy silently fetched a lined pad she had bought earlier.

Milo produced a pen and drew a circle in the centre of the page, writing *Avril Todd* in it.

"The murder occurred at about twenty past eight, didn't it?"

Lexy nodded.

"We know for a fact," Milo said, adding a satellite to the circle, "that Avril was sending letters to your neighbour, Edward de Glenville, who lost his father in an accident, and to the local vet, Guy Ellenger and his sister, what's her name? Hope – " he added more satellites, " – who lost *their* father in an accident. The letters suggest foul play in each case, perhaps intended to flush out some hidden truth, as you say. It's also a fair bet that Avril sent letters to the vet's nurse, Sheri-Anne Davis, on a different theme, something tangible and juicy that she had obviously uncovered. This ended in an attempt to blackmail Sheri-Anne, which would have worked if Avril hadn't been killed two days before the cash drop. Sheri-Anne made the drop anyway, so we can assume that she didn't kill Avril."

"Not unless she's clever as well as devious," said Lexy.

"She got on the phone to someone straight after she made the drop," she went on. "Told them she'd put the money in the tree. Then she told them Avril had died. So we could assume that whoever she was talking to didn't know Avril was the blackmailer either."

"We need to find out who that was." Milo made a note. "Say we rule out Sheri-Anne Davis and the mystery person for now, that still leaves us with several am-dram players whose movements we should check for the Friday night. And we can include any other players, like Avril's husband. There's a chance that the poison pen letters might not have been the motive. She wasn't exactly a popular woman, by all accounts."

Lexy nodded. "I've done a bit of ground work there." She ticked people off on her fingers, while Milo steadily wrote, looking up at her from time to time.

"Roderick Todd – he was in Lincoln at an old boys' reunion. That's probably been verified by your lot…"

Milo nodded. "I'll see if I can check that one out on the QT."

"Edward," continued Lexy, "was having a lovers' tiff at Peter's shop in the high street, which ended up with Edward being taken to Lowestoft nick on Friday night. He told me that himself on Saturday morning."

"OK – that's another one to check."

"I honestly can't see Edward having killed her," objected Lexy.

"Nevertheless, we check *all* alibis."

"Hope Ellenger." Lexy drew a deep breath. "She says she was at home on her own on Friday night." Lexy made a tippling motion. "She seems to have a drink problem at the moment."

"Can we check she was there at the time of the murder?"

Lexy sucked in a reluctant breath. "I can try her neighbours."

"Good. And her brother?"

Lexy swallowed quickly. "I'm not sure. I think he was in the vet's surgery all evening with Sheri-Anne Davis." She paused. Nice one, Lexy. Here she was, glibly supporting the vet's alibi, even when she had overheard Sheri-Anne Davis herself saying she was at a barn somewhere on Friday night. Still, Lexy had her own reasons for keeping that one quiet. But, once again, where did it leave Guy Ellenger?

"What about the rest of the cast?"

"It was supposed to be the annual am-dram company dinner on Friday night, but from what I could gather only Maurice, the director, and a couple of stage hands and extras went. The main cast – Guy and Hope Ellenger, Edward, Peter and Sheri-Anne Davis blew it out. Oh, and the Caradocs didn't go either."

"Caradocs?"

"Tristan and Tammy. They live next door to Guy Ellenger, and they loom large in the am-dram society."

"Tammy Caradoc." Milo's eyes took on an unexpectedly hazy quality. "I remember her when I was young. She was in *Bergerac*, wasn't she?"

"You used to watch *Bergerac* when you were a kid?"

"I wanted to be a policeman. What did you watch?"

Lexy thought back to the portable telly in the caravan. "*The X Files*. I wanted to be Agent Scully."

He looked around the cabin. "Not exactly living the dream, then?"

"And you are?"

He smiled thinly. "Right. Alibis. What have you got on the Caradocs?"

Lexy thought. "Tristan Caradoc was doing a ghost walk on Friday night – you know, terrifying the tourists with grisly tales of ye olde Clopwolde."

"What time?"

"I can tell you that exactly." Lexy fetched the poster Tristan had presented her with. "There's an eight o'clock walk, then a ten o'clock one."

"Has to work for his money, then."

"I actually saw him on the way back from the ten o'clock session on Friday night." She wasn't going to add that Tristan had helped her to restart the Panda.

"What about Tammy Caradoc?"

"Tristan said she stayed in. She's distraught about losing her cat – that's why they didn't go to the am-dram company dinner."

"Her cat?"

"You can't have missed the posters all over Clopwolde."

"Oh – that cat."

They sat in silence for a while, Milo staring at his notes, Lexy staring at the ceiling.

"One of the things I really can't figure out is what Avril was doing in that field," Lexy said suddenly. "It can't be where she was getting people to drop off cash. Much too dangerous for her. Even her husband couldn't understand what she was doing out there. He said she didn't like the countryside."

"Kind of unfortunate that she drew her last breath there, then. So, if she wasn't collecting her blackmail proceeds, what was she doing? Meeting someone?"

"Guess so. But not someone she was blackmailing – again, too dangerous."

"What if it was a woman?"

"Do you think it might be, then?"

Milo shrugged. "From the evidence at the scene, we're looking for someone strongly built, but not necessarily a man. The blow that killed her had been delivered with substantial force, though," he mused.

"When I heard Avril call out, her voice sounded weak," said Lexy. "Not like at the vet's – she was really strident then."

"The sedative had probably kicked in by that point." Milo doodled on the paper. "Is there anything else we need to take into consideration?"

Lexy squeezed her eyes shut, trying to think. "I spoke to one of Avril's neighbours on Saturday morning – an old dear. Bit weird this – she said she'd seen Avril come up the hill and go into her house at half-seven on Friday evening. But her next door neighbour reckons it was at a quarter past."

"Also an old dear?"

"Not as old as the first one, apparently."

Milo's mouth twitched. "It happens all the time – trust me. People are incapable of agreeing about the time, and the older they get…"

"I still might check it out."

"Whatever – we've got a few other things to go on, as well. Let's do some digging and get together again? I'll call you."

Milo pushed himself up and went to Lexy's phone, taking the number. "If you think of anything else – well, you know my number. Call any time."

"Don't you ever sleep?" asked Lexy.

"No – not lately."

He left abruptly, and got into his car.

Lexy watched him go. Why was he so… she searched for an appropriate word to describe Milo. Pompous? No, not exactly. Arrogant? Not really that, either. Disquieting – yes, that was it.

Why was DI Bernard Milo so disquieting?

17

News of the Costello's warbler was spreading fast. When Lexy awoke from a fitful sleep and pulled open her tattered curtains she discovered a small army of avian anoraks assembled in her garden.

At least it was a quiet invasion; in fact any sound at all, apart from the hallowed warbling, was heavily frowned upon.

Acutely aware of this, Lexy took Kinky along to the heath for his morning constitutional, all the while thinking about the methodical way Milo had pulled together the strands of the case the previous evening.

Why was he so keen to solve this murder? He was on convalescent leave because of some unexplained accident, but he wasn't exactly taking it easy. He seemed determined to do his job, whether the police force wanted him to or not. And he was working alongside Lexy whether she wanted him to or not. But only in the matter of Avril Todd's murder. He wasn't going to get near her other assignment. That one was worth money. There was a substantial reward for the return of Princess Noo-Noo.

That afternoon, Lexy and Kinky went into Clopwolde, Lexy sporting the nearly new collection she'd bought the previous day. First she was going to do some sleuthing, just to fulfil her obligations. Then she was going to call into every pub and shop in the village to look for a sensible job.

When she reached the newsagent, Lexy checked the rack out-side. The news of Avril's death hadn't made the front pages of the nationals, but a couple of them ran the story inside. The local papers wouldn't be out until later in the week. Lexy quickly read through the accounts. As Milo had confirmed, the only mention of her was as a passer-by with a dog. She heaved a sigh of relief.

Then she remembered that her next port of call was the vet's. "This is going to be painful," she said to Kinky, as they turned into the alley where the shabby surgery resided. He was all for giving it a miss, but Lexy was resolute.

Hope was behind the reception desk, looking as if the slightest noise would shatter her into a thousand pieces. There was no one else in the waiting area. As soon as she saw Lexy she came out from behind the desk.

"Come in here – we can talk." She led Lexy into Guy's surgery and Lexy put Kinky on to the examination bench, where he sat apprehensively.

"Are you going to go to the police?" Hope was on the edge of tears.

"You remember everything, then?"

"I know I told you about Guy. I wish I hadn't."

Lexy wished she hadn't, too.

"Look, I'm… just going to pretend I didn't hear anything." Lexy made herself meet Hope's eyes. "It's your own business. If what you say is true, Guy did what he did to save your mother. If there's any more to it, I guess your conscience will tell you what to do. Mine does. It's on at me all the time. Nag, nag…"

Hope gave a small wail and unexpectedly put her arms around Lexy. She felt as frail as she looked. It was like hugging balsawood. "You and your brother need to move on," Lexy told her.

"I know." Hope pulled some tissues from a box. "But the letter writer…"

"I told you – you won't be getting any more."

"How do you know?"

"Trust me – I know."

Lexy and Kinky left thankfully, albeit for different reasons. The visit had had a twofold purpose: to get that business with

201

Hope out of the way and also to ensure that the receptionist was at the surgery, rather than at home, because that was where Lexy was going next.

She left Kinky tied to a railing out of sight around the corner, jammed her old baseball cap firmly over her cropped hair, and walked up the steps to Hope's neighbours at number two, carrying a large plastic bin bag.

A buxom thirty-something woman opened the door and gave Lexy the hostile but resigned glance that people usually reserve for door-to-door salespersons. At least she didn't recognise her from the evening before last.

"Hello. I'm collecting old clothing for charity," Lexy said smoothly.

The woman visibly relaxed. "I'll see what we've got."

She turned and gave a call. "Vince – they're collecting clothes for charity. Where's that old suit of yours?"

"Back of my wardrobe. I'll get it."

"You should have given us some notice – I might have been able to find some more bits and bobs. I seem to have grown out of everything just lately."

"I usually call Friday evenings," Lexy lied. "But there didn't seem to be anyone here last Friday. Or next door."

"We were here," said the woman at once. "All evening. We hardly ever go out on Fridays now. My husband likes to cook instead – thinks he's Jamie Oliver."

"Sounds all right to me. How about next door?" Lexy pointed to Hope's house.

"Let's see. She went out, I think. About half past seven it was. She had a big bag with her so she was probably going to the surgery. She's the vet's receptionist," she added.

"Here we are." A chubby man appeared toting a shiny grey suit.

"Oh, brilliant. Thanks so much."

"Hope went out Friday night, didn't she, Vince?"

"Was that the night I made seared carpaccio of beef with parsnip mash? Followed by strawberry vanilla cream tart?"

His wife nodded, a tad ruefully.

"Yes, in that case, and I remember the crash at midnight when she got back." They gave each other a significant look.

Lexy scooted off with the awful suit and collected Kinky. She retraced her steps with a horribly lucid vision of Hope Ellenger out and about on the night of the murder, carrying a large bag in which a weapon might have been concealed.

If Hope had driven straight to Nudging, it would have taken her about fifteen minutes. Seven forty-five. She would have had to hide her car a couple of miles away from the scene of the intended crime, as her getaway plan would have involved using Avril's Volvo, and walk to the field. At a brisk pace, two miles would take about half an hour. She would have just about been in place before Avril arrived around twenty past eight, and…

Lexy drew to a sudden halt, remembering Kitty's words to Hope in the café the other day.

How are the driving lessons going, dear?

Hope was only on her third lesson. Lexy nodded grimly. So that was her off the prime suspect list. But perhaps not off the hook altogether.

Lexy made her way to Windmill Hill. She needed to nip up to number fourteen without being seen by Roderick Todd, the police or the old dear who thought Kinky's name was Keith.

Apologising profusely to Kinky, she left him tied up to a lamp-post and jogged up the road, still carrying the large plastic bag, which now contained the shiny grey suit. Number fourteen was almost opposite the Todds' house. Lexy slunk up the garden path and rang the bell.

A spry-looking woman with a grey bun answered. Budgerigar-type squawks emanated loudly from the interior of the house.

"Hello – just collecting some clothes for charity," Lexy smiled.

"What charity?" the woman demanded.

"RSPCA."

It was the right answer.

"Why didn't you say?" She bustled off. More whistles and squawks. "Now, now, Murgatroyd, don't be rude."

Lexy checked swiftly behind her. The Todds' house looked drawn and quiet, as if it were itself in mourning. Horace the cat was sitting solemnly in the front window.

"It's not much, I'm afraid." The woman with the bun had returned. Was she having a laugh? Lexy was going to need a wheelbarrow. She packed the pile of shapeless woollen items into the plastic bag on top of the suit, murmuring appropriate words of thanks; then she said, "Oh – do you have the right time please? My watch gave up the ghost earlier."

"Wait a moment."

The woman disappeared into her living room.

"Ten to three, exactly," she said, with a brief but smug look at the house next door. "I always make sure my carriage clock is set to Greenwich Mean Time. Unlike some people."

Lexy returned to Kinky, staggering under the weight of the clothing. "Looks like number twelve and number fourteen are going to have to agree to differ on the time that Avril came home on Friday," she told him. "But at least I tried."

After a visit to Oxfam to donate clothing, Lexy returned to Otter's End. She needed to give a bit of thought to her other investigative job – the one she would be tackling that evening. If she pulled it off, she was going to make several people very happy. The Caradocs, Hope and Guy Ellenger, and anyone else who cared about the fate of Princess Noo-Noo. It would mark her first and – she reminded herself – last success as a private sleuth.

It would also make certain other people very angry and upset.

She'd do well to bear that in mind.

At seven o'clock, Lexy collected her camera, a penknife, and a fleece. Just in case she was in for another late one. Her hand was on the door handle, ready to leave, when a knock made her jump back.

She peered through the net curtain, then gave a grin and pulled the door open.

"Hello, lovie," said Edward. "Who are those odd people crouching at the bottom of your garden? I trust they're not doing something unsavoury."

"Long story," said Lexy.

"Do tell later. Look, I've bought you a little treat. Proper coffee." He handed Lexy a paper carrier with the name of a posh grocer on it. "And some choccies to go with."

"Wow – that's very kind. Is it my birthday?" asked Lexy.

"If you want it to be. Actually, darling – this is an excuse for *me* to have coffee and chocolates, and to talk about *you know what*. I had two policemen at my place yesterday, you know. Very attractive ones, too, in full uniform – it was quite thrilling." He gave her a sidelong glance. "And on my way out last night, I just happened to notice a lean, tall man driving down from *your* place. Could he have been a plain-clothes policeman, perchance? He left very late – you must have had a good long interrogation."

Did nothing pass him by?

"Did you tell them anything you shouldn't have?" Lexy asked, checking her watch surreptitiously.

"Of course not, sweetie. It's all over the papers today, anyway."

"Listen, Edward, believe it or not, I'm just on my way out," Lexy said. "I have to go back to the police station, actually. It's a real drag." She really was going to have to stop lying.

"Oh – let him wait ten minutes." Edward waltzed into the kitchen and put the kettle on.

Lexy checked her watch again and winced.

"OK – just a very quick one," she said.

"Story of my life," he trilled. "Look – violet and rose creams – yummy."

Lexy tried to smile.

Edward lifted a small cafetière out of the bag, and opened a sachet of Javan coffee. "So, do you have any more juicy details? Tell me all."

Lexy screwed up her face. "Not really. They think Avril had taken some sort of drug before going out."

"Oh, please tell me it was ecstasy," begged Edward. "The scandal would be endless."

"Sorry to disappoint – it was just a sedative." Again, Lexy wondered how Avril could have driven as well as she did under the influence of a tranquillising drug. She must have had a cast iron gut, to match her features.

"She was probably depressed, poor cow."

Edward pushed the plunger into the cafetière and poured the coffee into two dinky cups which he also pulled out of the carrier.

"Milk in the fridge, is it?"

"There's some soya milk, but it curdles in coffee," said Lexy.

"Nice. Well, black it is then."

He passed it over to her.

"Ta," said Lexy. She threw back the hot liquid as quickly as possible.

"My word, you are in a hurry." Edward watched her replace the cup. "Violet or rose?"

"What? Oh – rose, thanks."

She took the proffered confection, picked off the pink candied top and smiled bravely at Edward as she popped it into her mouth.

"Have another one, lovie, you need fattening up. Although, I deduce from the foil containers in your kitchen that someone's been treating herself to a takeaway."

Lexy gave him a weak smile. "Fragrant Garden."

"Best Thai restaurant in Clopwolde," Edward proclaimed.

"It's the *only* Thai restaurant in Clopwolde, isn't it?" said Lexy.

"Well – yes." He pushed his chair back. "I can see that I'm not going to get anything out of you until you've had another tête-à-tête with the dashing detective."

"He's not exactly dashing," said Lexy. "More grim. Anyway, he's not on this case." Although you wouldn't believe that if you knew him.

"Ha – I was right! Your long, lean visitor is one of our boys in blue."

Lexy cast her eyes up.

"Now – remember to pop into mine on your way back tonight," said Edward. I simply *have* to know what's going on. TTFN." He blew her a kiss, let himself out, and gave the bird-watchers, who were just packing up, a coy wave for good measure. "Now that's what I call a telephoto lens, lovie."

Lexy waited until Edward was out of sight, then rounded up Kinky, who looked alarmed to be going out in the Panda again.

She drove straight to a garage on the outskirts of Clopwolde, put a fiver's worth of petrol in the car, bought a newspaper, drove back into the village and located Bartholomew Lane. Thankfully it was short, with only a dozen twee red-brick houses. Lexy occupied a parking space conveniently vacated by a Land Rover about halfway down.

She slouched down in her seat and shook out the newspaper. Now all she could do was wait, and hope her instincts were correct.

The minutes ticked past. Eight-thirty came and went. A number of cars drove past – the lane was obviously a rat-run of some sort. But it wasn't passing cars Lexy was interested in. Methodically she scanned the houses, watching for movement at the front doors.

Twenty to nine. Had she missed her chance? Lexy began to fidget. She was going to have to go back and call Milo. Tell him what she knew. And he wouldn't be pleased she'd been holding out on him.

Quarter to nine. Right. That was that. Over to the boys in blue. Or rather to the suspended policeman who wouldn't give up. Lexy chucked the newspaper into the back of the car, pushed herself up, and started the engine.

Then she saw her. Running down the drive of number nine, checking her watch, dressed in jeans and a fetching cotton top. She jumped into a yellow Mini, which, as luck would have it, was facing the same way as Lexy's Panda. All Lexy had to do was slide the Panda into gear and follow Sheri-Anne Davis.

Ten minutes later they were deep in the countryside. Sheri-Anne had turned down a series of increasingly small lanes that snaked through parched-looking heathland ringed with dark conifer woods. Lexy followed at a distance, only just keeping Sheri-Anne in sight. Eventually the Mini turned into a farm entrance, and bumped up a track. Lexy didn't dare to follow. She parked the Panda just off the lane in a small copse and, leaving Kinky to guard it – at least that's what she told him – she darted back to the gateway. Dusk was beginning to fall, and she kept to the shadow of a hedge, camera at the ready. It felt horribly reminiscent of the Friday night just gone, moments before she had heard Avril's dying scream. She rounded a corner, and saw two cars parked next to an old barn in a dingy yard garnished with stacks of used tyres, rusting car parts and rotting bales of hay. A dilapidated farmhouse stood nearby, clearly uninhabited.

Lexy slipped behind a tree and looked at the cars. One was Sheri-Anne's yellow Mini. The other was one she had seen very recently.

She crept nearer to the barn and made her way around to the

back, climbing up a precipitous mound of rubble to reach a crack in the wooden slats through which light filtered from inside. A familiar sound made Lexy grin and nod. She put an eye to the hole.

Gotcha…

She watched for a moment, straightened up and took a step backwards – into nothing.

The pile of rubble had a sheer edge, over which Lexy had toppled. She dropped down several feet, with an involuntary gasp, and fell back hard against the unyielding trunk of an elder tree, her head striking it with a dull thud.

A thin trickle of blood began to seep slowly into the earth.

18

When Lexy awoke all was whiteness. Must be heaven, but why did it hurt so much? Clouds were meant to be soft and fluffy. Perhaps she was lying on her harp.

A smooth, pink face loomed over her, the mouth open.

With a gasp, Lexy tried to push herself up.

Gentle pressure held her down.

A pair of ice-grey eyes swam into view. Definitely not heaven, then.

"Venus de Milo." Her voice was croaky.

The lips twitched. "That's me."

"What happened?"

"You're in hospital."

"Yeah – I already worked that one out." Forming the words was a real effort, like she was drunk. "What's wrong with me?"

"You've got concussion. Not badly. You've obviously got a skull of granite."

Lexy grimaced, put a tentative hand upwards. She felt a bandage that seemed to encompass most of her head.

"How long have I been here?"

"Since last night. You've been sleeping for hours. You must have been exhausted."

Since last night? Lexy searched his face. "Was I in an accident?"

"Sort of. You fell and hit your head."

"Where?"

He frowned. "Round the back of an old barn. At a farm out on Mellowsham Heath. Back end of nowhere."

Lexy gazed at him. "What was I doing out there?"

He looked carefully across to the open door, then bent towards her. "Don't you remember? You were following Sheri-Anne Davis."

210

Lexy squinted. "Yellow Mini?"

"That's the one. Remember following her cross country through the heath? Big, dark conifer plantation in the distance?"

She screwed up her face. "I kind of remember following her car along some twisty lanes. Were you bloody following me again?"

He nodded.

"Why?"

"Didn't trust you. I knew you were holding something back."

"Holding something back from what?"

He gave an irritated exclamation. "Our investigation. Avril Todd's murder. You remember that, I hope?"

Lexy stared at him.

"You do, don't you?" He was starting to look alarmed.

She grinned. "Yeah. I remember."

He gave her a weary look.

"But if you were following me last night," Lexy said slowly, "didn't *you* see anything?"

"I missed all the action – again. Lost you about a mile from the farm. I had to drive around for at least ten minutes trying to find you. It was just a lucky guess I checked up on the place, and saw your car parked in that copse of trees. I didn't see Sheri-Anne's car – she must have gone by the time I got there."

"Not very good at following people, are you?"

His eyes narrowed. "I am normally. Trying to keep up with you is proving unusually difficult."

Lexy suddenly winced. "Ah, my head – it's killing me."

Milo pressed a button above Lexy's headboard and almost immediately a dark-skinned male nurse appeared in the doorway of the little side ward. "I see you've woken her up."

"No – she came round of her own accord," he replied coolly.

"Well, you're not to start making her answer a lot of questions."

"Naturally."

"Yeah, right. You're a policeman. That's what you lot do, ask questions."

"Speaking of questions, has anybody got a painkiller?" groaned Lexy.

The nurse studied the notes clipped to the bottom of her bed. "I'll go and get you some paracetamol." He whisked away.

"I was thinking more elephant tranquilliser. Did you actually tell him you were a policeman?"

"Yes."

"You just left out the bit about being suspended?"

"Your memory's not that bad, then."

"It is." She made a face. "I don't remember getting out of the car at all, but I must have done if you found me by this barn. One moment I was driving along with Kinky and then…" She broke off, staring at the detective in sudden horror.

"Kinky – where is he?" She struggled to sit up.

He held her down. "It's OK. Take it easy. He was in your car. He tried to kill me when I opened it, but when he saw the state of you he consented to come to the hospital with us in my car."

"Didn't you call an ambulance?"

Milo shook his head. "I brought you here myself. Quicker."

"Where's Kinky now? At your place?"

"No. I took him down to the vet's. Guy Ellenger. He said he'd look after him."

"Oh, right. Thanks." An image swam into Lexy's mind of Guy Ellenger's face, with his melting toffee eyes and perfect teeth. Setting up an alibi for himself on the phone. Pushing his dad down the stairs. Lexy felt her heart give a sudden violent pump. She saw herself creeping up the path towards the barn. There had been two cars.

"Here's the doctor." Milo withdrew, moving to the window.

Lexy gave an exclamation of frustration.

A sleek, middle-aged consultant sporting an inappropriately

jolly bow-tie breezed in self-importantly, followed by a gaggle of medical students who grouped themselves tightly around her bed.

The consultant plucked her notes from the bottom of the bed and scanned them rapidly.

"Ah, yes – concussion. Any memory loss?"

"Yeah," said Lexy. "I can't remember what I did yesterday evening."

"Neither can I," mouthed one of the male medical students. Lexy smiled faintly.

"It's all right – it will come back," the consultant predicted. "Feeling OK otherwise?"

"Just a bit of a headache." Like World War II was a bit of a squabble.

He beamed. "Very good, then." He turned to leave.

"Er… when can I go?"

"Tomorrow," he threw over his shoulder, "if you're sensible today and do as the nurses tell you."

"Tomorrow?" Lexy turned back in anguish to Milo when the throng had left. "I can't wait until tomorrow. I've got to get out of here today."

"What's the hurry? Remembered something, have you?"

She couldn't meet Milo's eyes. She didn't remember the make or colour of the other car that had been at the barn. But she remembered *why* she was following Sheri-Anne. And she remembered what she'd seen in the barn – exactly what she'd expected.

"It's just that I need to get Kinky."

"He's with a vet. He'll be all right."

Guy Ellenger's face rippled into view again. Lexy tried to push herself up. Milo held her arm down, regarding her with his usual impenetrable expression.

"Don't be stupid. You've got quite a dent in your head, you know."

Lexy eyed him. "So… er… you found me unconscious behind this barn?"

"Uh-huh."

"Guess you saved my life?"

He nodded.

"Thanks," she said gruffly.

They sat in silence for a moment, Milo studying a poster on the wall, Lexy studying his profile.

"Do you ever smile?" she asked.

He regarded her impassively. "I smiled when you woke up."

"I missed it. Do it again."

"I'm out of practice."

"Why?"

"You don't want to know."

"I do. I want to know why you act so weird."

"Weird?"

"Look." Lexy gritted her teeth against the pain in her head. "I just need to know one thing in particular, OK?"

He nodded warily. "OK."

"Do you recognise me?"

"Eh?"

"You heard. Do you recognise me?"

"You're not that badly hurt."

Lexy made a gesture of impatience. "I mean from the show."

"The show?"

She rolled her eyes, even though it hurt. "I *knew* you recognised me." She was aware of her voice gaining volume. "Right from the start, when we met at the vet's."

The policeman went very still. They stared at one another.

His voice suddenly cut in, quiet and conversational. "My wife died six months ago. She was a police sergeant, killed on duty. I was there. I tried to resuscitate her but I couldn't. When I saw you at the vet's on Thursday, just for a split second I thought she'd come back. That's all. Don't feel sorry for me," he went on quickly, seeing the change in Lexy's expression. "I'm getting over it. Although we still haven't tracked down the killer. But I'm working on that."

They were silent for a while. Lexy lay back, stunned. Far from recognising a girl who briefly used to provide the eye candy on an early evening DIY show, Milo thought his dead wife had come back. The wife he'd tried to resuscitate. No wonder he tried so hard to bring Avril Todd back to life. Lexy suddenly found herself wondering if Milo had given *her* mouth-to-mouth outside the barn. She felt a warm flush spread across her cheeks.

"Are you all right?" Milo enquired.

"Yeah, I'm fine." She tried to push herself up again. A nurse came in, told her to lie still, took her blood pressure and hurried off to the next patient.

"Do I really look like your wife?" Lexy asked.

"The more I see of you," Milo said, soberly, "the less you look like her. Especially in the turban. Anyway, what show?"

"Doesn't matter. I was barking up the wrong tree." That was for sure.

"You have a visitor." The nurse's rich Caribbean voice cut in from the doorway. "I told him five minutes only."

Lexy focused dazedly on a huge bunch of pink flowers flouncing towards her, clutched by a well-manicured hand with a gold and diamond ring on the pinkie.

"You *poor* little lamb! I ran into Hope in the village – not literally of course – and *she* said Guy had told her you were in hospital."

"Hello, Edward," said Lexy weakly. "This is DI Milo, from Lowestoft CID." Well, in a manner of speaking.

"Edward de Glenville," said Edward, thrusting his hand at Milo. He turned to Lexy. "Is this your exceedingly grim policeman? He looks all right to me."

Lexy tried not to look at Milo, who had stiffened.

"Well – what happened?" Edward demanded. "You weren't whacked over the head by Avril's phantom killer, were you?"

"No, I fell and got concussion," Lexy said.

"What? In Clopwolde?" Edward looked so outraged that Lexy almost laughed. "That bloody council really need to get their act together about the high street paving stones. Nearly went flying myself the other day."

He groped in a large leather satchel. "I brought you some highbrow reading matter." He stacked them on the bed. A copy each of *Hello* and *OK!*, a pile of lurid fashion magazines and a *Daily Mail*.

He smiled at DI Milo. "I always get the *Daily Mail*, just to annoy them."

"Annoy who?"

"The general readership, sweetcakes."

Lexy had to turn away to hide her broadening smile.

"I'm in the process of asking Ms Lomax a few questions," said DI Milo levelly.

"Don't worry. I can see I'm not wanted." Edward gave Lexy an outrageously suggestive look. "Just wanted to check she was all right. Bye-bye for now, sweetie. Be brave."

"Thanks for the flowers and… Edward – you couldn't do me a favour?"

"Just name it."

"Check on Kinky for me? He's at the vet's house. Kittiwake. It's in …"

"Gorse Rise. Next to the Caradocs' vision in white," Edward finished for her. "I'll do it as soon as I can. When are they letting you out?"

"Tomorrow," said Lexy.

"When you get your discharge papers I want you to call me up and I'll come and get you." He delved in his pocket and pulled out a piece of paper, scribbling on it. Here's the number."

"Thanks. I owe you one. Two."

"Forget it. See you on the morrow." He leaned over and dropped a kiss on Lexy's cheek, then turned to DI Milo. "Be gentle with her, Mr Policeman."

Lexy gave him a wilted wave, and turned back to Milo.

"Sorry about…"

"Is he the one who was getting poison pen letters from Avril Todd?" Milo gazed after Edward. "The one who's father died in a fall?"

"That's him. Only one Edward de Glenville in Clopwolde." Lexy glanced wryly at the huge bouquet. "He did have an alibi for Friday night, in case you forgot," she added, seeing Milo's humourless countenance. "He was in Lowestoft police station."

He nodded. "While we're on the subject, did you have any luck checking alibis before this… incident at the barn? Roderick Todd's checked out – he was definitely in a hotel in Lincoln at the time of the murder."

"Oh, yes – I was going to call you," Lexy said. "I found out from Hope Ellenger's neighbours that she went out on Friday evening at half-seven, and she didn't come back until midnight."

Milo sat up. "That's very interesting. So she wasn't home alone, like she said?" He pulled out a notebook – not his police one, Lexy noticed.

She shook her head. "But if she was our murderer, she'd have needed to get over to the field, and in position, as it were, in pretty good time."

"And?"

"She doesn't drive. She only just started learning."

"Ah."

"I also looked into that matter of the story about the time difference noticed by the old ducks in Avril's road," Lexy went on. "You know, when one saw her coming up the hill at

217

seven-fifteen, and the other at seven-thirty.

"And?"

"It remains a mystery. The second woman was just as adamant as the first that her clock was always right."

"Told you." He checked his watch, stood up. "Right, I'm off."

Lexy turned her head painfully to watch him go. "Where are you going?"

"I'm going to take Floppy for another visit to the vet's. See if I can get talking to Ms Ellenger." He slipped something out of his pocket and indicated the telephone on the bedside cabinet next to her. "I got you a phone card, in case you want to call anyone. Here's my number. Oh – and here are your car keys. I left it parked outside your place. I'll see you later. Try to get some rest."

The door snapped closed before Lexy could say 'thanks'.

She sank back into her pillow, trying to think above the dull throb of pain in her head. The wall clock said eleven-fifteen. If she was going to follow up this business at the barn, she needed to get out of the hospital as soon as possible. She shifted, tried to push herself up, then lay down again quickly as the door opened. A nurse came in and checked her bandage.

"Do you want one of these?" She passed Lexy one of the magazines Edward had left on the end of the bed. Lexy tried to read while the nurse busied herself over at the sink. Her headache made the words blur, but she also found she wasn't as interested in fashion as she had been last week. Last week when she had been Alexandra Warwick-Holmes. It felt like years ago. Certainly felt like she'd aged years in the last few days. She dropped the magazine back on the bed, feeling her eyelids flutter.

An insistent racket brought Lexy out of her sleep. The phone on her bedside table was ringing. She reached out and put it to her ear.

"Hello?" she mumbled.

"Lexy? Is that you?" She thought she recognised the voice, but she could hardly hear it.

"Speak up," she said.

"I can't, sweetie. I'm hiding."

"Edward?"

"Listen – I'm in Guy Ellenger's garden. Behind the ceanothus."

"Ceanothus?"

"It's a shrub. I'm in his shrubbery."

"Is there any point asking why?" Lexy found herself unaccountably whispering too.

"I came to pick up Kinky for you, like you said. Guy wasn't in, but I could hear the dogs, so I came round the back." The phone crackled, and Lexy heard yapping. "Shut it, you noisy little…"

"Edward – are you still there?"

"*Yes*. Which one is Kinky?"

"Sorry?"

"Lexy – there's five ruddy chihuahuas in this garden. Which one is Kinky? And don't say the brown one."

"He's the one with the little stitches in his ear."

"I haven't got my flipping reading glasses with me."

"Let me talk to them," Lexy hissed. She looked up sharply as the door opened. The nurse came in and gave her an interrogative look.

"Won't be a sec," she told him.

"What do you mean, let you talk to them?" Edward's voice was a low scream.

"Hold the phone down near the dogs," she murmured, aware of the nurse's penetrating stare.

"Right, I'm doing it," she heard Edward say. "Quick. This place is swarming with coppers."

Coppers? What was he on about? "Kinky," whispered Lexy lightly into the phone. "Come here, boy."

The nurse pursed his lips.

"Louder," she heard Edward mutter.

Lexy drew a deep breath. "Kinky," she yelled. "Come to the phone. Come to Lexy."

"That's got it. Up you come, matey-boy."

"Ahem," said the nurse.

"I'll ring you back in a minute," Lexy said, relief flooding through her. At least the mutt was safe now. Safe from what, though? She didn't really know.

"Sorry." Lexy put the receiver down, her face reddening. "That was my dog…"

"I see." The nurse regarded her closely.

"Chihuahua," Lexy babbled. "Very intelligent breed."

"May I examine you, please, Ms Lomax?"

"Of course. Think I'm all right now. In fact I'm feeling fine."

"I'll be the judge of that."

"I wasn't *really* talking to my dog."

"Lie back please."

When he'd gone, telling her in no uncertain terms to rest, Lexy reached for the phone again, punched out Edward's mobile number from the piece of paper he'd left her.

"Edward – where are you now?"

"On the way back to my place. Kinky is reclining on a cushion on the back seat."

"What's this about the police? At Guy's?"

"As far as I could make out from my hidey hole, he's been arrested."

"What?"

"Perhaps he's the Clopwolde Clobberer."

"*No.*" Lexy shook her head. Not Guy Ellenger.

"I know he's handsome, darling, but that doesn't mean he's good. Got to go, or I'll be arrested myself for gassing into my phone while driving. Give me a ring later. And don't worry about Kinky. He'll be treated like royalty. I'm off to Peter's. Bye-ee."

Lexy swore softly. What the hell had Milo done? She picked up his card and dialled his number, but his phone was switched off. She called Edward again.

"Listen – sorry – but can you come and get me now?" she said, lowering her voice even though the door was shut. "They've discharged me. Need the bed, apparently. Told me to go home and take it easy."

"Charming. It's a bit soon, isn't it, sweetie?"

"Oh… please just come and get me, Edward," Lexy begged. "I've got to get out of here."

"What's the time now – half one. I'll be there at two."

"Thanks. I'll wait for you outside," gasped Lexy.

As soon as she had put the phone down, Lexy began unwinding the bandage from her head. She wouldn't be able to sneak past the nurses' station looking like a Sikh.

She spent the next ten minutes gently easing herself up, and dressing. She checked herself in the mirror, recoiling in shock. She was as white as a skating rink. The wound she had sustained from the fall was on the back of her head, but the dressing felt like it was taped firmly in place. Taking a deep breath, Lexy picked up her bag, took a few steps forward and quietly opened the door.

The nurses' station was temporarily deserted. Lexy tottered out and within moments was in the lift being borne swiftly to the hospital foyer. She smiled weakly. Piece of cake, sneaking out of hospital.

But as she weaved across the foyer, trying to resist the urge to sink down and cradle her throbbing head, she spotted a most unwelcome sight stalking through the front entrance. She tried to dodge behind a pillar but it was too late.

Milo loomed over her.

"What the…?"

"Why did you have Guy Ellenger arrested?" she demanded, hoarsely.

His eyes narrowed. "His alibi didn't check out. His sister told me that she was in the surgery alone all Friday evening, sorting out the computer records. That's where she was going when she left her house at seven-thirty on Friday evening."

"*Hope* was at the surgery on her own all Friday evening?"

Lexy felt herself becoming even paler than she already was.

Hope must have been the person who Guy had been speaking to on the phone when he was setting up an alibi for himself. That call made sense now.

"*…you know you were at the surgery yesterday evening? If anyone asks, I want you to say that we were there together. All evening. Do you understand what I'm saying? What? Yes, I'm really, really grateful. You know I am. You're an angel. Bye-bye for now.*"

Hope must have already had a few drinks when Guy spoke to her. When Lexy asked Hope the question later that evening, after she'd had still more to drink, Hope had suddenly become very still – as if she were trying to think hard. *Yes,* she'd said slowly. *I was here all night on my own.* She had nodded emphatically. Hope had forgotten what Guy had told her to say – got it wrong.

Lexy's shoulders drooped. "So you went to see Guy?"

"No – that would have blown my cover. He was out on a call when I spoke to Hope, but I put in an anonymous tip-off to the station, and they must have collared him on the way back, at his place, from what you say. He's probably being questioned now."

Lexy regarded him dismally, wondering how much Guy was going to let on.

"Sheri-Anne Davis is next on my list," Milo went on. "I want a few words with her about what was going on last night – seeing as you can't remember."

That wasn't good. Lexy needed to get back to that barn before Milo got to Sheri-Anne.

She made to move past the detective. He blocked her way.

"What are you up to now?"

"Going home," she replied. "I got discharged."

"And I'm the Pope," he said steadily. "You're coming back to that ward with me."

"No way. I told you, I'm out of here." Lexy veered to one side, trying to push away an image of Milo in Papal regalia.

He moved in front of her. "You're up to something again."

Lexy felt a sudden bolt of anger. He was like a dog with a bone. "I'm not up to anything. I just want to go home. God knows I didn't want to be involved in any of this in the first place! I came down here to be *incognito*. That's a joke, isn't it, with you following me everywhere like a bloody... bloodhound." She felt her hands grip her t-shirt as if she were about to rip it in half. "If I had only just borrowed the bloody money in the bloody suitcase in the first place..."

"What bloody suitcase?"

"Stop asking stupid questions," she snarled.

"I'm a policeman," he snapped back. "That's what I do – ask stupid questions. Well... questions, anyway."

They glowered at each other.

Lexy tacked determinedly towards the exit.

"How are you getting home?" He drew level with her.

"Someone's picking me up," she said, staring straight ahead.

"You're unbelievable."

"Well, believe this – I'm about to throw up all over your Hush Puppies."

He took a hasty step back. "They're Wranglers, actually." He pushed her on to a nearby chair. "Deep breaths. I'll get you a... receptacle." He strode off.

As soon as he was out of sight Lexy got to her feet and, gritting her teeth firmly, finally escaped. The pneumatic front doors hissed shut emphatically behind her.

Edward, behind the wheel of his Jaguar, was waiting on the service road.

223

"You all right, sweetheart?"

"I am now," said Lexy. "Felt a bit queasy a moment ago, but it passed. Hey, Kinkster!"

The chihuahua had jumped out of the car and leapt joyfully up at her.

"How have you been, boy? Sorry I passed out on you."

She slid into the car, holding Kinky. "Oh, no." She ducked her head down. "Edward – drive."

"What… oh, I see."

The Jaguar accelerated smoothly on to the main road.

Lexy took a quick look behind. Milo was standing outside the hospital holding a cardboard hat, looking both exasperated and vaguely forlorn.

19

"So are you going to tell me why I've just had to kidnap your dog and bust you out of hospital?" Edward enquired.

"Another long story."

"You're full of them, lovie. Did your tall policeman, from whom you now appear to be on the run, tell you what's been going on with our friendly neighbourhood vet? Like why's he been arrested?"

Lexy shook her head. "I don't know what to think. DI Milo said Guy's been taken in for questioning over Avril's murder, because he'd lied about his alibi for last Friday."

Edward gazed at Lexy, his mouth forming a ludicrous 'O'.

"Watch the road," she snapped.

"Oops." The Jaguar swerved to avoid an oncoming motorcycle. "But they've got hold of the wrong end of the stick," Edward protested. "Guy Ellenger's no murderer."

"I agree," said Lexy. Apart from having killed his father. That old chestnut again.

"But if it wasn't Guy, who else could it have been?" Edward reached for a pair of shades on the dashboard, and slid them on.

"Someone else from the am-dram?" Lexy said.

"Maybe – Avril certainly knew how to rock the boat." Edward glanced at her. "Take Sheri-Anne Davis for starters. Avril threatened to expose her grubby little affair with one of the cast members. I overheard them speaking in the foyer the other week."

Lexy turned to him, sharply.

"Didn't catch with whom, to my annoyance. But it's so much fun speculating. I do so want it to be a woman – wouldn't it be delicious if that got out?" He sighed wistfully. "It's got to be someone with money – have you seen Sheri-Anne's shoes?"

"Yeah – I used to have a pair like them. Six hundred quid and they hurt like billy-o." Lexy stared into space.

"That's fashion, darling. No gain without pain. Where am I taking you, by the way? Home, I hope."

"No – I actually need to go to a barn in the middle of nowhere."

"I might have known."

"Can you turn left up here? I'll have to try to remember the way."

Edward indicated, giving her a sideways glance. "Are you *sure* you don't want to go home, lovie? That knock on the head might have sent you doolally. In fact…"

"No – I know what I'm doing. Right here, and then down that lane through the heath."

"As long as you're sure."

Oh, yeah. She was sure. She just hoped they'd get there in time.

A short while after, the Jaguar was bumping along the track that led to the disused barn.

Edward parked, switched off the engine, and regarded Lexy dubiously. So did Kinky. "Better leave him here." Lexy pushed open the car door, clutching momentarily at her aching head.

"This is where I fell over and concussed myself last night," she said as they walked towards the barn.

Edward recoiled. "Why on earth did you want to come back?"

"I have my reasons." She led Edward to the barn door. It was locked. "Bollocks." She gave it a weak shove. "Got to get in."

"Can't." He pointed to the shiny padlock.

"It's a matter of life or death."

"Here we go again." Edward rolled his eyes. "Seeing as I was arrested only last week for criminal damage, I might as well add breaking and entering to my repertoire, although God knows why you want to get into…" He eased her to one side, and pushed his shoulder hard against the door. The rotten wooden panelling split obligingly, and the door swung open.

They were greeted by a small wailing sound.

"Hello, Noo-Noo," said Lexy.

"Well, I'll be jiggered." Edward stared at the cat in astonishment. She was in a strong metal cage, with a blanket-filled box at one end. A litter tray, food and water had been provided, together with a pile of cat toys, but Princess was clearly delighted to have some human company. And she was looking rather smug.

"How on earth did you…?"

"I followed the cat-napper yesterday."

Edward watched her, eyes goggling. "Who was…?"

"Our very own trainee veterinary nurse – Sheri-Anne Davis." Edward gasped.

"And someone else," said Lexy. "Presumably her mysterious lover, but I didn't see him. Or her," she conceded. "There was another car here when I arrived, but I can't remember the make or colour. Sure I've seen it recently, though."

Lexy, holding her throbbing head with one hand, reached down and picked up a wicker cat basket. "Noticed this when I was looking in yesterday evening," she said through gritted teeth. "Now, all we've got to do is get Princess in it. And I happen to know she's an acrobat, so let's make doubly sure she doesn't give us the slip."

Lexy undid the metal clasp on the cage door. Edward stood behind her, knees bent and arms spread like a goalkeeper, and Lexy opened the door and put the basket against the aperture.

Princess Noo-Noo was far too curious not to creep into the basket to examine it, and as soon as her whip-like tail followed the rest of her in Lexy slammed it shut.

"Sorry and all that," she said, as the cat writhed and scrabbled in her wicker jail. "But we're not going to chase you halfway across Suffolk. Not with you in that condition. Speaking of which – now for him." Lexy pointed to the other end of the barn.

Edward jumped. A large black tom cat with infuriated eyes was sitting in a similar cage, half hidden behind some bales of hay.

"He lives at the farm just down the road," said Lexy. "He'll find his own way back. Stand aside."

Edward leapt on to a bale of hay. The cat made a ghastly low growling sound as Lexy approached. Princess meowed fearfully from her basket. Lexy spoke to the tom gently, flipped the metal clasp, and watched him shoot out of the barn like a furry black bullet without a second look at the Caradocs' cat. Typical male, she thought.

"Right, I think we should follow his example, although less quickly." Head throbbing, Lexy picked up the wicker cat basket, and the three of them made for Edward's car. An apprehensive-looking chihuahua watched them approach from a side window.

Both Caradocs were home when Edward and Lexy arrived on their doorstep at half past three.

Tammy answered the door, looking haggard.

"What are you doing here?"

"Special delivery." Lexy produced the cat basket from behind Edward.

For a moment Tammy just stared disbelievingly at her cat.

Princess Noo-Noo peered back at her through the wire front mesh of her prison, her pink, heart-shaped mouth producing the same ear-splitting yowl that had accompanied Lexy, Edward and Kinky all the way back from the barn.

Tammy's drawn, exhausted face underwent a transformation. For a split second Lexy glimpsed the glamorous young actress

DI Milo had admired twenty years ago.

Fingers shaking, face flooding, Tammy unfastened the plastic catch. Princess leapt straight out and attached herself to Tammy's large front.

"Oh, bless – I'm welling up here myself," said Edward, fishing out a hanky and dabbing his eyes.

Tristan appeared. "What's going on? Did I hear…?" He gave a theatrical gasp. "Princess! She's back!"

He staggered forward, putting out an incredulous hand to the cat-limpet.

"How…?"

"It was Lexy," said Tammy.

"You *found* the little mite?" Tristan, copper-coloured eyes brimming with tears, stared at Lexy. "How in the…where was she?"

"It's a…" Lexy gave them both a tired smile. "Can we go and sit down?"

Edward, Lexy and Tristan went into the living room. Princess gave the sofa a joyful clawing while Tammy poured champagne in the kitchen.

Tristan gazed fixedly at the cat. "I just can't believe she's back. It's a dream come true. I… dammit!" He jumped up. "I'm meant to be meeting Al Cromarty at the pub – you know – the actor? Lives down here now. Good friend of mine. Better tell him I'll be late – won't be a moment."

"Name dropper," snorted Edward, when Tristan had left the room. "And look at this place – I mean, *look*!" He swept an arm around at the legion of photographs. "Don't they get tired of looking at themselves? I'm sick of the sight of them alrea…"

"Ssh," said Lexy, as Tammy came in with a tray, tears still cascading down her face.

Edward adopted his previous pose, smiling mistily and clutching his handkerchief.

"I don't know how we're ever going to repay you," Tammy sniffed.

Lexy gave her a sharp glance. With money, hopefully.

Tristan returned at that moment, and when the glasses were handed around and chinked, Lexy found all eyes on her.

"Come on, lovie – spill the beans." Edward's equilibrium seemed to be returning; he threw back his champagne enthusiastically. "How did you pull this one off?"

"It was just an idea in the back of my mind," Lexy began. She turned to Tammy. "It was when I saw the photograph of Princess and you told me how you'd rescued her. You see, years ago, I heard a story about an odd-looking kitten born in a litter of farm cats in Cornwall. Turned out that he was a genuine mutation, and after some… er… *in-breeding*, he sired two curly-haired kittens. This was the origin of the Cornish Rex – a new cat breed. A similar thing happened in Devon."

"So, are you saying that our Noo-Noo is a Rex?" Tammy gazed down in amazement at the clownish cat, who was pummelling her ample chest slowly, eyes half-shut, like a punch-drunk boxer.

"I'm saying she's a Suffolk Rex," said Lexy. "The first of a new breed. Very significant in the cat world."

The Caradocs and Edward leant forwards. "So – whoever stole her," said Tristan, slowly, "knew exactly what they were doing."

"Yup. They saw her potential to make money. They tracked down Princess's father, the big tom cat that lives over on Mellowsham Farm, waited until Princess was – well – just mature enough to, you know… rock the Kasbah, and got the two of them together."

Tammy looked horrified. "They let Noo-Noo's father…? That's…"

"Disgusting," supplied Tristan. Even Edward looked shocked.

"It was the only way to create more little Suffolk Rexes," said Lexy, matter-of-factly. "And each of them is going to be worth a fortune."

"Really?" Tristan looked at his cat with new respect. "Er... where did you find her?"

"She was being kept in an old barn out near Mellowsham Farm."

"How did you find that out?"

"Lucky guess," Lexy lied. "I was following...some leads."

Edward shot her a glance.

"Who did this?" said Tammy, ominously. "Who stole her?" Tristan put his hand comfortingly over hers.

Lexy rubbed her chin. "I'm not sure. I'll need to do some more digging." She stood up and cleared her throat. "Was there some mention of a reward...?"

"Tristan! Haven't you given her anything yet?" Tammy jerked her hand from her husband's. He obediently produced a wallet and began peeling twenty-pound notes from it.

"And if you've got any sense, you'll go straight to bed, now you've done the fairy godmother bit," Edward harangued on the way back to Otter's End.

"It's five o'clock in the evening," Lexy pointed out. She had counted out the bundle of notes Tristan had given her. Two hundred pounds. That was better than a poke in the eye with a sharp stick. A lot better.

The Jaguar turned up Cliff Lane, making the steep ascent to Otter's End. They got out and walked up to the front door of the log cabin together, Kinky leading the way with a proprietary air.

"You know that little cow Sheri-Anne stole the cat," said Edward. "Why didn't you just tell them?"

"I want to find out who her accomplice was first."

"Any ideas?"

"That's the trouble. I'm not sure. It could be her boyfriend, Lance. His dad owns Mellowsham Farm."

"Oho," said Edward.

"But I think we're looking for someone with a few more grey cells."

They went into the airless cabin and through to the small kitchen.

Edward reached for the coffee and cafetière he had bought Lexy. "Got anything to eat?"

Lexy opened the formica cupboard. "Lentils, couscous, stuff like that."

Edward made a face. "I'm off, then."

"OK," said Lexy, torn between relief and pique. "You've been the best today – I can't believe how much of your time I've taken up. And I've got Kinky back. Thanks ever so much. For everything."

"You don't need to make an Oscar acceptance speech," snorted Edward. "I'm coming straight back with some decent nosh. Did you seriously think I was going to leave you on your own in your condition?"

He swept out of the door.

Lexy stood in the now familiar living room, uncertain what to do next. Her first instinct was to go and check that the suitcase was still under the bed. It was. Lexy regarded it with mixed emotions. She needed to offload it without any more delay. Things were due to get pretty hot around here soon, and if the police were going to catch up with her, she wanted to make sure the five hundred grand wasn't still sitting under the bed to complicate matters. She'd just have to make the money Tristan had given her last as long as possible.

As she passed back into the living room, Lexy was brought up short by a small flashing light. It was the telephone answering machine. Someone had left a message. Two messages.

Might be a couple more jobs. Not that she ought…

She fumbled behind the sofa and pressed the play button.

"It's Milo. Listen – I can't find Sheri-Anne Davis – no one seems to know where she is. Can you call me if you see her?"

The phone kicked into the next message.

"Hi, Lexy – Guy Ellenger. I'm in Lowestoft police station. There's been some kind of mix-up. They seem to think I'm involved in this Avril Todd thing – no idea why. They swooped on my house earlier and took me off with my arm up my back. Unbelievable. Thankfully, no one was around to see – the neighbours were out. Anyway – I'm really sorry to get you involved like this but I didn't have a chance to sort the dogs out before I got bundled off. My lot are inside, but Kinky didn't come in with them when I called, so I guess he must still be in the garden."

Lexy grimaced at the phone.

"When you pick up Kinky, can you drop in and feed them? I can't ask Hope – she'd want to know where I was, and it would all be a bit awkward. But I know I can count on you to be discreet. The back door key is under the mat – original, eh? I should be back soon, anyhow, when the police realise they're barking up the wrong tree." He laughed nervously. "I hope you get this message. See you later. Yes, well, thanks in advance."

The answering machine clicked as he rang off.

Lexy stared at the phone, imagining Guy being questioned in an interview room. "Barking up the wrong tree," she said, half-aloud. "Is that what I've been doing? Getting hold of the wrong end of the stick?" Then, more thoughtfully, "Like a dog with a bone." A series of images suddenly ran through her mind – Kinky having his ear stitched, Kinky sniffing at a stick, Kinky, somewhere, trying to find a bone. Dog's DNA in the wound…

"Hello, sweetie. Are you all right?"

Edward had a Miu-Miu bag dangling from his arm. He went

straight into the kitchen, and began laying packages on the table.

"Now then, English muffins, strawberries, cream…"

"Edward," Lexy said. "I'm really sorry about this, but – I need to go out again."

He put his hands on his hips. "I'm starting to think you don't like civilised food. Is there another problem?"

"Yeah. Guy Ellenger's still at the police station."

"Still?" Edward looked at his watch. "It's half five. He must have been there for four hours. That's not good."

"He wants me to go and feed his dogs."

Edward's neatly barbered eyebrows shot up. "Honestly. Doesn't he know you've only just got out of hospital?"

"I don't mind – won't take me long to drive there and back. Come on, Kinky."

The chihuahua took one look at the bunch of car keys Lexy was dangling and dived under the sideboard.

"Don't be silly – I'll take you," said Edward.

"There's no need –really. Come *here*, Kinky." Lexy added, with some force.

"Never a dull moment with you, is there?" Edward strode out of the kitchen. He was holding a long-handled broom. "And I thought San Francisco was non-stop."

"Er…what are you doing?" Lexy moved towards the door.

"You want him to come with us, don't you?" Edward knelt beside the sideboard and gently eased Kinky out with the aid of the broom head. "Quickest way I know. Works with small children, too."

He smiled indulgently at Kinky. "Poor little pooch. You're still trying to get over the trauma of having to share a car with a cat that makes more noise than you do, aren't you?"

He held open the door. "Right – come on, what are we waiting for?"

Soon the Jaguar was bumping back over the ruts of Cliff Lane in the direction of Clopwolde. Lexy and Kinky sat in the front passenger seat, Lexy staring silently ahead, Kinky looking back longingly at the cabin.

"I hope Guy's not having as bad a time as I did," said Edward. "When I got taken in for questioning after the old man went over the cliff last year, they were positively rude. Brutal, even."

"What happened?" Lexy asked distractedly.

Edward sighed. "Dad had this habit of taking Nimrod out for a constitutional at about eleven every night. Poor old Nimrod couldn't go through the night otherwise – prostate, you see. Curse of the male gender. It was windy and cold and the old man must have gone too near to the edge." Edward shook his head. "He should have known better. We've lost nine log cabins, several outbuildings and at least three locals over the last fifteen years."

"Nine log cabins?"

"Yes, lovie. We need to talk about that. Anyway, a couple of fishermen found dad's body on the beach early the next morning. First I knew of it was when I got woken up by the police after an hour's sleep, having been out on an absolute bender the night before. I'd got in at about three-thirty and I just assumed the old man was asleep in bed. When I was rudely awoken from my alcohol-drenched slumber to hear he'd been found on the beach I flew into a rage and started calling him every name under the sun for going near the edge. God knows what the Old Bill thought." He smiled wryly. "Actually, it was startlingly obvious what they thought. They asked me to get dressed straight away and accompany them to the station to give a statement. Shocking, it was. I didn't get a coffee until about ten o'clock, and that was a vending machine one. Vile." He shuddered. "But at least they were happy with my version of events. Verdict – accidental death. Anyway, these log cabins…"

Minutes later, the Jaguar pulled to a halt outside Guy Ellenger's house. Lexy was looking rather pale. They saw a curtain flick at the Caradocs' window next door.

Lexy left Edward in the car and, followed by Kinky, let herself into the garden, and down the side of the bungalow to the back door. The sound of chihuahuas in full throat reverberated from the house. Kinky stood stock-still, his nose quivering.

Lexy located the key.

"All right, boys – it's me," called Lexy, gently. "Come to give you your dinner."

"Thank heavens for that!"

Lexy recognised the fruity voice as Tristan Caradoc's. He was obviously standing behind the high wall that divided the two bungalows.

"I thought I saw your svelte form disembarking from Edward's car," the voice went on. "The little buggers have been barking in there ever since we got back this afternoon. We were starting to get worried."

"Guy says sorry," called Lexy. "He's been detained."

"Is there a problem?"

"No. He's got a family… thing… to attend to. Well, must feed these dogs."

She unlocked the kitchen door and found herself in a small canine sea. They swarmed in the direction of a larder, where Lexy found a bag of dog biscuits and a stack of small stainless steel bowls. She carefully ladled a pile of biscuits into each bowl, with an additional one for Kinky, and put them down in a row, smiling at the column of waving tails.

She didn't even hear the back door open.

"Wha' you doing here?"

It was Hope Ellenger. And she was slurring again.

"Hi," said Lexy, brightly. "I ran into Guy. He asked me to pop over and feed the dogs. He's tied up with an emergency – near my place."

"Why didn' 'e call me? He always calls me."

"His batteries are flat. In the phone."

"But he should've asked you to come to me."

"The main thing is, they're fed," said Lexy.

"And yours, too."

"I couldn't let him stand by and watch." Lexy tried an engaging grin.

"I'll take over from here."

"Fine. C'mon Kinky."

Lexy led an indignant Kinky outside. She looked back at the door. Would Hope be all right on her own? Somehow or other Lexy would have to get a message to Guy now, to let him know that his sister was waiting in for him, and she wasn't best pleased to have been passed over in favour of a scruffy newcomer. Lexy pondered uneasily for a moment.

"Are you still there?" It was Tristan's voice, speaking quietly on the other side of the wall.

"Yes."

"Can you pop round quickly?"

Lexy rolled her eyes. Now what? "OK. I'll see you in a sec."

She went out of Guy's gate. "Just got to see Tristan. Five minutes."

Edward groaned.

"I'll let him know you're waiting with the engine running."

"It's what I tell all the boys."

Lexy slipped into the Caradocs' neat drive. Tristan met her at the door, looking red and flushed with what Lexy hoped was excitement at getting his cat back.

He beckoned her into the hall, after she had told Kinky to stay put outside. "Tammy and I have been on the Internet finding out about Rex cats. Absolute fortune she's worth."

A phone rang from another room. "Wait a tick," he said.

Lexy caressed Princess, who was slaloming around her legs,

and studied the photos again. There was one of Tristan dressed ludicrously as Margaret Thatcher in a tight blue two-piece, alongside someone dressed as Ronald Reagan, in a cowboy outfit, and…

Tristan reappeared. "Alternative panto in Lowestoft last year," he murmured.

He handed Lexy a much larger roll of notes than he had earlier.

"What's that for?" She couldn't tear her eyes from the photo.

"Finding Princess, of course."

"You've already given me two hundred pounds. I can't take any more."

"You jolly well can, young lady." He wrapped Lexy's fingers around it. "Just an extra token of our appreciation. If she's expecting, we'll be set up for life. Tammy's been down at the travel agents already." He grinned easily. "I've been down the pub. Tammy must have come back, and gone straight out again – probably to raid the delicatessen this time."

"Thanks. I'm j… just glad Princess is back," stammered Lexy. "I'll… er… see you…"

"At the ghost walk next Friday?" His eyebrows worked humorously.

"Yeah, yeah. I'll be there. Tristan – you – er… haven't seen Sheri-Anne Davis this afternoon, have you?"

His smile became guarded. "No. Why would I?"

"I… no reason. Well, best be off. Thanks for this."

Lexy pocketed the money and walked quickly back to the Jaguar, aware of Tristan still watching her from the doorstep.

She ducked in. "I think we've got a problem."

"God 'elp us, not another?" Edward's face became serious at her expression.

"Need to find Sheri-Anne."

"Why?"

"I'll just feel happier if we can."

Edward started the engine. "Village?"

"Yes – quick."

Edward put his foot down.

"Did you see Hope go into Guy's place?" Lexy clutched at the dashboard as Kinky shot into the back seat.

"No."

"She scared the bejesus out of me in there. She must have come in the back way."

They pulled into the high street. "Where to?"

"Let's start at the village hall."

There was a parking space right outside.

"Have you got a key?" Lexy was already jumping out.

Edward groped in the glove compartment. "I wish you'd tell me what's going on."

"I'm not completely sure myself."

"A small snippet would suffice." He unlocked the door and stood aside to let Lexy into the foyer.

"Where are all the costumes kept?" she demanded.

"In the wardrobe room of course."

"Show me." Lexy felt urgency grabbing at her in a distinctly over-friendly way.

Edward, still grumbling, flicked a couple of light switches and took Lexy through the double doors into the hall, and up some stairs to the left of the stage, Kinky at their heels.

"It might be locked. Don't make me break the law for the third time in a week."

But the wardrobe room door had been left ajar. Lexy gave it a push, and they went inside. Rails of garishly coloured theatre costumes lined the walls, and an open cupboard stood in a corner full of wigs, folded scarves, hats, bonnets and gloves.

Watched quizzically by Edward, Lexy quickly flicked through the clothing on the rails and examined the accessories in the open cupboard, before turning away, disappointed. Then her eye fell on an old trunk that, judging by the tracks in the dust, had recently been pushed under a wide shelf.

"Help me."

Edward sighed. "It's only going to have some mangy old costumes in it from *The Importance of Being Earnest*. Now, there was a good play. My finest hour, in fact."

They heaved the trunk back through the dust. Lexy flipped the catches and pushed the lid back.

Kinky began to whine.

A blue skirt and blue fitted top, size 22, lay inside, spattered with dark red stains, together with a piled-up wig that had been dyed the colour of rust.

20

"*That* wasn't in *The Importance of Being Earnest*…"

"I know. It featured in a different drama. A real-life one. *Come on!* We really do need to find Sheri-Anne."

Lexy was already heading back down the stairs. She heard Edward bang down the lid of the trunk and shove it back under the shelf, Kinky still whining insistently. He must have smelled the blood.

Edward and Kinky caught up as she strode through the silent hall.

"You're making me very nervous now, sweetie," Edward panted. "Why have we got to find Sheri-Anne?"

"I think she might be able to shed some light on Avril's murder. And because of that she's in danger. Let's just get out of here. I'll tell you when we're somewhere safe. I feel like someone here's listening to us."

They burst into the high street. A passing group of tourists looked at them askance.

Edward locked the door, fumbling with the key.

"Where's your mobile?" Lexy snapped.

"It's in the car. Who are you going to ring?"

"Milo." She pulled the detective's card from her bag and prodded out the number on Edward's phone. It went straight to voicemail. She cursed.

"It's me. If you get this, can you come straight to Clopwolde? I think Sheri-Anne's in danger. We're just going over to the vet's surgery now to look for her." She pushed the phone back at Edward and, grabbing Kinky, began to cross the road.

"Oh-oh, there's Tammy." Lexy pulled Edward down behind a parked car. "Don't want to get caught up with her again."

"Why did you have to pick a bloody Mini to hide behind? I'm much taller than you, in case you hadn't noticed, and my knees aren't what they used to be. And people are looking at us."

"Shut up and pretend you've lost something." Lexy peered through the car windows at Tammy's ample, receding form.

"OK – she's…" Lexy stared down at the car. "Edward – this is *Sheri-Anne's* Mini. She must be in the surgery."

They darted down the narrow alley to the vet's.

"Looks closed." Edward checked his watch.

"She's been known to work late."

Lexy tried the door. It was unlocked.

She and Edward exchanged a glance.

"I'm going in," said Lexy, "but can you stay out here? Let me know if anyone turns up?"

"Who's likely to turn up?" Edward said, exasperated.

"I told you – I'm not sure – yet."

"You owe me a very large Pimms in the pub later."

"Done." Lexy walked into the waiting room. Kinky followed reluctantly, and hovered by the door, one slim paw raised, ready to dash out at a moment's notice.

"Sheri-Anne? You in here?" Lexy crossed to the reception desk. There was an empty vodka bottle at the back of the shelf. Presumably what Hope had been knocking back before she went over to Guy's bungalow earlier.

Outside, she heard Edward start to warble *Some Enchanted Evening*. Very appropriate. This was shaping up to be one of the least enchanted evenings of her whole life.

Lexy checked the small office behind reception. Empty. There was a door at the back. She walked over and opened it. It led to the drug room at the back of Guy's surgery.

Remiss of someone to leave the place unlocked. Lexy walked through, opened the back door of the vet's surgery and went in.

Edward's singing filtered in through a small, high window –

open a fraction, but barred. Obviously designed to prevent escape bids by panicking pets. Lexy glanced up at the gruesome, yellowing St Bernard's femur on the wall. She remembered looking up at that same bone when she had brought Kinky in to be stitched up.

Except there was something different about it now.

Lexy walked around the examination bench and took a closer look. The bone had been taken down and put back the wrong way round. The heavy knuckle end was now balanced precariously on the smaller of the two brackets.

In the waiting room beyond, she heard Kinky give a small growl.

"*Fools want to tell you, wise men never TRY…*" Edward was working up to a crescendo. Kinky barked. Lexy was surprised he wasn't howling.

She opened the door to the waiting room.

"*SOME ENCHANTED EVENING…*"

But there was a different voice singing alongside Edward's. Right behind her in the surgery.

Lexy spun around.

"Christ! You scared the life out of me!"

Tristan Caradoc shook back his mane of hair. "I'm mortified, darling. I didn't think my singing was *that* bad."

"Did you just arrive?" What was Edward playing at? Apart from trying to deafen everyone within a five-mile radius of Clopwolde.

"I was here already, actually. That's why the front door was open." Tristan swung a key from his hand. "So – did you find Sheri-Anne?"

"No. But we think she's in some kind of trouble."

"She will be when I catch up with her. I've been looking everywhere for the little cow."

"This is serious," Lexy snapped. "If she's not here, we need to get out there and look for her."

"Not you, Lexy Lomax. Oh, no. You've caused me quite enough trouble today. What *you* need right now is a nice little sleep."

Tristan brought his right hand up. In it he held a syringe full of a colourless liquid.

Kinky, now standing in the half-open doorway, gave a low growl.

"Don't make me laugh, you little prick." Tristan made a sudden darting move around one side of the examination bench, slamming the door shut on Kinky and forcing Lexy around the table, effectively trapping her against the back wall.

Kinky immediately set up a volley of barks on the other side of the door.

"Charming," remarked Lexy, her eyes flickering around the room. She gave an involuntary glance up at the bone, now balancing on the edge of the bracket above her head. That door slam had very nearly brought it down on top of her.

The drug room was on her left now. Through the small barred window opposite came the rousing strains of *Bloody Mary*.

"Edward!" Lexy suddenly screamed at the top of her voice. "Ed-ward!"

But Edward was in full flow and didn't miss a beat.

Lexy's eyes met Tristan's.

"Didn't you know?" he mocked. "The motto of the De Glenvilles is *Me First*. He's far too enchanted with his own magnificent voice to hear yours. Which is just as well."

Lexy tried to smile. "So, when did *you* first realise that Princess was something far more significant than an odd-looking litter runt?" she asked, conversationally.

Tristan eyed her. "So you've cottoned on at last?" He gave her a lop-sided smile. "It was dear Avril who spelt it out to me, actually. Lucky – she might have told Tammy first, then things would have been quite different. As it was, Avril popped round to see Tammy one morning – it was quite some months ago – something to do with a raffle, I think. It wasn't long after we'd got Princess. Avril, being a cat person, noticed something familiar about our little bundle of joy that she couldn't quite put her finger on. Not at the time, anyway. But a day or two later, the penny must have dropped. So she collared me in the high street. *Did you know you might have a new breed of cat there, Tristan?*" He did Avril's flat, penetrating accent very well. "*A Rex?*"

Tristan flicked his hair back. A small drip of liquid fell from the syringe.

"I popped into the library. Checked it out for myself. The woman was right. And when I dug a little deeper, I realised that, far from having the runt of the litter, we had the jewel in the crown."

He drew a self-satisfied breath. "Just think. A new breed of cat. She would command thousands. And if she was bred back to her daddy – well…" He shrugged. "World was my oyster."

"Just *your* oyster? What about Tammy's?"

"I wasn't going to tell *her*. Truth is, Tammy and I haven't been getting along too well since the old girl's stage career fizzled out, and, most unfortunately, her looks with it. Even with black leather and lace it was becoming a struggle."

He gave Lexy a salacious smirk. "I had to look elsewhere. A lot of young women go for the more mature man. Especially in a backwater like this."

"And especially if he takes them to bistros and buys them Prada shoes."

"Quite. Anyway, the money I'd been throwing around was our retirement savings, so the news about Princess was timely, as you can imagine. I had been rather hoping to continue living in the style to which I'd become accustomed. But somehow I needed to organise things without Tammy twigging. And I also needed Avril to keep her trap shut. So I told her I was going to get Princess registered as a new breed on the QT, and then surprise Tammy with it on our wedding anniversary."

"Very romantic," said Lexy, trying to keep her eye on the syringe. She had moved an inch further along the wall to her left.

"Avril realised, as quick as a tick, what I was up to, and said she'd be delighted to keep my little secret, as long as I made her a regular monthly payment."

Tristan gave Lexy a wry look. "Even so, it was still worth it. But I needed someone competent around animals to help put my little plan into action. So I took the lovely Sheri-Anne into my confidence. We worked everything out very carefully. Chose a date when Princess would be receptive to a male cat and tracked down and swiped the only one who would do – her own father." He frowned. "Still find that distasteful. Also Sheri-Anne had to seduce that thick lump Lance, in order to get close to the tom. Oh, well. All was going fine though, until Avril caught Sheri-Anne and me together in a little wine bar, making plans to move away on the proceeds of our venture. Can't imagine how she knew we were there – I suppose she must have followed us. Bitch. So the monthly payments went up."

He glanced up at the window as Edward went straight into *Happy Talk*.

Lexy eased herself two more inches to the left. If she got out of this in one piece she never wanted to hear the words 'South' and 'Pacific' again. If she got out.

"But you were nearly there," she heard herself say. "Avril being paid off, Princess ready to rock, Tammy none the wiser."

"Yes – apart from the problem with Avril, everything else was as smooth as silk. Until she had the idea of a large cash payment." Tristan's eyes hardened. "At which point I was starting to think that she would be better off out of the equation altogether."

Lexy stiffened. He was going to confess. And she thought the ghost walk on Friday night had been such a strong alibi for Tristan. She should have checked…

"But someone beat me to it."

Huh? Lexy's eyes opened wide.

Tristan gave a rich chuckle. "When I heard that Avril had been bumped off I had to stop myself leaping up and punching the air! First thing I did was nip back and grab the blackmail money Sheri-Anne and I had left for the old witch."

Lexy's lips twisted. Milo's uniformed colleagues would think that they'd been sent on a fool's mission when they turned up at the village hall.

She drew in a breath. Milo. If he picked up her message he could be here any moment. *Quick as you like, Venus,* she prayed.

"Anyway, Operation Catnap had gone like a dream," Tristan was saying. "We'd got the male cat caged up and ready in the barn. Sheri-Anne had to do a bit of work to get them both in the mood, but the violins and candlelight paid off in the end." He sighed. "We *were* going to collect Princess from the barn this evening. Take her with us to the States. Got her passport and everything. Flights booked. Then sell the kittens, except for one of the male ones, of course, and… start all over again." He glared up at the window. "Doesn't he ever shut up?"

Lexy flexed herself. "So – you must have been really pleased to see me and Edward this afternoon, complete with Princess Noo-Noo?"

"I thought I hid my towering rage very well," said Tristan. "It helps so much to have a stage background. But I have to admit you've messed things up quite badly. Now I've got to steal the bloody cat all over again." He snorted. "When I find Sheri-Anne, that is. In fact I don't even know why I'm wasting my time telling you all this…"

"So – Sheri-Anne's OK?" Lexy interrupted.

"Fit as a fiddle. We had a little rendezvous at the village hall earlier."

Lexy curled her lip distastefully, then gave Tristan a challenging look.

"What's in the syringe?"

"Just a bit of sedative. You'll have a nice snooze in the back of the surgery, Hope Ellenger will come in and find you tomorrow – shock, surprise – and Tammy will be waking up at home at about the same time. Meanwhile Sheri-Anne, Princess and I will be a memory. But one they'll be talking about in Clopwolde for years." He visibly preened himself.

"So what are you going to do about Edward?"

Tristan thought for a moment. "I'll have to give him an armful too, won't I?" He looked up at the window again. "A merciful release for us all."

Lexy found herself almost agreeing with him.

"Have to call him in when I've dealt with you." Tristan rubbed his chin. The syringe dripped again. "Tell him you've fainted or something, and when he's bending over you – bosh! As they say." He grinned.

"But if *you* didn't kill Avril," said Lexy, still trying to keep her voice even, "who did?"

"No idea. Now – let's get this over with."

Lexy tried desperately to make sense of the series of images flitting through her head. A blue, tight-fitting outfit. Rust-coloured wig. Avril walking up Windmill Hill at a quarter past seven on Friday evening. And Avril walking up Windmill Hill at seven-thirty.

She suppressed an exclamation. *Both* the old dears had been right! Which meant…

"Tristan – I don't think you're going to find Sheri-Anne." Lexy eyed him urgently.

"What?" He waved the syringe impatiently. "Not at this rate

248

I'm not."

"*Get a load of Honeybun TONIGHT!*" Edward really knew how to belt them out.

Lexy flicked her eyes, led him forward another inch. He had reached the centre of the wall now and she was within a metre of the door to the drug room.

"I think someone else has already found her."

"Rubbish. Now… I advise you not to struggle. Don't want to put this in the wrong place – I'm not a doctor, although I've played plenty in my time. Here we go, one, two…"

"I mean it. She's double-crossed you."

He faltered. It was all she needed. Lexy launched herself at the open door to the drug room, grabbed the handle and yanked the door towards her as hard as she could. It slammed shut so violently the whole room shook.

She found herself involuntarily ducking as the huge St Bernard femur bounced from its bracket and crashed down straight on top of Tristan's chestnut mane.

He staggered forward, cracked his head on the edge of the examination bench and slid to the floor, the syringe still in his hand.

The other door burst open, and DI Milo skidded in, followed by Kinky, with Edward bringing up the rear, goggling in disbelief.

At least he'd stopped singing.

"You cut it a bit fine," said Lexy to Milo. He was already on his mobile.

"Ambulance, please. Clopwolde village veterinary surgery. A middle-aged IC one man unconscious with head wound…"

"Where did he spring from?" Edward pointed hysterically at Tristan. "He didn't come past me, I swear."

Lexy picked up Kinky and hugged him briefly. He glared at Tristan's prone form. "He was already here," she said. "We were having a cosy little chat, and the bone just chose that moment to fall off the wall. Knocked him off balance, and he hit his head on the examination bench." She smiled grimly down at Tristan. "Bosh! As they say."

Tristan gave a low moan.

"It can't have hit him too hard," said Milo. "He's coming round."

"What's that?" Edward was staring at the syringe.

"Oh, that was meant for me," said Lexy. "Animal sedative, I think. Tristan was intending to put me to sleep for a few hours. Then he was going to come for you."

Edward looked so horror-struck that Lexy burst out laughing.

Milo was kneeling beside Tristan. She squatted next to him. "Thespian boy here's the least of our problems," she said, quietly.

Milo gave Lexy a sidelong glance. "So he's not the killer?"

Lexy shook her head. "But I've had a chance to do some thinking. Astonishing how the mind is concentrated when some jerk starts waving a syringe in your face." She paused. "You see, I think I now know why Avril Todd went to that field."

Milo raised his eyebrows. Edward leaned on the examination bench, looking from one to the other.

"And she wasn't there from choice," Lexy declared.

"What do you mean?"

"Remember that problem with the old dears and the time Avril walked up the hill?"

"Huh?" said Edward.

"That again?" Milo shifted irritably.

"Yes. The thing is – they were both right."

"What – so Avril came home, and went straight out again, then came back up the hill a few minutes later?" Milo gave her a weary look.

"No", said Lexy, patiently. "They both saw Avril walking up the road at exactly the time they said. Except that the Avril who walked up the road at seven-thirty wasn't the real Avril Todd.

250

It was someone dressed up to look like her." She drew a deep breath. "Someone who had carefully planned to kill her."

21

Edward emitted a low whistle. In the distance, a siren wailed.

"The first part of the plan must have been to get into the house dressed as Avril," Lexy said. "The impostor either had a key, and snuck in, or else barged past the real Avril when she answered the door. They must have known that Roderick Todd was going to be away last Friday, so it would have to be someone reasonably well acquainted with Avril."

Lexy was aware of Edward staring at her so intensely that his eyes seemed about to leap from their sockets.

"Once inside," she went on, "my guess is that Avril must have been overcome somehow and injected with the sedative that was found in her system at the post-mortem. The killer intended to take Avril to the field in Nudging and do away with her there, probably because they assumed she wouldn't be found for a while."

"Reckoned without you, then," said Milo.

"What about the murder weapon?" said Edward.

Lexy thought back to what the old lady had seen at half past seven. "The impostor was carrying a tapestry bag just like Avril's. Whatever it was must have been concealed in there, along with a change of clothing."

"As we know," she went on. "The Todds have an integral garage, so this impostor got the real Avril into the back of her Volvo, concealed her under a blanket or something, then shortly after, got the car out of the garage, still dressed as Avril, and went out. So it looked as if the real Avril Todd was going out at her usual time, alone."

"It would certainly explain the mystery of how she'd been able to drive doped up to the eyeballs," interjected Milo. "And, of course, as the impostor was leaving the house, you turned up, expecting to follow the real Avril."

"And you turned up," said Lexy, "intending to follow me."

"Confused? *Moi*?" Edward moaned.

"Go on." Milo threw a quick glance at Tristan, who had also given a moan.

"OK. The impostor must have known Avril might wake up, so they had to drive hell for leather to the field, get her out of the car, and dispatch her properly while she was still half asleep. That's why Avril sounded so weak and confused," said Lexy.

"And they used Avril's own car as a getaway, and left it in a ditch where it could be easily found." Milo supplied.

"Yes – it was a safe bet, because as Avril tended to use her car as an unpaid taxi for the am-dram, a jumble of DNA and prints would be all over it anyway." Lexy spoke quickly, aware of the ambulance siren getting closer, her mind falling over itself. "I reckon this person changed from the Avril disguise into dark clothes, and *walked* back to Clopwolde cross-country."

Milo nodded. "Of course. If they were used to walking and knew the path it would only have taken an hour or so."

"And when they got back," continued Lexy, "they slipped into the village hall and put the clothes and wig in an old trunk, intending to dispose of them properly later. Except Edward and I found them. Perhaps the murder weapon's in there too."

"What about the tapestry bag?" Edward chimed in.

Lexy gave a swift shrug. "I'm guessing the murderer left it at Avril's house. If Roderick Todd is like most men, he's not going to find it strange that his wife had two shopping bags. If he even notices."

Tristan moaned again.

They heard the ambulance pull into the alleyway. Within minutes, Tristan was being loaded into the back, while Edward spoke to the paramedics.

"Yes – I was walking past and I heard a noise. I found him unconscious when I came in to investigate. The bone must have fallen off the wall and knocked him against the examination bench."

Tristan opened his mouth soundlessly.

"Shouldn't he be arrested, or something?" said Edward, as they watched the ambulance depart.

"He'll keep. At the moment we've got bigger fish to fry." Milo headed for the high street.

"Where are we going?" Edward asked.

"Gorse Rise. The vet's place."

Lexy felt herself going pale. "Do you know something we don't?"

"Just a hunch."

They sat in Milo's estate car outside Guy Ellenger's bungalow, silently watching.

Dusk was falling, and next door in Amalfi the curtains had been drawn. Every couple of minutes a feline shape swung on one or other of the drapes. They heard a sharp remonstration at one point, and a bulky figure loomed and disentangled the shape.

Guy Ellenger's curtains were still open. They could see the vet pacing around his living room. Hope was sitting on a chair near the window.

"So – you think Guy did it?" Edward asked.

"I'm actually wondering if they did it between them, some-how," Milo said.

"Only one of them is big enough to dress up as Avril."

"Well – nevertheless, I want to get them both in for questioning. Although the vet's not going to like it – especially as he's just got back from the nick. He might prove a bit…evasive."

"I know how to get round Guy's the back way, if that's any use," Edward said. "In case there's a problem."

"Yes, all right – go for it. I'll give you five minutes to get in place."

Edward let himself out of the back and loped out of sight along Gorse Rise.

"Can you go and tell Tammy about her loser of a husband?" said Milo. "We'll deal with Guy and Hope."

"I can look after myself in a…" Lexy began, but Milo shushed her. His phone was ringing.

"It's the station – better take it." He flipped it open. "Milo."

Lexy watched his face freeze into disbelief as he listened.

"OK." He snapped it shut, gave her a helpless look.

"What?"

"Edward doesn't have an alibi for Friday night."

This was so not what Lexy wanted to hear.

"But he was at Lowestoft nick. After the scene at Peter's shop."

Milo shook his head. "That scene must have been during the afternoon – he was bailed by six o'clock, with no charges pressed. He had plenty of time to dress up as Avril, drive her out there and kill her. He had a good enough motive."

"No!" Lexy tried to push aside the vision of Edward shredding his poison pen letter. The old stick leaning against the wall in his kitchen, the one that Nimrod the retriever used to chew. The way he had been offering to help her at every turn.

"I'm going to have to pull him in," said Milo. He swore under his breath, tapped out another number on his phone.

"But he's my friend," whispered Lexy. "I trusted him."

"Appearances can be deceptive." Milo peered out into the dark road. "I'd better get out there or he'll think something's up. Go and tell Tammy about Tristan…"

"But…"

"… and stay there until the police arrive."

"But…"

"Lexy – don't argue. Just get out there and do it."

Lexy let herself and Kinky out of the car. She watched Milo run quietly down Guy Ellenger's drive, then opened the Caradocs' gate, feeling sick at heart. Far away in the distance she heard a growl of thunder.

She pressed the bell.

"You'd better stay out here," she told Kinky. Having met Princess Noo-Noo, he was happy to agree.

"Lexy! This is unexpected."

Lexy stood awkwardly in the hallway of the Caradocs' bungalow. Princess scampered lightly up to her, jumped against her leg, then shot off again.

"She's gone totally scatty," said Tammy, with a fond smile. "I thought she might be a bit more quiet and thoughtful after the weekend she's had." She paused. "You haven't seen Tristan, have you? I've been trying to ring him, but his phone's switched off."

Lexy took a deep breath, forcing herself to concentrate and not think about what might be happening next door. "Actually, Tammy, he's had to go to hospital – that's what I came to tell you. But it's nothing serious," she added quickly, as the woman's eyes widened in shock. "Just a knock on the head."

"Knock on the head? How?"

"He was in the vet's surgery. You know that big bone on the wall?"

The other woman nodded. She had gone completely still.

"It fell off, hit him on the head and he knocked himself out on the edge of the treatment bench."

Tammy broke out into a storm of laughter.

Lexy gave a faint smile. Tammy must be one of those people who have a nervous reaction to bad news. The sort who burst out into giggles when they hear someone's died. Either that or she appreciates irony, said an unbidden voice in her head.

She shot a glance at Tammy, and wished she hadn't.

It was the latter.

Tammy was laughing because Tristan had been hit on the head with the very weapon that had killed Avril.

And now Tammy knew Lexy knew.

"Would you like a lift to the hospital?" said Lexy, pleasantly.

"I don't think that will be necessary." Up close, Tammy was large. About the same size as Avril, in fact.

"You know, Tristan was about to run away with that trollop, Sheri-Anne." Tammy leaned her wide behind on the wall, as if settling in for a comfortable chat.

"Really?" said Lexy, trying to sound concerned. It wasn't difficult.

"Yes. Not that I gave a toss about that. What really made me see red was the fact that they were taking my cat with them." Her eyes hardened. "I only found out this afternoon, when I discovered the passports in his jacket pocket. One for him, one for Sheri-Anne, and one for Princess. After all I'd done for the bastard."

She turned to a picture of Tristan on the wall. The one of him dressed as Margaret Thatcher, in the tight-fitting blue number.

"When I discovered Avril was blackmailing Tristan, I thought it was because of his pathetic little affair with Sheri-Anne. I had no idea about all this cat business until you told me this afternoon." She petted Princess, now draped around her neck. "He was giving Avril a large amount of money every month. I was almost flattered to think he would pay that much to keep me from being hurt. But I couldn't have him throwing away our life savings." She gave a sudden harsh laugh. "Put me in a bit of a dilemma. I didn't want to tell him that I knew. Because if he knew I had found out about the affair, things could never be the same again between us." She looked sadly at Lexy. "I just wanted everything to be like it always had been. When we were young and beautiful. *Eternity was in our lips and eyes, bliss in our brows.*" Her mouth set. "So I came up with a plan to put Avril out of the picture."

"Ah," said Lexy.

Tammy sighed. "It took some careful planning, but it went like a dream on the night. It was Tristan's ghost walk evening, so I knew he'd be out of the way. He always leaves the house early so that he can get a pint in first. As soon as he left, I nipped down to the village hall the back way via the vet's surgery, with my walking gear in a tapestry bag just like Avril's."

Lexy nodded to herself, but the fact that she had guessed right was no comfort at that moment.

"I disguised myself as her, then I walked quickly around the corner and up Windmill Hill." Tammy paused. "That was the risky part – I was praying I didn't run into any of her neighbours."

Lexy wondered how worried Tammy would have been if she knew she'd been spotted by one of them. "How did you know Avril would be at home?" she asked.

"Because I called her earlier. Part of the plan. Said I wanted to speak to her about an am-dram matter. She told me to get there before eight as she was going out."

Tammy smiled. "When she answered the door, I knocked her out with a little whiff of chloroform from the surgery, and gave her a shot of sedative to keep her from struggling. Then I got her into the Volvo, drove her to the field, and…" She gave a wry shrug. "I thought I was so clever using that dog bone as a murder weapon." She paused, frowning. "I wasn't expecting anyone to find her for days, not right out there. I dumped the car, changed into my walking gear, got back to Clopwolde and hid the clothes in the old trunk"

"Then you took the bone back to the surgery the following morning, inside the rolls of canvas for Hope," Lexy supplied.

Tammy gave her a nasty smile. "And your bastard little mutt could smell it, couldn't he? Anyway, despite running into you at just the wrong moment, I thought I'd got away with it. The body was found a little sooner than I would have wanted, but I saw

Tristan's look of relief when Maurice from the am-dram called to tell him Avril was dead, and it was all worth it." She reached up a plump hand to stroke Princess. "My only problem then," she went on, "was the loss of my poor Noo-Noo. I knew that someone must have stolen her, but I'd never have dreamed it was my own husband." She stared bitterly at the photo of Tristan again, then turned to face Lexy.

"When you brought Princess back today I thought my life was complete, especially when we found out her… *circumstances.*" She caressed the cat again fondly. "It was my reward for rescuing her in the first place. I went straight down to the travel agents and booked a cruise."

Then her face hardened. "Then I came back here and found the passports. The ones I wasn't meant to see."

Lexy shifted uncomfortably.

"Tristan had gone out – said he'd gone to the pub. I went to have it out with him. But when I got to the high street, I saw him coming out of the village hall, very furtively, with Sheri-Anne." She drew a deep breath. "And I saw Sheri-Anne go back inside. I thought that perhaps I'd have it out with her instead. So I sneaked in after her."

Lexy swallowed.

"She was in the locker room. She didn't even see me come in. I picked up a coconut and cracked her on the head. She collapsed immediately. Stone dead. I'm rather good at that. I picked her up – she was as light as a feather, the little bitch – and I put her…"

"Don't tell me," said Lexy, quietly. "You put her in the old trunk in the wardrobe room, a few layers down, underneath your Avril disguise."

"How did you…?"

"Just a lucky guess." That's why Kinky had been whining. Sheri-Anne must have still been warm when Lexy opened the trunk.

"Tammy – we need to make a phone call."

"I'm afraid not."

Lexy backed towards the door.

"You see – now that Princess has her own little passport, I thought that she and I might go for a journey. Seeing as Tristan and Sheri-Anne aren't going any more."

Especially Sheri-Anne.

"I booked the flight when I got back this evening." Tammy looked at her watch. "In fact, we really should get going. I was going to wait until Tristan got home, and make sure he didn't go anywhere else for a while. But it looks as if fate has already arranged that for me." She gave a short, manic laugh, dislodging Princess. The cat ran up the stairs. "So, I suppose all I have to do now is make sure that *you* don't talk."

Tammy bent into the alcove where the boots and coats were kept, and selected a stout walking stick. Lexy immediately groped for the door handle and managed to pull it half open.

"Oh, no you don't."

Lexy ducked. The stick smashed against the thick glass panel, shattering it, and slamming the door shut again – but not in time to stop a chihuahua dodging in.

Tammy let out a scream of pain. Kinky had fastened himself to her ankle. She raised the stick again.

A second later, the door was kicked open from the outside so hard that Lexy was knocked sprawling. Edward leapt over her and brought Tammy to the ground in a flying rugby tackle. They rolled about on the carpet among the broken glass. There were shouts and curses. But Lexy barely noticed. It just seemed like something unimportant playing in the background.

Before Tammy had been overcome, her last blow had landed on Kinky.

Lexy dragged herself into a kneeling position, shook him incredulously.

"Wake up, pal." It seemed such a daft thing to say. She even gave a half-laugh. "You'd better not be winding me up here, Kinks."

Then she saw the blood soaking into the carpet underneath him.

"F...!" Lexy scrambled up.

Edward and Tammy froze in a horrible parody of the missionary position.

Lexy stooped, grabbed up the bloodied walking stick and advanced on them. "Out of the way, Edward."

Edward landed Tammy a punch in the throat, jumped up and wrestled the stick from Lexy's hand.

"Not the answer, sweetie," he panted, standing over the coughing woman.

Princess sat at the top of the stairs, looking, for once, grave.

Lexy turned back to the small caramel-coloured body on the floor. She bent and scooped the dog up, cradling him to her chest, and stepped awkwardly over the ruins of the door. She ran up the gravel drive, feeling Kinky's limp body thud gently against her at each step. She barely noticed that Milo's car was empty.

Within a minute Lexy was hammering at the vet's door.

Guy Ellenger pulled it open, frowning in surprise.

Mutely, she offered Kinky, his head lolling.

The vet took the dog, lay him on the hall floor, kneeling over him. "What happened?"

Lexy choked out the explanation.

Guy Ellenger's hands ran gently over Kinky. He gave Lexy a quick, serious glance.

"I'm sorry..."

Hope was now standing behind Guy, looking dopey but concerned.

Lexy felt herself backing away. "I have to go... I can't..."

She turned and ran blindly out of the drive, down Gorse Rise towards the high street, fighting an urge to drop to her knees on

261

the roadside and curl up.

A minute later she heard footsteps running behind her. She sped up. "Lexy – it's me. Hey – stop, will you." Milo grabbed her arm, spun her around, and steadied her. "What's going on? I can't find Edward anywhere."

"Edward's not the murderer. He saved me. He's in with her now."

"Her?" Milo bent his lanky frame to catch his breath.

"Tammy Caradoc. She killed Sheri-Anne too. Put her in a trunk in the village hall."

Milo closed his eyes. "How did you…?"

"Edward will tell you."

"Where are *you* going now?"

"Home."

"You can't. CID are on their way," said Milo.

"And that's a good thing?" Lexy carried on towards the high street.

"You can't just walk away. They'll need a statement for a start."

"How's this for a statement?" Lexy found she was shouting uncontrollably. "My dog's been killed."

22

Lexy walked up Cliff Lane, through the silent heath. The air was thick enough to slice and the track was only just visible in the last light of dusk. Another rumble of thunder sounded, much closer this time. She was less than halfway when a squall blew up, swatting her face with fat raindrops.

Within five minutes the storm was upon her. Lexy was soaked through, her short hair flattened to her skull. The sky was livid with forked lightning, and the whole landscape seemed to be raging with her at the injustice of life.

It became a vast struggle to climb the last stretch of road to the cabin. Trees, silhouetted in the lightning flashes, bent like limbo dancers under the force of the wind. She ploughed, head down, through the last hundred metres, then raised her dripping face and rubbed her eyes.

The cabin wasn't there.

"Sh…!" Lexy ran forward, stumbling over pieces of broken wood, debris and clods of torn-up earth. The entire building had slid back several yards, the veranda ripped from the ground, broken struts like a row of drunks on a tightrope.

Lexy clambered frantically up to the warped front door, a single thought in her mind.

She kicked the door open and groped for the light switch. By some miracle it was still connected. The living room sloped at a crazy angle, the chintz sofa and sideboard both slammed up against the far wall along with everything else that wasn't screwed down.

The whole place was slipping down the cliff.

Lexy crept along the hall, trying not to listen to the tortured creaks coming from the very fabric of Otter's End.

The bedroom had already begun to split away from the rest of the cabin, setting off on its final journey. Rain splashed through a jagged hole in the roof. The bed was jammed on its side against the far wall, and under it was wedged the suitcase.

"*Bollocks!*"

Holding on to the door frame with one hand, Lexy slid on her backside down the soaking carpet until she was leaning against the bed. She tried to move it with her feet and legs, but it refused to budge.

She flinched at a particularly loud squeal of protest from the cabin. With an ear-splitting crack, the back edge of the bedroom split open. The bed itself slowly turned over and crashed out of the cabin, then bounced absurdly out of sight down the dark cliff.

It was so nearly followed by the suitcase.

Lexy, lying on her back with one hand still clinging to the door frame, had wrapped her legs around it. She lay helpless for a few seconds, gathering what remained of her strength, then gripping the suitcase handle for dear life with her free hand, she began to inch backwards up towards the door. Her arm nearly ripped out of its socket.

With a muscle-wrenching effort she gained the bedroom doorway, and dragged the suitcase up the buckled hall floor. But just as she reached the living room door, a massive clap of thunder shook the cabin, and she began to slide slowly back as the entire back half of Otter's End disintegrated.

She gave an almighty yell, seized the suitcase with both hands and hurled it through the door into the sloping but still intact living room.

It shot back towards her, then took a lucky bounce and came to rest hard behind the door. The lid swung open and the bank notes burst out like a flock of startled pigeons.

Her hands now free, Lexy pulled herself into the living room.

She shoved the door closed on the dark vista of open cliff and sea, and crouched on the slope trying to grab at the notes and stuff them back into the suitcase.

The sound of splitting wood made her look up, alarmed, from her crab-like pose. The front door burst open, creating a whirling through-draft, and the bank notes flurried even more furiously through the air. A figure balanced on the threshold.

"Shut the bloody door!" she bawled. "And help me!"

Milo stretched out a hand towards her.

"No, you idiot – get the money." She plucked a handful of fifties from the air.

"Where did this come from?" Even in this situation, Milo was acting the cop. He reached out a hand to grasp at a passing note.

"I stole it," Lexy yelled. "All right?"

Milo dropped the note as if it were a poisonous snake. It whirled up in a sudden gust, and stuck to his wet face.

Lexy gave a wild bark of laughter. He peeled the note from his cheek, and stared at it.

"Help me get them back. They're not mine," she yelled again.

"No way – we need to get out of here. It's about to go. Give me your hand."

"I'm not going anywhere without this money," Lexy bellowed.

The two of them frantically collected as many notes as they could and stuffed them back into the suitcase, then Lexy scrambled out of the remains of her front door, and Milo, holding the suitcase to his chest, clambered out straight after. They ran for cover just as the remains of Otter's End collapsed and tumbled down the cliff face towards the beach.

"Edward warned me this might happen," Lexy remarked, with dangerous calm.

"Get in my car," said Milo.

"Seats'll get wet." Lexy looked down at her soaking jeans.

"Doesn't matter. Get in."

Lexy slung the suitcase in the back, and slumped into the passenger seat.

The detective jumped in beside her, shut the door, and turned to her.

"I'm sorry about Kinky," he said.

Lexy was glad that Milo had called Kinky by his name. Even if it was a stupid one.

She blinked rapidly.

"OK. Now, what's the story with that?" He jerked his head back at the suitcase with its soggy cargo.

Lexy contemplated the money. The reason for all her problems. The reason she was homeless, dogless and alone.

"Since you ask, my arsehole husband recently stole a previously undiscovered Lowry painting and sold it on the black market."

"Oh, God," moaned Milo.

"He was doing a valuation for a house clearance after an old man died. The man – Gillespie was his name – had left instructions that all the proceeds of the clearance sale were to go to charity. Gerard found the Lowry in the loft, among a load of ordinary, low-value paintings. Identified it immediately. He must have thought his ship had come in." Her eyes hardened. "He donated five hundred quid to English Heritage – his idea of irony – and sold the Lowry to a dealer for half a million. Cash. When I discovered that he'd taken the proceeds and stashed them in his safe, probably to provide himself with a tax-free pension, I took the money myself." She looked steadily at the detective. "I'm going to give an anonymous donation to the bird sanctuary down the road. I've heard there's a pair of warblers that could do with some help."

Milo regarded her for a long moment.

"You are a rather remarkable person," he stated softly.

23

"So you've decided to move on?"

Lexy and Guy Ellenger were sitting at a wooden picnic table outside a fisherman's hut. Four chihuahuas frolicked in a rough patch of grass nearby. Lexy watched them pensively.

"Thought it would be for the best," said Guy. "Start a new life in the Yorkshire Dales, take on some fresh challenges, expand into cattle and sheep, that kind of thing."

"You're starting to sound like James Herriot already." Lexy kicked at the sandy soil beneath her feet.

"I'll miss Clopwolde, obviously." Guy smoothed out a sheet of paper in front of him, not looking at her. "But I thought it would be best to get Hope into a completely new environment." His voice dropped. "How much did she tell you, by the way? That evening when you were at her place?"

"Not much." Lexy attempted a shrug.

"Everything, then?"

She nodded.

"I thought she must have done. Explains a few things." He glanced swiftly at Lexy. "You're the only other person who knows. Avril Todd just took a wild guess about the way our father died, but it was obviously close enough to send Hope over the edge. As soon as you told me that Avril had been killed I thought Hope had done it. She'd been acting so strangely lately. That's why I called her straight off and told her to say she was at the surgery with me on Friday night if anyone asked. Gut reaction. I'd got so used to protecting her."

"Protecting her?"

Guy Ellenger gave her a complicated look.

"Listen – I would never have gone through with that false

alibi if Hope had really murdered Avril." He paused. "I mean, an eight-year-old kid pushing a vicious drunk down the stairs on the spur of the moment is one thing, but an adult murdering someone in cold blood… Believe me, I do appreciate the difference."

"Hang on – I thought you were ten when you did it?"

He gave her a curious look. "Is that what she told you? That I did it?"

Lexy nodded.

"And you believed her?"

Lexy stared out across the flat, watercolour Suffolk landscape without answering him. She might have known that a brilliant vet who looked like God's gift to women and could cook and multi-task couldn't possibly have a dark side. And now he was moving to the Yorkshire bloody Dales.

Guy pushed the sheet of paper towards her. "My new address and phone number, in case you ever happen to be in the area."

"Thanks." She pocketed it. He'd have a wife before the year was out. Northern women weren't daft. "You know where *I'll* be."

They looked up at the sturdy wooden hut behind them, built on high stilts in the old Suffolk tradition. "Edward was using it for a beach hut, would you believe."

A few yards away a slow-running river meandered past on its way to the sea. The sea itself was a good five-minute walk away over a high shingle bank. Lexy had made sure of that – one cabin sailing off into the sunset was enough. A distant view of the sea from the front window was enough for her. From the back she could look out over an endlessly changing vista of reed beds and water meadows.

It was a good base for a private investigation business. Plenty of opportunity for uninterrupted thinking.

They watched as a white estate car rolled slowly along the rough stone path towards the hut and pulled up outside. The door slammed.

"Look out," said Lexy. "It's Robocop."

DI Milo removed his shades and gave Lexy a weary glance.

He had been reinstated. Mitigating circumstances. Lexy privately reckoned that as no one could stop Milo being a policeman, the chief constable thought it would probably be simpler to give his warrant card back.

He took a seat, fitting his legs with some difficulty under the picnic table.

"Is that another one for frappé and profiteroles?" Edward's face appeared at an open window above them, Peter beside him.

"Just a tea, thanks."

"*Philistine…*" The faces withdrew.

Milo raised a querying eyebrow at Lexy.

"We're having morning coffee," Lexy explained. "Edward likes to do things properly. According to him, tea is an afternoon drink."

"Not for me, it isn't," said the detective.

Before long they were all seated around an elaborate tray of coffee and pastries.

Milo took an awkward sip from a bone china teacup with pink rosebuds on it.

"How's business?"

"Quiet," admitted Lexy. "But I only moved in last night."

"Didn't stop you last time."

"Don't remind me. On my first morning in Otter's End I'd agreed to follow a cheating wife and find a lost cat before I'd so much as unpacked my toothbrush."

"And neither of those cases turned out quite the way you expected." Guy gave her a rueful smile.

"It certainly took me a while to work out that they were linked. I just wish I'd got on to Tammy earlier. But it could have been a lot worse. I'm really grateful that Edward got to Tammy before she got to me."

"Think nothing of it, sweetie," said Edward. "It was just fortunate that I spotted Kinky in the Caradocs' front garden while I was…" He hesitated; they hadn't told Guy about DI Milo's intention to haul him off to the police station again that evening. "Anyway, I thought the little mutt had given you the slip. I pinned him down on the front door mat and that's when I overheard good old Tammy giving you chapter and verse inside. Couldn't believe my shell-likes."

"I was grappling with reality myself," said Lexy. She glanced at Milo. The two of them had also kept quiet about their last-minute suspicions concerning Edward.

"Thanks to you I was becoming something of an expert at breaking down doors by that point," Edward continued.

"Odd, that. It's not as if you're usually the violent type," Peter remarked, dryly. "Except where my Clarice Cliff collection is concerned."

"What happened to Tristan after Tammy was arrested?" Guy interjected.

Lexy shrugged. "He got discharged from hospital and he's recovering at a relative's house in the west country. Don't think he's intending to return to Clopwolde."

"Is he facing any charges?"

Lexy glanced at Milo. "No – when all's said and done, he didn't actually commit any crimes. He was just having a mid-life crisis *extraordinaire*. He couldn't really be done for stealing his own cat. Or having a fling with an eighteen year old."

Guy snorted. "He threatened you with a syringe-full of pet tranquilliser."

"I agreed not to take that any further," said Lexy. "He's got enough problems, what with his wife on a charge of double murder. Anyway, he did give me a nice present before he left Clopwolde."

"Yes – we need talk about that, lovie," Edward cut in. "That animal is destroying my ancestral home. You should *see* my Liberty drapes. Ruined." He selected a cinnamon pastry.

"Well, I can't keep her here," said Lexy, reasonably. "Anyway – I've seen the way she and you look at each other. When she's wrapped around your neck."

"She won't be able to do that for much longer – she'll be far too fat. In fact, she's already trying to find somewhere suitable for a nest. I'm just hoping it won't be my Louis XIV *armoire*."

"Do cats nest?" enquired Milo.

"Suffolk Rexes do," Edward informed him knowledgeably.

"Are you going to keep any of the kittens?" Milo asked Lexy.

Edward replied before she could. "With a horde of American cat-fanciers in a bidding war over them? I don't think so, dear. Lexy's got to pay me rent for this place somehow or other, and that's before we even think about the Liberty drapes. To say nothing of my washed silk Chinese rug, which looks like a big pile of hamster bedding now. Pets, eh? More trouble than they're worth."

"He won't let me sell the kittens," Lexy said in a stage whisper to the others.

Edward sipped his coffee primly, then suddenly choked. A solid white bird had emerged from a mound of reeds beside the river and stood several yards away, glaring at them.

"Bit close for comfort," remarked Peter.

"Yes – I don't like the look of that beak. Shoo." Edward made an ineffectual flapping motion with a napkin.

The group of chihuahuas surged forward, with shrill barks.

Guy banged on the table.

"Chico, Gomez… come here NOW! All of you."

The dogs rushed as one towards the swan.

It stretched up, beat its massive wings and hissed like a punctured tractor tyre. Everyone immediately struggled to get free of the picnic bench. Coffee cups and pastries rolled in all directions. The four chihuahuas scattered.

Evidently pleased with this effect, the swan took a ponderous step towards them.

Lexy glanced back towards the hut. "Can someone shut the…"

But it was too late.

A fifth chihuahua had appeared.

He was so heavily bandaged that he appeared to be part dog, part mummy. But that didn't stop him limping with astonishing rapidity from the hut doorway, straight at the swan, growling like a miniature Harley Davidson.

"Oh, crap," said Lexy.

COMING SOON FROM
CRÈME DE LA CRIME

From Gordon Ferris

THE UNQUIET HEART

Private eye Danny McRae battles with black marketeers, double agents and assassins in 1940s London and Berlin.

Lovers by night, gang-busters by day…

Danny McRae, struggling private detective. Eve Copeland, crime reporter, looking for new angles to save her career.

The perfect partnership…

Until Eve disappears, a contact dies violently and an old adversary presents Danny with some unpalatable truths.

His desperate search for his lover hurls him into the shattered remains of Berlin, where espionage and assassination foreshadow the rise of political terrorism. The ruined city tangles him into a web of black marketeers and double agents - and Danny begins to lose sight of the thin line between good and evil…

ISBN: 978-0-9557078-0-3   £7.99

Praise for _Truth Dare Kill_, Gordon Ferris's first Danny McRae adventure

… a believable world of desperate people… will keep you turning the pages…
- Catherine Turnbull, Dursley Gazette

…dark atmosphere… a riveting read…
- Gloucestershire Echo Weekend

… populated with a carnival of misfits… an exciting debut
- Crimesquad.com

From Adrian Magson
NO KISS FOR THE DEVIL

Riley Palmer and Frank Palmer are back – and this time it's personal.

A young woman's body is found dumped in the Essex countryside.

Investigative reporter Riley Gavin recognises her as Helen Bellamy, a former girlfriend of her colleague, PI Frank Palmer.

Ex-military policeman Palmer is accustomed to death, but this is different; this is the brutal murder of someone he was once close to. He knows only one way to deal with it: find the killers.

Meanwhile, Riley's next job is a profile of controversial business-man 'Kim' Al-Bashir. She soon realises that there are sinister forces working against him, and if she doesn't tread carefully she could end up losing her assignment.

And, like Helen, quite probably her life.

ISBN: 978-0-9557078-1-0   £7.99

Praise for previous books by Adrian Magson

…strong echoes of the classic prickly relationship between Modesty Blaise and Willie Garvin… Gritty and fast-paced detecting of the traditional kind, with a welcome injection of realism.
 - Maxim Jakubowski, The Guardian

The excitement carries through right to the last page…
 - Ron Ellis, Sherlock magazine

You'll no doubt read (it) as I did in an afternoon.
- Sharon Wheeler, Reviewing the Evidence

From Roz Southey
CHORDS AND DISCORDS

Music may be the food of love, but it doesn't fill an empty belly…

Winter is not a good time for jobbing musicians in early 18th century Newcastle. The town has emptied for the season, and Charles Patterson, harpsichordist, concert arranger and tutor to the gentry, is down to his last few shillings.

But Patterson has another talent: solving mysteries. When an unpopular organ builder thinks his life is in danger and a shop-boy dies in dubious circumstances, the offer of a substantial fee persuades him to seek answers to some difficult questions.

Like, who stole the dancing-master's clothes? Why is a valuable organ up for raffle?

And will Patterson escape whoever is trying to kill him?

ISBN: 978-0-9557078-2-7   £7.99

Praise for Roz Southey's first gripping Charles Patterson mystery:

… points for originality… absorbing… unhackneyed setting
- Alan Fisk, Historical Novels Review

A fascinating read and certainly different
- Jean Currie, Roundthecampfire.com

… wonderful background… complex plot … the quality of the writing hurtles one along
- Amazon

From Maureen Carter
BAD PRESS
Detective Sergeant Bev Morris tangles with the media

Is the reporter breaking the news – or making it?

A killer's targeting Birmingham's paedophiles: a big story, and ace crime reporter Matt Snow's always there first – ahead of the pack and the police.

Detective Sergeant Bev Morriss has crossed words with Snow countless times. Though his hang-'em-and-flog-'em views are notorious, Bev still sees him as journo not psycho.

But a case against the newsman builds. Maybe Snow's sword is mightier than his pen?

Through it all, Bev has an exclusive of her own… a news item she'd rather didn't get round the nick. DS Byford knows, but the guv's on sick leave. As for sharing it with new partner DC Mac Tyler – no, probably best keep mum…

ISBN: 978-0-9557078-3-4   £7.99

Praise for Maureen Carter's earlier Bev Morris books:
confirms her place among the new generation of British crime writers.
- Julia Wallis Martin, author of *The Bird Yard* and *A Likeness in Stone*

Many writers would sell their first born for the ability to create such a distinctive voice in a main character.
- Sharon Wheeler, Reviewing the Evidence

… Maureen Carter's likeable and feisty anti-heroine is a delight…
- Amazon